Only once will they heed your call.

They had stood on this very spot: her mother, tall and willowy, with a shock of sunfire hair and eyes greener than a cat's, holding the girl's hand and pointing to the rough hewn trunk of the giant oak.

"This is where I come from, Daughter," she had said, her voice thick with a honeyed pride that made the girl squirm.

"The faires will help you should you ever have need of them," her mother had continued, her voice the timbre of silk. "You have their blood in your veins and that will be enough. Though only once will they heed your call—so use the gift I give you wisely."

Now that she stood at the entrance to the Sídhe, the world hidden behind the majestic oak tree beckoning her forward, uncertainty overwhelmed her. Up until that very moment, she's been so sure of herself and her plan; now she felt lost. The idea that there would be no going back once she'd put the thing into motion had not worried her in theory, but to hand the child over to the fairies when one was actually doing the deed was a very different thing.

"I know it's for the best," she whispered as she pressed her lips to the babe's ear. "I know it."

—from "The Green Man" by Amber Benson

Also Available from DAW Books:

Boondocks Fantasy, edited by Jean Rabe and Martin H. Greenberg
Urban fantasy is popular, but what if you took that modern fantasy and moved it to the "sticks," with no big city in sight? Trailer parks, fishing shacks, sleepy little towns, or specks on the map so small that if you blink while driving through you'll miss them. Vampires, wizards, aliens, and elves might be tired of all that urban sprawl and prefer a spot in the country—someplace where they can truly be themselves without worrying about what the neighbors think! With stories by tale-spinners such as Gene Wolfe, Timothy Zahn, Mickey Zucker Reichert, Anton Strout, Linda P. Baker and others.

Zombiesque, edited by Stephen L. Antczak, James C. Bassett, and Martin H. Greenberg
Zombies have long stalked and staggered through the darkest depths of human imagination, pandering to our fears about death and what lies beyond. But must zombies always be just shambling, brain-obsessed ghouls? If zombies actually maintained some level of personality and intelligence, what would they want more than anything? Could zombies integrate themselves into society? Could society accept zombies? What if a zombie fell in love? These are just some of the questions explored in original stories by Seanan McGuire, Nancy A. Collins, Tim Waggoner, Richard Lee Byers, Jim C. Hines, Jean Rabe, Del Stone Jr., and others. Here's your chance to take a walk on the undead side in these unforgettable tales told from a zombie's point of view.

After Hours: Tales from the Ur-Bar, edited by Joshua Palmatier and Patricia Bray
The first bar, created by the Sumerians after they were given the gift of beer by the gods, was known as the Ur-Bar. Although it has since been destroyed, its spirit lives on. In each age there is one bar that captures the essence of the original Ur-Bar, where drinks are mixed with magic and served with a side of destiny and intrigue. Now some of today's most inventive scriveners, such as Benjamin Tate, Kari Sperring, Anton Strout, and Avery Shade, among others, have decided to belly up to the Ur-Bar and tell their own tall tales—from an alewife's attempt to transfer the gods' curse to Gilgamesh, to Odin's decision to introduce Vikings to the Ur-Bar . . . from the Holy Roman Emperor's barroom bargain, to a demon hunter who may just have met his match in the ultimate magic bar, to a bouncer who discovers you should never let anyone in after hours in a world terrorized by zombies. . . .

Courts
of the Fey

*Edited by Martin H. Greenberg
and Russell Davis*

DAW BOOKS, INC.
DONALD A. WOLLHEIM, FOUNDER
375 Hudson Street, New York, NY 10014

ELIZABETH R. WOLLHEIM
SHEILA E. GILBERT
PUBLISHERS
www.dawbooks.com

First Printing, November 2011
1 2 3 4 5 6 7 8 9

DAW TRADEMARK REGISTERED
U.S. PAT. AND TM. OFF. AND FOREIGN COUNTRIES
—MARCA REGISTRADA
HECHO EN U.S.A.

PRINTED IN THE U.S.A.

Acknowledgments

Table of Contents

INTRODUCTION

Russell Davis

There is an old saw in publishing about there being only seven or twenty or thirty-six or maybe only three basic storylines. I suppose if you're a deconstructionist, this kind of thinking makes sense. I'm not. Deconstructing a story in that manner is a little like going to a Criss Angel or David Copperfield show and looking behind the curtain. As a writer, I don't want anyone peeking back there unnecessarily at my work; as an editor, it feels cheap, like I'd be devaluing the work that goes into creating the magic that is a good story.

I've been a co-editor (with Martin H. Greenberg) on a good handful of DAW Books anthologies over the years, and back in 2004, we did one called *Faerie Tales*. People seemed to like it, which is very important, and I had a lot of fun putting it together, which is not quite as important, but still . . . these are the kinds of projects we do for love. No one is retiring off a theme anthology any time soon, but that's not really the point. The point, at least for me, is to try and come up with a theme that allows the writers a lot of freedom to create their own unique story and at the same time, works to constrain the overall theme of the book so that readers broadly know what to expect, but get some surprises along the way.

Now, I might be accused of double-dipping. People like faerie stories, and since it worked once, well . . . maybe I just skipped on back to the well, bucket in hand and a song in my heart. If memory serves, there are at least one or two writers in this anthology that had a story in that one. And maybe that accusation of double-dipping is true. But I don't think so.

Courts of the Fey, unlike the first faerie related anthology I did, is a bit more constrained, for one thing. The stories all had to relate to the Seelie or Unseelie Courts in some fashion, and while the writers in this volume took that in all kinds of directions I couldn't have imagined on the front end, no one took the obvious escape route and did a contemporary political story where Glenn Beck is set upon by angry fey creatures sent by the Queen of the Seelie Court, which happens to be situated on a hidden mound beneath the Supreme Court of the United States. (I admit I'd been sort of looking for that one, but maybe it's better that they avoided the more obvious political implications for this particular volume.)

The other thing that makes this one different *is* obvious. No two magicians create an illusion or a magic trick in the exact same way. This is true for writers as well. I could ask a hundred of them to write a story specifically about the death of the Fairy King and I would get a hundred different stories. Interestingly enough, I could then ask that same group to do it again, and get another completely different set of stories. That is why this volume is different than the last, and that is why it's not double-dipping at all. What writers create is magic and illusion and each time they put pen to page or hands to keyboard, the good ones come up with something different.

This also explains why those theories about how many (or rather, few) storylines actually exist is so much hooey. Because a story is more than its plot and more than its characters——it is the sum of all the craft *and* the writers vision, style, and voice that makes each story a unique glimpse into a world that never was or might someday be.

In *Courts of the Fey*, you'll find stories from the incredibly talented Lilith Saintcrow to the beautifully poetic Michelle Sagara; from Amber Benson, who moved on from *Buffy the Vampire Slayer* fame to her own special gifts as a writer; to Sarah Hoyt, whose worlds have encompassed Shakespeare and beyond. Stories from Rob Thurman and Dean Wesley Smith and Mary Robinette Kowal and more. Twelve writers in all, award winners and bestsellers and maybe a couple you're reading for the first time ever, conjuring new visions of the worlds of the faerie for your enjoyment.

I hope that you find walking the paths of these worlds as magical as I did. Step into the mushroom circle, friends, and be transported into the *Courts of the Fey*.

GALLOW'S RESCUE

Lilith Saintcrow

He sat straight up in bed, the marks normal humans would mistake for tribal tattoos writhing on his arms. They hurt, a fierce sweet pain, and a bolt went through him from crown to toes.

Jeremy. Her low contralto making the word sweet as caramel. *Jeremy Gallow.*

She had said his name.

The only light was from a weak quarter-moon peering blearily through his blinds. The window was open slightly, and frost traced patterns on the glass, reaching in with tiny insubstantial fingers. He always slept with it open, now.

Just in case a small brown bird should come fluttering by.

"Robin?" he whispered.

Nothing but the moonlight, pale and thin as skimmed milk, soaking through the venetian blinds.

Sometimes, on nights this cold and clear when Daisy was alive, he would leave his mortal wife sleeping in their bed and slip out to the field behind the trailer. The lance would spill into his hands from the tattoos, silver shading into iron as he willed, its blade cleaving night air with a low sweet sound. He was slightly less than Half, so the cold iron, deadly as it was, didn't bar him or poison him.

No more. Daisy slept under a bed of earth, and Robin had left him.

Jeremy. A hopeless whisper, her sweet voice blurring. Another shock ran through him, the sort any fae would feel when his name was truly spoken.

After all, he'd given his oath. *If you ever need me, call. And I will come.*

But Robin had merely looked at him, those blue eyes sharp and cold as a knife behind the screen of welling tears. *I will never need you, Gallow,* she'd said, and swept out into the spring sunshine.

Need would have to be dire indeed for Robin Ragged to say *his* name.

Jeremy was already off the bed and moving, the marks on his arms itching and tingling as they ran. He denied the lance its freedom and it subsided— but only because they both knew he would need it again. Later, or, if Robin were in danger, sooner.

He would prefer sooner.

To oblivious human eyes, he looked like every other skinny-hipped construction worker just barely on the sunny side of forty, old enough to know there were no more options but still with enough juice left in him to sling bricks or take heavy duty. A lean, tensile male, maybe looking for a fight, or maybe just looking for his next bottle of brewski and game caught at the corner bar. The clothes helped—who would expect to find a fae wearing Carhartts?

But fae, even Tainted or Half, would smell the stench of cold iron on him, the salt-sweet breath of mortal blood, the fume of murder, and besides, his face would be known to no few of them. A Queen's Armormaster, even one who had turned away from the Summer Court, was not one to bandy words or blades with.

So when he slid through the swinging door into Goodfellow's Reste, there was a breath of silence and an uncoordinated but graceful drawing-away. Smoke wreathed the roof timbers, and it was probably Goodfellow's joke that the whole place looked like a tourist dive impersonating a seventeenth-century English tavern. Right down to the many-fingered dryad birchgirls in black vests and low-cut white blouses, their shallow breasts plumped by the tight lacings and the swish of their long greenish-gray skirts like the sough of wind through branches. Kobolding at the back table peered through the smoke, their broad warty faces slack and dull, tankards piled on their tables. Others of the Bright and the Little Folk stared or pretended not to, including a dripping kelpie in biped form, his broad white teeth bared.

At the bar slim brown Goodfellow paused, wiping at the shiny wood with a snow-white cloth. His dark eyes narrowed, and if his tanned hands dropped out of sight below the bar, Jeremy decided, he would kill the mischievous free fae and take his chances elsewhere.

A tide of whispers followed the clumping of Jeremy's yellow workboots; he stepped as heavily as a human out of long jobsite habit. Mortals didn't like it when they couldn't hear you.

Besides, the more noise he made, the greater the advantage would be when he chose not to.

Goodfellow very carefully rested both his hands on the bar's surface. Oak, polished to a high sheen. It vibrated, and Jeremy paused before he was tempted to touch it or the brass resting-rail along its foot. Behind Goodfellow, ranked bottles gleamed in jewel tones or umber shades. Some of them were even full of alcohol.

The free fae's catslit pupils widened a trifle, the high sharp points of his ears poking through a frayed silken mat of nut-brown hair. The leather and homespun he wore were all shades of rough bark and mud; it would be easy to mistake him for a tree-spirit. White teeth showed as his V-shaped smile rose.

Sometimes, when the Puck smiled, you could see his true age. But not often.

"Gallow." A nod, his sharp chin dipping. "What ale do you wish to ail yourself with?"

For a moment Jeremy's voice wouldn't work. It was always a shock. No matter how long he stayed away, how he surrounded himself with mortals and fell into the rhythms of the mortal world, it only took a breath of the fae to make him feel . . .

. . . at home.

"Goodfellow." His jaw threatened to crack. "Where is she?"

It was perhaps a mistake not to observe etiquette.

The Puck tilted his head. His smile had fallen away, a discarded leaf. "There are many *shes*, Gallow, and I keep no track of your lightskirt business."

Wrong answer. The marks twinged, Jeremy moved, and the entire bar went dead-quiet, not even the scrape of chairs against rough wooden flooring.

The lance extended, a solid bar of silver, vibrating on the edge of substantiality against Jeremy's palms. It was a column of cold moonlight, but the blade at the end was now long and leaf-shaped, dull cold iron resonating as it sensed fae flesh. A low hungry sound stitched itself into the silence; Goodfellow pressed back against the shelves of bottles and the lance twitched as it sang.

"I am not going to *ask* again," Gallow said, softly. "Robin. Robin Ragged. *My* Robin."

Goodfellow's callused brown hands were up, a parody of harmlessness. The snarl drifting over his boyface was probably the last expression his human victims ever saw. "The Ragged cares naught for anyone, Gallow, and for thee least of all. I would have told you for proper payment, or maybe for the mischief of watching her break thy—"

The lance flickered, sweeping laterally. Jeremy stepped aside, the contours of a battlefield flashing through him and the lance keening as it showed him the next few moments, time and choice interlocking to produce the pattern of the battle. Once seen, the pattern could be disrupted.

The old Armormaster who had trained Gallow in the lance's use had never mentioned this gift, and sometimes he wondered why.

The big black doglike creature howled as the lance bit, quicker than a snake's tongue. The blade rang silver for a moment, striking to wound instead of kill, and the gytrash thumped onto the floorboards, greenish blood spurting. Goodfellow snarled again as the lance flicked back, the point suddenly cold iron again and pressed against his throat, even though the boy-shaped fae was now crouching on the bar's shining surface.

Jeremy said nothing. A whispering ran through the fae, under the gytrash's sobbing for breath.

"Fenwicke Station." Goodfellow's shoulders dropped. "Along the third track, the north wall. Her home is there; 'tis all I know. The Ragged has not come for her glass of wine since last halfmoon, and you are not the first to ask questions of her."

And now I cannot ask who else has come looking. Gooseflesh rose all over him. Goodfellow was a bad enemy to make. "Thank you." He even managed to sound sincere. "I'll return, Puck."

"Don't." Goodfellow tensed, muscle by muscle. "There is no amends for this, Gallow."

"Sweet nothings," Jeremy replied, and backed away. They whispered even more as he left, and the rain outside was just as cold as the sick feeling under his breastbone.

*   *   *

Robin, where are you?

She was a creature of the Summer Court, and they loved air and light. So why would she make her home here, in a hole cut into the north wall of the tunnel leading uphill from Fenwicke Station? The subway roaring past at intervals was not conducive to quiet dreaming.

But it was hers, there was no question. There was a low armchair in just the shade of blue she wore in eye and dress, the peacock-shade of a summer sky just as dusk first unloosed its mantle. A narrow pallet and bits of colored glass strung on the weeping concrete wall. Cobwebs in the corners and one lone black high-heeled shoe right next to her bed, the covers thrown back as if she'd been pulled loose by force.

He only had a doublewide trailer, but it was better than *this*. "I wouldn't have touched you," Gallow murmured, only half aware of speaking. "You could have just . . . " *Lived with me. In my trailer. Christ. When you were used to the Summer Court's luxury, even if you were only Half.*

And with memories of her dead, purely mortal sister lingering in every corner, would any woman, fae or human, consent to stay? Especially after . . .

You did not treat her well, Jeremy.

Yes, she had been treacherous. What else could he expect from the Seelie Queen's plaything? Ragged Robin, a full Half-fae, taken to Court after a child-hood of neglect as her mortal sister's shadow, seeking a chance of escape.

So treacherous.

But *he* had been downright cruel.

He ran his fingers over the back of the chair. How many nights would Robin have sat here, her legs drawn up, and watched the trains rumble past, spilling their diseased yellow light?

Under the tang of iron and concrete, exhaust and pollution, there was the warm perfume of spice-pear. He filled his lungs with it, and the markings ran with fire on his arms. The lance was unsatisfied, and his own unease added to it.

Unease? Call it what it is, Gallow. Fear.

There. A glint on her tumbled bed. He approached, cautiously, and looked at the silver coin, half hidden under the threadbare sky-blue sheet.

The quirpiece gleamed as he tweezed it delicately free with two callused fingers. Memory threatened to swamp him—she was a Realmaker, her craftings not vanishing into leaves and sticks like other fae's. Was this the same piece she had left to break her trail the night he met her?

It didn't matter. For shoved further under the sheet was another small, stray gleam, a thin gold chain, smelling of truemetal but broken now, as if it had been violently yanked free. He slid the quir into his pocket and lifted the necklace, turning it to catch the faint illumination from the mouth of the hole, fluorescent glare from Fenwicke Station slipping wearily down the tracks to creep into the corner here.

He remembered clasping it, Robin holding her

redgold hair aside, the scent of her filling his lungs and bright spring sunshine gilding his bedroom window. The supple curve of her naked back and how the pear-spice of her had lingered on the sheets after she left him.

I will never need you, Gallow.

A shrieking clatter tore through the memory; he was in an instinctive crouch before he realized it was merely another subway train. It flashed past.

Who was she punishing? Or was she hiding? From whom? Me?

"Robin," he breathed, and the thin golden chain twitched, tugging against his fingers. The necklace would lead him to her.

And then God help whoever had torn it from her throat.

Dawn was rising in veils of gray as Jeremy drew the shadows over himself and bit back a curse. The necklace tugged insistently in the hollow of his palm.

The entrance to Craigie Park held a high-crowned pair of gates, set in a chunk of ivy-festooned wall that only stretched for ten feet in either direction. Mortals probably thought the rest of the wall had been pulled down as the city grew, pressing in on the little bit of tamed wilderness full of thorny bushes and crazy-looping jogging paths. They wouldn't guess that the walls simply stepped *sideways*. Disappearances in the park were blamed on human criminals.

Some of them might even be guilty, for all Gallow knew. He eyed the unlocked gate, its spikes slick with dew and the ancient padlock dangling from a length of chain probably older than the city itself. Both sides of the gate were drawn back and perhaps rusted that way, for all that the metal wasn't cold iron.

The Seelie Queen closed the gates of her garden in fall and reopened them to unloose the spring, but Unwinter always stood waiting. When the Wild Hunt rode forth, this would be the gate they used, and when they brought their struggling prey back, the threshold would receive first blood.

A shudder worked its way down his body. No wonder she had called his name, if the Unseelie had her. Was she prey for a Hunt? Not likely; his Robin was too quick, and she could sing her way free if she had to. He'd seen her singing unleashed and the destruction that followed . . . but there were ways to incapacitate a Tainted fae, even a full Half. She had been running from a plague-scored Unseelie rider the night he'd met her.

The quirpiece trembled in his pocket, too. Jeremy hunched his shoulders under his work jacket. They would miss him at the jobsite this morning.

He could always find another job. Maybe roadwork, and that would take him out of this city. Still, there were always entrances to Summer or Unwinter, if you knew where to look.

I will never need you, Gallow.

He was well within his rights to leave her there. Perhaps she was already dead.

But the necklace quivered, and he saw her face when he had thrown the words at her, each one a wound. *I loved your sister because she was mortal, fae. You're a dalliance, and a traitorous one to boot.*

She was white as milk, her blue eyes darkening and the pulse beating in her throat above the necklace's gleam. The thin crystalline sound of a heart breaking, and his own acid self-loathing. He had been foolish enough to think her dead Daisy's replacement. The truth was, Daisy was the shadow and Robin the light that cast it.

And still, afterward, she had stood at his back when the Seelie Queen's part in the making of the fae-killing plague had been revealed. The Queen and her mortal scientist lover, mixing their poisons to kill Unseelie fae—but the Seelie themselves took ill as well, and there were those who had broken free of the Queen's hold when all was revealed.

Robin's quick thinking and the threat of her song unleashed on the very Court she had always served had saved Jeremy's worthless life.

He had stupidly thought it meant she had forgiven him.

Gallow faded further into the shadows. If he intended to slip into Unwinter, he would have to do it before dawn rose further.

But he did not have to stroll in through the Hungry Gates and announce himself. There were other ways.

With his hand against venous ivy over chill granite stone, he was glad of his flannel shirt and work jacket. The cold of Unwinter settled against skin and hair, his breath plumed, and the world became gray-misty, the Keep rising above him on a spur of rough stone.

The Summer Court was white stone and fluid lines, golden light and bright shade, jewel tones and sparkling eyes. Unwinter Keep was . . . otherwise, a hungry collection of piercing towers, barred windows, a gated maw across a black-metal bridge tarred with filth, the moat roiling gray smoke over a fluid too thick to be water. The necklace scorched against his palm, and bloody accents in the gray and black mass above him showed through.

Unwinter was colorless save for the rubies and red glass. Some Unseelie fae said the colors were too subtle for those born in the Summer Court to see.

Jeremy examined his surroundings carefully, eased one foot forward. The yellow of his workboots had faded, parchment now instead of sunshine. The thread of gold in his palm was richer and brighter, elemental metal showing its truth.

The lance itched and burned, scenting the danger around him. He slid free of the small entrance set in a long ivy-grasped wall and set off around the edge of the moat, moving silently as he could.

If he remembered correctly there was a small secret stair on the east side, coming up through the donjons. The Keep did not change much over time, and entry was normally easy.

It was the leaving of Unwinter that was difficult.

Robin. Be alive, I'm coming.

Silence filled dusty halls. Unwinter would be settling for the day, drowsing as the mortal world ploughed through its sunlit half. Once, to avoid a small group of trow as they cavorted through knee-high dust, he clung to a cobweb-wrapped chandelier, his left boot braced on a carved frieze and his right held high in empty air, work-hardened muscles protesting. He had lost very little of his flexibility.

He had visited the Keep as an envoy and once or twice as an assassin, both honorable enough missions. What was he now?

The necklace tugged, drawing him deeper and deeper into the Keep's gloom. The quiet was unnatural. He should have seen more fae before now—spreggan and more drow, kelpies and the dark brughnies leering, leprechauns with their clubs and their claws, the Hunt's tall lords in ragged silks with their dark or silver-chased armor laid aside for the day.

And the hounds. Don't ever forget the hounds.

It was a trap, of course. But he followed the necklace's burning twitching, wrapped around his wrist now, and tried not to think of the possibilities.

The chamber was round and thick-walled, the stone floor patterned in a compass rose, black and gray interwoven with thin threads of crimson. Jeremy eased into the room, the necklace tightening on his wrist, and was not surprised in the slightest when the door thudded shut and the roof folded back, huge clockwork gears grinding. The floor bowed, the rose became a dish, and he leaped sideways for footing, finding himself braced against the wall.

"*Welcome,*" a cold, lipless voice echoed, and Jeremy stared up. His boots slipped as the floor turned slick, the gears grinding with unlovely screeches. The King of Unwinter, his high horned helm a cup of shadows lit only by two red-coal eyes, glared down from the gallery above. His spiked shoulders, cold silver-chased plate armor glinting in the dimness, held the rags of a tattered crimson cloak, and his gauntleted fists rested on the lip of the gallery's balustrade.

Around the gallery's rim, other Unseelie clustered. Barrow-wights leered, their chill gray robes belted with pale gold and their rings chiming as they drummed fleshless fingers; *beansidhes* clutched at themselves, their mouths moving with silent screams and their long gray hair moving in runnels; the drow clung to rafters and peered down, their eyes lit with bloody glints. Seawater and freshwater dripping from kelpie hooves and their tossed manes dribbled down the wall, smoking with ice. The leprechauns rattled their clubs, and dark pixies crawled over the King's shoulders, tiny unhealthy foxfire glimmers under their fluttering wings. Other Unseelie of every shape and size crowded, jostling for a look as the gears kept grinding and cracks showed in the floor, the compass rose dilating.

Whatever was underneath it was bound to be

nasty. The marks on his arms burned, the lance struggled for freedom, but he kept looking. Where was she? She *had* to be here, she must be—

"*Stop!*" The cry rang like cold glass, shivering into pieces on a fullmoon night. It tore the air, flushing it with chill, and she vaulted the gallery's rim with sweet grace, her blue skirt fluttering and bare battered white feet dangling briefly. Her bleeding feet came up, pushed against the wall, and she was airborne.

Jeremy *moved*, sliding against the tipping, heaving, cracking floor. She was falling, her curling hair a russet flag, and the Unseelie set up a belling, baying scream that could stop a mortal's heart.

The floor juddered, his boots finding purchase, and she obviously had not expected him to catch her. They almost went over in a tangle of arms and legs, but he had his footing at last and broke her fall, shoving her behind him. The lance burst free, a column of truesilver, and he expected them to come leaping down behind her.

The King laughed.

The assembled fae cowered under the lash of that chill, deadly amusement. One of the brughnies toppled over the balustrade, twisting as she plummeted, and hit the cracked, sloping floor with an unhealthy, meaty sound.

It's stopped moving. Jeremy's ribs heaved, his breath pluming on iron-frosted air. The gears had quit grinding. *Now we see what the game is.*

"*Stop!*" Robin cried again, and her voice sliced

through Unwinter's laughter. "Or I'll drop and break it, I swear I will!"

The sudden stillness was eerie. The lance quivered in Jeremy's hands. He could hold a bottleneck for a very long time, but here on uncertain footing with someone to protect . . . well. And the Unseelie were not known for single combat.

It was then that he noticed the patches of green-black corruption smoking on several of the fae. The brughnie's twisted body sent up thin tracers of acrid steam as it rotted, a foul stench escaping it in a gassy whisper.

The plague was here. It had broken Unwinter's walls at last.

His skin chilled, reflexively. Those Tainted by mortal blood did not take the illness—yet.

"Gallow." Robin's hand was on his shoulder, her fingers digging in. "What in the name of Stone or Throne are you doing *here*?"

His throat was dry. The lance sang hungrily. "You called," he managed, staring up at the crimson gleams of the King's eyes, deep in the twisted helm's shadow. "What are *you* doing here, Ragged?"

And he could have kicked himself, because he sounded disdainful. Instead of . . . his heart knocked against his ribs. *We are about to die, Gallow, and that is all you can say to her?*

"You called *me*." She squeezed his shoulder, as hard as she could, her fingernails pricking the tough cloth of his work jacket. "And *he* said to bring it, for your life. The serum."

"And do you have it, Tainted songbird?" The King's words split like gravel and the Unseelie writhed under that lash. A *beansidhe*'s open mouth worked like a fish's, her sightless eyes rolling up until the gray-webbed whites showed, and she slumped against her sisters as the spots of greenblack danced on her pale skin.

Robin stepped delicately forward; her dress flapped, torn and stained with various fluids. Her feet left bloody prints on the twisted compass rose, but she didn't flinch. Jeremy hissed a warning—*are you mad, woman? I cannot protect you if—*

Her slim, beautiful fingers flicked. He studied her profile greedily, taking little sip-glances, unable to stop himself. The same long nose and sculpted mouth, the same high gloss of sidhe beauty over a face that was not, in the end, very much like her sister's. Similar to Daisy's beauty, but all her own.

How could he ever have thought them alike?

She held up a long, thin crystal ampoule, the colorless liquid inside sparkling as it moved, sluggishly. "I held a phial of vaccine back, yes." Her voice shook, but only slightly. "You will not have it if you harm him, Unseelie. And I will sing thee into thy grave besides, on my name and my voice."

Jeremy all but flinched. "Robin—" A strengthless whisper.

"Threats, little Tainted bird. Hand over the cure, and we shall perhaps let you live." The King was deadly serious now, and the Unseelie rose, scrabbling forward. They would press down into the cup of the

small chamber, and he would kill as many of them as he could, but—

"Gallow." She cast him a sidelong glance, and he saw the bruise spreading up her white throat. "You should not have come."

She drew back her arm, and hurled the crystalline ampoule upward. Unseelie crowded forward, each of them shoving the others aside in their haste to catch the cure, and the King roared.

Jeremy stepped aside, the lance's blade singing happily as it buried itself in the piebald kelpie's stomach. The fae went down in a welter of half-horse, half-human, hooves scraping stone, and Robin's voice trilled behind him, a low descant of unearthly beauty that struck the knot of *beansidhe* threatening to descend on them and peeled inhuman flesh back from spongy, blackened bone.

"*Run!*" Jeremy screamed, and backed up, using his bulk to move her along. The music coming from her throat didn't falter, spiraling up into a sustained note of chill glass murder, but Robin fell.

The lance braced itself in his right hand; he bent and found her arm with his left, hauling her up. "God damn you," he yelled, the blasphemy scorching the Keep's wall next to him, "*Run, Robin!*"

No longer singing, somehow she was on her feet again and stumbling, bloody prints left behind. He had a vague memory of kicking the door to the compass-chamber down as the Unseelie fought for the ampoule, even the King's flickering, murderous gauntlets unable to restore order. Unwinter shook with rage, the fae turning on each other, and Robin's head came up, her russet-gold curls tangled and tumbling as she pitched forward, leading him down a dust-choked hall.

"Should be here," she choked, somehow audible through the massive noise, and Jeremy snapped a glance over his shoulder. They were free of pursuit for the moment, but that could change when Unwinter restored order to his subjects and came a-hunting. The Hounds would be loosed, and the knights of the Wild Hunt would be given their names, and—

Robin plunged aside, her feet almost tangling. He kept her upright by yanking on her bird-thin arm, and the thought of the bruises he would leave on her sent another bolt of hot self-loathing through him. She half-fell through a narrow casement, wood splintering as she forced it wide, and the Keep shuddered on its foundations again. The noise behind them cut off, deadly silence rising like a shark for the legs of an unwary swimmer.

"Here!" Robin coughed, and the window swung wide. "Best way. Jeremy—"

He shoved her out, his boot catching the windowsill, and launched himself into empty space as the silver whistle of the lord of Unseelie calling his hounds pierced the Keep, a deadly thread through the eye of a frozen granite needle. They fell, and the lance shivered as it shredded into insubstantiality. His arms closed around Robin's warm living weight as they plummeted free of Unwinter.

*   *   *

The phone shrilled, but he ignored it. It was just another job lost. He could find work anywhere.

Her feet were a mess. He dabbed them with iodine; she hissed in pained breaths and leaned back, her skirt falling away from bruised knees. Crouched on the bathroom floor, he glanced up at her drawn, flour-pale face and her messy, glowing curls. "Sorry."

"I don't know why you're bothering. They'll heal. And there's a blood trail leading them here."

"Let them come." He smeared the antibiotic cream as gently as he could, wiped his fingers, and reached for the gauze. "We won't be here."

"Gallow—" Another hissing breath, she flinched.

He glanced up again, his jaw setting itself. "Or, maybe Unwinter won't come, having what he wants." It sounded unreasonably hopeful even to him.

"He doesn't have what he wants." Robin's shoulders hunched. Her arms were bruised, too. What had she suffered before he'd arrived? "I told the truth—I *did* reserve a phial of the vaccine. He didn't stop to ask if what I showed him was that particular vial."

Of course. "What was really in it?"

"Holy water." She gingerly took her foot back as he finished.

He cupped her other heel, lifted it, examined the damage. "You are dangerous, Robin Ragged." Blessed water would either do nothing or it would burn fae flesh. Most likely the latter, since they were Unseelie.

"Isn't *treacherous* the word you want?" She moved as if she would free her foot from his grasp, but his fingers tightened. "I should go."

Not yet. "You're not going anywhere. Why were you in Unwinter?"

"I *told* you." An aggrieved sigh. "I heard you—*ssss*, that hurts. I heard you calling."

"And you came to rescue me?"

"There were also Unseelie chasing me. I thought . . . "

But she didn't say what she thought. Instead, she leaned back against the toilet tank, alarmingly white, blue eyes half-lidded and her throat working. She was gaunt, her collarbones standing out, and his chest hurt. If fae were susceptible to cardiac arrest, he might think he was having one.

"You thought to rescue me. Funny. I thought to rescue *you*." The necklace glinted, wrapped around his wrist as he cleaned the shredded flesh. "An Unseelie trick, perhaps."

She jerked her foot back. "If you're accusing me of being in league with Unwinter—"

"Shut up." He yanked on her ankle. "And settle down, so I can bind these. Where are your shoes?"

"Lost one when the barrow-wights came for me; lost the other when a group of spreggan—*ow!* What are you doing, whittling the cuts deeper?"

"No, just cleaning them. Unwinter will hunt us for this, Robin."

"They won't care much for you. In any case, it matters little. They're *plagued*." A dismissive shake of her tangled curls. "If I stay free long enough, there will be few of them left to hunt me. Or Unwinter will go to Summer for the vaccine, and nobody will care about *me*."

"You are an optimist. The Queen has reason to hunt you too."

"Which makes this an excellent time for me to begin a-wandering, as soon as you're finished torturing my feet."

"We."

"What?" She shook her head again, like a tired horse. "Gallow, cease. I should be going."

"*We* are going a-wandering, Robin. Not *me*, not *I*, but we. If you mean to stay ahead of Unwinter's hunt, and free of Summer as well, you'll need me." His throat was oddly dry, so he focused on her foot, the iodine sting-smelling and staining. More antibiotic cream, and she was silent as he finished and reached for the gauze.

"I don't need you, Gallow." A whisper, as if her own throat was dry as well. "I've stayed free so far."

"And they tricked you into thinking I needed you, and you came." He wrapped the gauze, taped it, and found the slippers he'd put on the bathtub's rim. Blue, with embroidered roses.

They had been Daisy's. They were slightly too tight, with the gauze, but they would serve to protect the bandages. She would only need them a short while. The Half healed quickly.

His hands moved independently of him, capping the iodine bottle, gathering the refuse of bandaging. "I'll cook you something. We can rest for a few hours, but before midafternoon we should be gone."

"Jeremy." Now she was hugging herself, palms cupping her sharp elbows. "I am not my sister. I'm not Daisy. I won't ever *be* her."

Is that what you think? That I want you to play her to me? "I never asked you to be." The lie stung his mouth. If she hadn't looked so much like his mortal wife, he would never have followed her that first night.

Or would he have followed, curious, and let the plagued Unseelie rider chasing her strike to kill? There was no way of knowing now.

The phone shrieked again. He hauled himself up, glancing at the bathroom mirror. It was speckled, and he was pale. His eyes burned, and he looked more fae than he could ever remember seeming. He unwound the necklace from his wrist, laid it on the counter.

"I'll repair that before we leave."

He was a fair cook, and they were both hungry. Robin said no more, but she didn't demur when he led her into the bedroom after a breakfast he could barely remember eating thirty seconds after finishing. He set his alarm for just past one and sank down next to her, pulling the blankets up over them both. He tucked her in, moved closer, and tried to ignore the stiffness in her when he slid an arm around her waist. Dawn had well and truly risen, sunlight striking the closed window and fingering the blinds.

"Relax," he said into her hair. "You're safe, Robin. I promise."

He still had his boots on, just in case. The Hunt did not ride by daylight . . . but still. The discomfort kept him awake for a full five minutes before sleep claimed him, and as the darkness covered him he realized she was still tense. Yet her hair still smelled of spiced pears under the tang of Unseelie, iron, and copperblood pain, and for the first time in months Jeremy Gallow slept without dreams.

He sat up in bed, blinking, the pillow next to his holding a dent from her head and something shining, a supple curve.

He grabbed the necklace. It was repaired, a Realmaker's skill still vibrating in the metal. His boots hit the floor.

His front door opened. He heard the familiar squeak and thump, and he crashed through his bedroom door and the hall. "*Robin!*"

The slippers were neatly placed next to his battered couch, the television's blind eye watching. He had once put his fist through that glass gaze, and remembered Robin kneeling in front of it, patting the shards and slivers back into place.

Her hair was combed, her dress was patched. The bruises on her arms were fading, yellow-green and shrinking instead of purple-red and fresh. Her hand tightened on the doorknob, and thin winter sunshine was a haze around her.

She stepped over the threshold. There was a swish of blue skirt, a puff of brown feathers, a flash of crimson, and Jeremy's knees buckled.

She was gone.

Dusk came in a glory of orange and red. Jeremy stood at the edge of the grove of trashwood, looking up the hill. The marks on his arms tingled and itched, alive with danger and sharp exhilaration.

Up the hill, the trailer gleamed. Smoke billowed, and the flames peeking out through the windows had a good hold. Sirens echoed in the distance.

It was a good way to break his trail, and hers. He waited as the sun sank, drawing back further into the grove and watching the struggle to combat a fae-laid fire. He'd been thorough; there would be nothing but ashes left. It wouldn't spread to his neighbors, at least.

Purple twilight gathered in corners, and through the mortal hubbub came another sound. Jeremy's head lifted, and he picked up the duffel at his feet.

It was a thin crystalline whistle, an ultrasonic hunting cry. Any fae within hearing would be frantically digging for shelter; the few humans who could hear it would shiver without quite knowing why and find a reason to stay indoors.

The Wild Hunt was afoot, and early.

Jeremy's lips skinned back from his teeth. He hitched the duffel onto his shoulder and turned away from the ruins of his mortal home.

The Hunt would find her, no matter how canny she was. All he had to do was follow them, and when they found his Robin he could strike.

And *they* would be the hunted.

The fire crackled and hissed.

Gallow vanished into the coming night.

AN ANSWER FROM THE NORTH

Sarah A. Hoyt

Along the perfect corridors of the glittering palace of air and light, the intruder came striding. Gloved and attired like the Lords of Fairy, in velvet and silver he came, dark hair glossy, every feature perfect, and his blue eyes sparkling like the ice that had once protected the children of magic.

Wherever he stepped, his iron spurs clinked against the tiles and left dark marks upon the polished marble floors. And behind him, the beautiful ladies of fairy grew a little paler; the singers of elfland grew a little quieter, and light flickered and faded just a little.—while magic seemed to flicker and waver, like a flame on the edge of extinguishing.

"To see Albric," he came, he said. "The High King of fairies," he said. "Or elves, or the bright ones, or whatever you call yourselves. For I care not. But I will see him, or else I will sit in your palace like a blight. I will not leave and I will not tire until you agree to see me and to meet my terms."

Behind their fans, the ladies of fairyland looked yet paler, their gazes long with fright, and a messenger, a puck, one of the humble woodland fairies, was sent to summon his majesty.

That was how King Albric sat with the stranger and heard from his rude human lips the conditions and terms laid by his race onto the fair ones, the shimmering ones, the blessed ones—the ones who'd married the land in her youth and espoused her in her splendor, those who harnessed her magic to their purposes, and looked over creation with a benevolent eye.

He was not old, not as his race reckoned it, but he remembered when ice covered all of the land, making it glitter like a jewel and sparkle with magic. Before human kind, before fire, before the poisoned iron that ripped open the womb of the land and poisoned it ever after for magic and fairy kind alike.

Then the humans had come, from the south—bringing plow and fire and war-like ways, and hastily built houses, and temples to their barbarous gods. They had no magic and they warred all the time—against the remaining ice; against each other; against their gods and against the world. Ephemeral creatures, the king had thought them. Passing. They meant nothing. They would be nothing. Nothing would mark their passage and after they vanished again, their iron would go with them and fairykind would resume its play upon the face of the Earth.

Instead they'd grown, populous and fractious, and now one of them was here. Right here, in the palace of fairykind, unafraid and demanding.

Albric came into the room, wearing his cloak woven of dark, starlit nights, his tunic spun from silken butterfly wings, and met the human who seemed to Albric to be more solid, more whole, made of finer stuff than Albric himself.

And when they sat together, the human commanded, as though he were the victor of some war that Albric wasn't aware of fighting, "You will leave all these lands to us," the human said. "every fertile field. Every pasture meadow. You do not use them and you do not need them. You can retreat to the desolate places, the rocky lands that will not admit plow. You may haunt the lakes and the dreary forests, but you will not," the human said, looking at the king with his icy blue eyes full of disdain, "you will not take woman or babe. You will no more replace our children with your mewling changelings, nor will you make it so that buildings collapse unless a blood offering is made."

Albric had opened his mouth to protest that he'd never done any of those things. Aye, women or babes his court might have taken, now and then, but only for love of the lost and abandoned or to prevent their dying a cruel death in the dark woods. But changelings and human sacrifice—or blood sacrifice of any kind—that he'd never demanded, never thought of. His kind lived of the natural-born grains, the natural-grown berries, the naturally spun magic of the world. The *others*, the dark ones, those ruled by the Queen of the North, might demand more even of the ephemeral, iron-bearing humans. His kind did not.

But then he realized protest would be for naught. The humans knew only two kinds: human and not; iron and magic; elf and not elf. They would not be swayed nor consider that within a kind many kinds subsisted, nor would they temper their hatred for one for the sake of the other.

Instead, he'd thought he needed to gain time. He needed to find if this man were a mere messenger or what his power was to deal with the king. And if he had the authority, Albric must sway him. "And who be you," he asked. "Who would dictate to the king of magic?"

The man smiled and looked up, unbowed. "I am Cedric," he said. "Ruler of my tribe and I speak for all humans who, after us, might live in this land."

"And what gives you that right? How can you dictate to us? What will you do if we throw you out and ignore your demands?" the king asked, and tried to ignore the feeling that came from the stranger, and the way the light dimmed and bent around him, as if he were not a mere ephemeral human, but something else, something new.

"Ah. I dictate by right of plow and iron. If you throw me out, I will come back."

"With warriors?"

"With plows," Cedric said, and smiled. "And I will tear your palace, and I will plow your land. And

I will sow it with iron-laced salt, so that your kind will be no more of this world nor of the next, but captured in between, caught and bent, and unable to live or die while you watch my kind thrive and grow and forget you."

"And how did you find our palace?" the king asked. Never before had a human been able to find it unless the elvenfolk wished him to, much less to come into it with iron spurs and ill intent.

But Cedric only smiled and bowed. And his blue eyes reminded the king of something he wished he could forget. His features reminded the king of his own, glimpsed before his mirror every morning. Albric thought and he thought but he couldn't remember any indiscretion with a human maiden that could have created this fierce foe.

Instead he turned his mind to more important thoughts—how to defend from the attack, how to thwart the enemy, how to get Cedric-who-could-violate-fairyland subdued or bought, or silenced. And then, now awake to the danger, Albric would think of a way to turn the humans from the door, to tame them, or to slow them. If they weren't going to die off, they'd need to be contained, so fairykind's magic would not die, so elves could survive.

It was the humans or the fey.

"Well, Cedric, I lay it upon you, while I think over your message, that you stay with us and share with us bed and board and ease. That you listen to our music, that you taste of our mead, that you be our friend before you are our foe."

He expected refusal or else confusion. Surely the man knew—by now they all knew—that tasting the mead of fairyland meant the mortal would leave no more. And if this Cedric who could walk in fairy and bring iron to the hallowed precincts were vanished, surely the other humans would take fright.

But Cedric only smiled and said, "Three days you have to think. Three days, three nights and not one more, oh king of those who ride the winds and dance at secret revels in the heart of moonlit nights. Three days I'll bide with you and drink your mead and taste your delights. Three days and not one night more."

In his room, the king called forth Peaseblossom, his attendant nymph and swift rider of the currents of air. Writing fast, in words of light upon a sheet made of dragonfly wings, he sketched a message to an ancient foe. *We are besieged, my lady,* he wrote. *By a human named Cedric, who commands a band of men bearing iron and fire, and who threatens to destroy and desecrate this our abode, unless we agree to be banished to the lands his people neither want nor need. Unless we agree to give up our magic dwelling upon this blessed land and retreat to desolation, he will make us less than ghosts and more than dead. I ask your help. Your people ever were better at fighting and destroying, at cursing and blighting. Now we need your magic to fight this man—to find how he can see our palace and violate our presence with iron. To find how we can make him and his people go away and torment us no more.*

He sealed the missive with his magic ring and

handed it to Peaseblossom, who looked back at him with wide, frightened eyes, and who seemed almost as colorless as the winds she rode.

"Take this," he said. "Over the bridge of air to the Queen of the Northern Lights. And tell her that it is urgent and not something she should delay, no matter what her resentment against me."

Peaseblossom had bowed, her fright glimmering forth from her like a frosty current, and then she vanished, running, towards the invisible bridge that extended between the bright court and the dark.

That he should have to ask *her* help rankled Albric, but nothing could be done on that score. If, for once, the queen saw the urgency and acted to save his people and hers all would be well. Could she doubt that, after doom befell him, his own fate would befall her?

He had a memory of eyes of glimmering ice, of dark, glimmering hair, of her red, red lips so soft, so warm, so yielding, and of her face beautiful like the visions of angels that men tried to sculpt out of clay. He remembered her touch and her smell and the perfume of her skin.

And he remembered he hated her.

The Lady Breena, fair as the sunlight, accounted prettiest in King Albric's court, looked at her lord in disbelief. "The human, my lord?" she asked, as though he'd ordered her to lay with a rough woodland creature and enjoy it. "You wish me to sit with the human at a feast?"

"Aye," King Albric said, sad to see fear and dismay

in the lady's eyes, but not knowing what else to do. Bed and board and rest the man had accepted, and until and unless the queen of the North came to the rescue, bed and board and rest were the best weapons the king could deploy against him.

The blessed court had neither army nor terrible magical curses with which to lay waste to the enemy. It had nothing but the weapons of delight with which to enslave the man and make him a willing thrall to fairyland. "Aye, you'll sit with him, and feed him honeyed cakes, and for him you'll play your enchanted harp, for you're as fair and bright as any in my kingdom, and your music is as captivating as the whispering rivers in spring, and your sweets more delightful than mortal kind can make. You'll play and you'll sing, and you will make him love you."

"But sire!" she said. Looking up, she met only the ice and command he willed into his eyes. She bowed her head, and knelt at his feet, and cried but did not beg. And rose, and left, to fulfill his command.

Cedric did not wear his spurs, the king noticed, when he came into the banquet hall. And in Albric's heart a flame of hope was kindled. For now the light didn't dim around the man and the bright palace of fairykind sparkled with its wonted brilliance, enough to dazzle mere mortal eyes unprotected by iron.

The flying fairies thronged the air, spreading flower petals like rain. The floral scent, as the petals were crushed underfoot, filled the hall with the sweetness of spring and the heady joy of a summer day.

Beneath this fragrant fall, lords and ladies of fairy-kind, dressed in their best, sat or reclined, attended by pucks, who refilled their shiny crystal glasses with mead-sweet and brought candied cakes to their idle lips.

Cedric reclined, and tasted of the mead and ate of the cakes, and yet his mind remained unbowed and his eyes clear, looking around as though to say that among his rude people he'd seen better and more magnificent sights.

And the king, sighing, saw that Breena's sacrifice would be necessary. He stood and he clapped his hands, and she came forth, from where she'd waited.

She was fair, oh so fair. For her five elven poets had spun a hundred delicate poems so beautiful that humans would die to hear them. Her face was as perfect as a jewel chiseled and polished in every detail, her emerald eyes shone with the green of new leaf, the joy of new life. And her skin was clear and bright as the petal of the rose before it's fully unfolded to the sun. She wore white, which made her cream and pink skin look yet fairer and her glossy gold and red hair yet brighter. As she stepped in, graceful in her white slippers, and approached Cedric with a bright smile, his mouth dropped open, and his cup fell, quite unnoticed, from his nerveless fingers.

Cedric rose and bowed to her, and he drank his mead by her side.

But late that night, when the high lords of fairy-kind had drunk themselves into stupor, his eyes remained clear, his mind remained unfettered, and when the king took his leave, Cedric said, "You have two days, Albric. And not one night more."

"Where is Peaseblossom?" the king asked the puck, who helped him remove his robes and don his night garment woven of spider-silk. "And is there an answer from the North?"

But the puck only bowed and spoke, with the voice of his kind which was rather like the rubbing of dry twigs or the grating of rocks, "No, sire. Peaseblossom has not come again, over the bridge of air, and there is no answer from the North."

The next day the court rode amid the meadows and fields, disporting themselves upon their fairy steeds. Three people stayed behind in the glittering palace: the human, who remained locked within his chambers as though fearful of trickery or attack, should he step out; the king, heavy with his thoughts, not knowing which would be worse, to ally with his northern foe or to be lost forever; and Lady Breena, who mourned her fate.

For years she had been as fair as moonlight, as joyous as laughter. If she thought to marry—as she supposed it must one day come—she'd expected to be picked by Albric himself. For who else would he choose from his dazzling court but the most beautiful?

But the years had passed and the king hadn't

asked. Indeed, he seemed to have no thought to creating that which after him must hold the throne, for though fairykind lived long, they were not immortal. But the king seemed content to watch season and year, decade and century, pass by with no thought of love, no delight in children, no desire for her.

Sometime, long ago, she remembered hearing he'd crossed the bridge of air, night by night every night, to sup with the queen of the bright northern lights. But that had been another time, and a sort of madness—for who could marry day to night or the gentle magic of the blessed to that of the night fairies? Who could join dark and light? Surely such a union would tear asunder and fracture the world caught in between the two lovers. No children could be born of such a match, or else, any born would die, in the instant of breath, the moment of first feeling magic. For how would their magic be? Neither dark nor light, neither blessing nor curse.

And so Breena had waited, and she'd dreamed, and spun a trousseau as bright as butterfly wings, as soft as the feathers of birds in the spring. She'd learned to play, and learned to sing against the day when Albric would make her his queen.

But now he ordered her, with force and with magic, to expend her enchantment on a mere, rough human? He would sacrifice her to save his kingdom.

All that was soft in her heart turned to ice toward him, ice as bright and glittering as the blue eyes of the man named Cedric.

*   *   *

That night, the hall shone brighter than ever. The captured light of a thousand stars was scattered across the glittering crystal ceiling that reflected the velvet-dark sky above.

When the Lady Breena entered, in her dress of the purest blue, the human, Cedric, rose and bowed to her, and bent low upon her hand to kiss it.

Then he stood by her, right near, as she played music upon her silver harp.

She played melodies that were as old as the ice that had one day covered all of the land that men had now taken. And as she played, frosty fingers seemed to touch the faces of those who listened—to caress hair, to kiss lips, to tease like a lover and play like a child, among the grand assembled company.

And Cedric stood and stared, and listened, and hung upon every note. When she sang the desolate songs of long-lost paradise before humankind, her voice as silvery as the notes of the harp, he shaped his mouth in wonder, and his eyes opened wide, as though he thought he'd been transported to paradise, and there was nothing more wanting in his life.

Albric thought that this time fairyland had caught the human. Now would Cedric stay, in thrall of Lady Breena, a shadow in the court, spending his all too brief mortality upon worshiping her in vain.

Yet when the singing was done and the court retired, the human told the king in unbowed tones, "You have one day and one night, king. And not a night more."

*   *   *

The puck, or another puck, as they all looked alike, and were all pieces of the same creature, part woodland and part fairyland, wood and bone together, looked at King Albric with the baleful look of a puppy who knows the master is displeased. "Nor has Peaseblossom returned," he said. "Nor is there, yet, a message from the North."

And the king paced, half the night long, wondering what the queen could mean, and why she would let both their peoples suffer for his old sins.

Not that it had been a sin, he thought, to leave her when he'd found that she'd meant to use her dark magic to bind him to her—no, the sin had been to fall in love with her. Oh, how he missed her midnight hair, her snow white skin, her red, red lips, and her body as passionate as his kind could never be.

And her heart full of treason.

But even traitors must know when they could not survive by themselves, without those they would abandon and watch die.

"Send Aster after Peaseblossom then," he said. "For I must have an answer from the North."

During the day, the king waited and thought. Like a woodland creature caught in a trap, he saw no way out but that which would cost him a part of himself. He rose every time he heard the sound of hooves. It wasn't like the queen of the North to travel by day, but his emissaries might.

She's been massing her armies, he thought. *She's been ranging her soldiers. The terrible Orcs, the fearsome redcaps shall soon come and descend upon Cedric's people and render all of it moot. They shall destroy and maim and so fill the humans with unreasoning fear that mortals will never again trespass upon the halls of fairykind or the glades sacred to our magic. The ones who survive will be fearful and small, and pour out a libation of milk every morning, to the kind elves who allow them to live. And no more will they build, and no more will they plow, and iron shall be banned forever more.*

He paced and thought, and he thought and he paced, and he twisted his hands together in distress, while his attendants stood by and watched, quiet and fearful. And part of him dreaded having asked her for help, for once she came, how was he to stop her? Her magic was cruel where his magic was kind, her magic killed while his magic protected, and when they were together there was no safe place to be and nowhere anything mortal or fragile could hide.

And what would the queen think of Lady Breena, whom Albric had thought to marry, someday soon, when he no longer dreamed of the queen's dark hair, of her skin of snow, of her red, red lips and that body that was like the heat of day, like the force of the sea, like the joy of life?

He thought and he paced, but there was no certainty and there was no hope, and there was no answer from the North.

Lady Breena would have to lie with the man named Cedric and endure his rough human nature and his crude natural ways.

*　　*　　*

Tonight the walls themselves shone as though sun-rays were captive within them. A million butterflies fluttered and sparkled in the air, filling the hall with the giddy joy of nature unbridled. All the ladies and lords of fairykind had dressed in their brightest, adorned with colored feathers and sparkling jewels.

The bards sat on gilded chairs at one end of the salon, clutching their golden harps and waiting for the Lady Breena, who now came walking into the salon, dressed all in red.

Red like the firelight was her dress, red like the spring robin her cloak. Her hair was caught up in a ruby sparkling with something like flames. And her feet were encased in shoes embroidered in thread that shone like more rubies.

Cedric rose and went to her. Beneath the glittering ceiling, amid the glittering pillars of the salon they danced. They spun like whirlwinds, in the arms of the music, perfect together, each step exact.

Her body molded to his, his steps assured, hers echoing them exactly as they flitted and flew, now fast, now slow, now sad, now joyful—a reel and a turn, a career and a winding down. In each other's arms, they sparkled and smiled.

And Albric thought perhaps this would do it. Per-haps no more would be required.

But after the dance, when even the glittering elves of the court of the blessed were tired and broken by their exertions and joys, yet Cedric remained un-bowed, untired.

He bent and whispered upon Lady Breena's ear, and then, with her by the hand, he approached the king. "Remember, O king. This is the last night of three. Tomorrow at dawn I will have your answer for what it's to be—exile or the plow, restriction or fading. You have this night to think. And not a night more."

Her sighs and his laughter, and the sound of kisses echoed through the palace and pierced through the magical walls. They branded like iron and they cut like a blade.

"Send Rosepetal," the king screamed, above the sound of sighs and the echo of kisses, his throat tight with grief, his eyes blurring with unshed tears. "Upon the bridge of air, to the Queen of the North, to beg for an answer, to beg for rescue, to tell her I'm hers to do as she please, to tell her that she can have blood and pain and fire and grief, but not to leave me waiting for an answer from the North."

And the servants cowed, and paled and hid, but Rosepetal sprang upon the bridge of air, running like the wind, determined to bring them succor from the North.

Morning dawned fair, the sky like the skin of a newly ripe peach and a little breeze bringing with it the chill of dew and the tinge of charcoal from the human village.

The king rose, as though he'd been long dead, dead and buried and gone. How fortunate they were, his father and forefather and those before him, who had not had to face a young crude race, full of harsh devices. They were dead and past suffering, one with the wind, and the glittering air, and the hope of spring—they knew nothing of the iron that poisoned the land and made its fruits inedible; they knew nothing of men who hated fairykind.

In the looking glass made of a perfect sheet of primeval ice, the king saw himself. His hair had turned white, his beard yet whiter, his eyes as light as the fog that clouds winter nights. His hands trembled and his lips sagged. He'd lost his way and nigh lost his wits.

The servants who'd looked after him for the millennia of his untroubled reign, now cowered in shadows and looked on him as though he might at any moment order them to destroy or kill or maim.

But his madness was past. There was yet no answer from the North. The Queen of the Dark, the Lady of Shadows thought she'd live on well and long with him. She had laughed at his messages. She'd scorned his desperate submission.

Only one thought remained, only one spark kept the king's heart from feeling as cold and dark as winter with no hope of spring—and that was that the Lady Breena's love had conquered the dark savage heart of the man named Cedric.

She woke in his bed, his arms around her, his heart beating fast, his lips searching her.

"Come with me," he said after he kissed her. "Come and be my wife."

For a moment she stared at him, her mind caught in his eyes like blue ice, his features so rough. She'd thought she'd hate him. She'd thought that to touch him would be to betray fairyland and her immortal kind. She'd thought she'd forsaken her ambition; she'd never be queen.

Now on waking it was as though she had been asleep, not just all the night, but her whole life long. The dreams and the thoughts of her life in the palace, the spinning of a trousseau, the playing on the harp, the songs and the waiting, how long had it been?

Centuries, millennia, and yet this morning, she was a maiden, young and fair and new, just coming alive, just learning of the world.

When Cedric touched her all of fairyland looked like a bubble, spun for a moment on the surface of the water and just as quickly lost.

"It will be hard," he said. "I won't lie to you. My people and yours are not alike. Your people are light, and air and wind; mine are the Earth and all that grows on it. We use iron to till, and we herd rough beasts. We live on coarse stuff, as coarse as we are." He looked at her, intent but kind. "And yet inside, you will always remember, being a lady of the air, a princess of light; and many a time you'll wonder why you left, for the hut of a farmer, the pain of birth, and the cry of the babes. I won't lie to you. I want you to come willing and knowing, and be my farm wife, and remain by my side, till our lives are told and the earth claims us."

She knew it was true—she'd heard them cry, the women who lived with men like Cedric and bore their babes and spun their clothes and wore themselves out in tending the fields. She'd seen them shiver in winter and swelter in summer.

But ah, she'd heard them sing in the spring, of love most strong, of two souls like one. She'd seen them smile at babes, newborn, and she'd watched them kiss their rough farming men. And until now, she'd never understood the joy in their eyes, the spring in their step.

"I will come with you," she said. "Wherever you go. But won't fairykind die in that world of yours?"

He'd laughed loud, and shaken his head, swift. "Not if you wish to live, for you must know that every human inside knows what it is like to live forever and to be magic and air. It is all in the mind, caught in the rough body, and if you find your joy in between, then you'll be one of us, and you'll belong with me."

"My lord, my lord, wake and attend."

The king woke and turned, in surprise and fear, to face his servants standing beside him: Rosepetal and Aster and fair Peaseblossom.

He sat up, his covers clutched to him. "Is it here at last? Has it finally come? Has the queen of the North sent her armies and bands, the horrible Orcs and the blood-mad redcaps? Will she wreak vengeance? Will she come and save us?"

Their faces were grave; they did not encourage

him to hope for much. But they had a letter, frail parchment, well folded.

Rosepetal knelt and handed it to the king with her head bowed, her eyes looking down. Was that a tear glittering in her softly shining eyes? Was the news so bad? Was all lost, then?

The king didn't know; he could not see. He broke open the seal of the dark queen.

Before he could read, a puck came in. "Milord, I have a message, from the Lord Cedric. He has dressed in his clothes, he's put on his spurs, he says he is leaving as fast as he can, and he needs your answer, or it shall be the plow, because he said, my lord, you get not a moment more."

"He leaves so soon? He wakes so bold? The fair Lady Breena didn't touch his heart, didn't bend his mind?"

"The Lady Breena is dressed and stands with him, ready to go to his world, to become his kin."

"But the iron in his spurs, the iron in heart?"

"She chooses to be human," the puck said. "Till death them part."

"I will come to him," the king said. "As soon as may be." And he opened the message from the dark northern queen.

His tears shone, between eyes and paper, and obscured his vision, and made it hard to read. Through them he could see no more than a few words, glittering at him in her slanted hand: *powerless* was one and *already surrendered* and *all lost* and *our sin* and *will scarce remember.*

He blinked. Hot tears ran down his face to his beard. And his sight became sharper and the words clear.

Albric, recall, it began without fear. *how you left me, it must be now a good thousand years. Oh, it wasn't our fault; we could not have lived forever together. Your magic and mine could never exist in the same palace, in the same people. Our brief, pleasing sin was loving the opposite. The day longs for night, but it should never meet. And night craves the day, with its light and its heat, but one destroys the other wherever they touch.*

Remember you left me to save all of you. And you left me behind to mourn all I'd lost.

But you left behind two slivers of you, two sparks of the day growing in the night. A boy and a girl, neither light nor dark. They could not live here, and they could not live there. They were left at the door of a poor human hunter, as humans used to be, all fear and all silence. I thought them gone, I thought them lost. I thought no more of them, nor of you, nor of love. I enjoyed my hunt, I craved my pleasure.

But they lived, they grew, and they married humans, and their children, bright, had more children still, till now every human born of clay and blood and of iron and fire carries within a spark of our magic, a hint of our love, a bit of the day, a shadow of night, the fire and the ice that should never meet unless they die. And yet they live, and yet they grow.

And it is our love that gives them force, which feeds their power that makes them create, that tames the iron, that helps them plow, that gives them the courage to challenge us both.

I've already surrendered, I've already agreed, to come no nearer men than to touch their dreams.

Farewell, my beloved. From now on we'll be like shadows that pass in the world of men, like fleeting illusions dancing on the wind. Our children will live, our children will grow, till they cover the world with their fire and their plow—a touch of night, a touch of day, a hint of enchantment and a taste for blood.

Ah, Albric, beloved, we've grown a fine brood.

GOODHOUSE KEEPING

Mary Robinette Kowal

The door to Grace's home office was open, the computer screen glowing with welcome. Next to the keyboard, a cup of tea steamed. She looked out of the corners of her eyes hoping to spy her house brownie, but Thistlekin was as elusive as always. When she sat, her cat Mallory leaped into her lap and settled down to watch. Stroking his head absently, Grace cleared the papers off a cushion on the desk for her client.

The visiting brownie stood uncertainly next to the chair. His capped head came barely to her knees and his large ears drooped with exhaustion. From the hole in his brown knee britches to the stain on his vest, he looked as though he had traveled far.

"Brownie, you may sit here if you'd like."

The wizened creature bowed and leaped up, flipping to land on the cushion. He sat with his legs crossed and his broom laid across his lap. She saw him eye the tea, but did not offer him any, lest he feel obligated to serve. She had too many houseless Folk in residence already. For many of them, she was the last place of refuge in the mortal world. One might say it was part of her job as the foster daughter of the Faerie Queen.

Grace picked up the cup and sipped it. Chamomile. She smiled; Brownie Thistlekin always knew when she needed soothing. She opened her database. "Now. We'll start with your house name."

"Briarwood House, Granny."

Grace grimaced; as her fortieth birthday loomed, the honorary title had begun to sound unpleasantly old. She typed in the house name and pulled up the file. "That's a very good house. Their family has kept the ways as long as they've had a hearth." But like many houses, the current goodwife kept the ways out of a sense of tradition, not because she believed in the housefolk. "And how are you called?"

The brownie stood up and leaned close to her. He smelled of dry leaves and embers. She bent her head, so he could whisper, "Brownie Nutkin."

"The Nutkins of Briarwood House." Grace smiled at him. "I know your papa. How is he?"

Brownie Nutkin the Younger twisted the broom. "Dog got him."

She drew in a breath and pulled back, as if recoiling would protect her from the news. "I'm so sorry."

He bit his lip, and worried the straws in his broom. Brownies were born old, their faces full of fissures from the womb, but this brownie looked as if grief would split his face in two. She suddenly realized that Brownie Nutkin was far younger than she had first thought; she had placed his father at Briarwood House only nine years ago.

Brownie Nutkin the Younger was too young to begin courting, so why was he here? "You can't be here for a placement."

"You can find us a new hearth and home."

"For your whole family?"

He shook his head, ears flapping. "All the Folk want to go. After the goodwife's man came. His nasty dog hunts us." He tipped his tiny head back and wailed. "It got Papa."

Grace yearned to pick up Brownie Nutkin and cradle him like the hurt child he was, but brownies were wild things. Her foster mother had taught her that. She let him grieve and listened to the quiet rustling as the Folk in her house came to bear witness.

When he finished keening and wiped his long nose on his sleeve, Grace asked. "Is this why you want a new placement?"

He nodded.

A thought occurred to her—the Folk were very particular about titles. "Goodwife's man . . . They aren't married? If he isn't her Goodman, why hasn't your family driven him out?"

"Papa tried."

"Oh."

"Unsanctified. Nasty man. Hits the goodwife."

Grace clenched her teeth.

The brownie hesitated. "She leaves the cream out. We don't touch it. Dog is waiting."

Grace chewed on her lower lip. She did not like to think of Briarwood House becoming bare and barren. She scanned the file again. Three brownie families, a hobgoblin, and five sprites called Briarwood House their hearth and home. Where could she send them all?

"Does your mama know you're here?"

Brownie Nutkin fidgeted on his cushion. "No."

He could not be more than five years old. A movement in the corner caught her eye. Brownie Thistlekin winked at her and nodded once. She sighed. "The Folk of this house will shelter you tonight. I will send Robin Redbreast to tell your mama where you are."

Brownie Nutkin stood, bowed to her, and jumped off the desk. Brownie Thistlekin took his hand and led him across the room.

And they were gone, into the byways and highways of the Folk.

Grace dumped Mallory off her lap and went to the window. Opening it, she let the October air cool her face with a brief illusion of peace. She whistled once, then waited. The moon silvered the grass and caught in the tree branches, turning them into filigree. A quick shape flew over the lawn and Robin Redbreast landed on her windowsill. His eye was dull with sleep and he gave one short peep to question her.

"I'm sorry, dear. I need you to go to Briarwood

House and tell Mama Nutkin that her son is with me."

He cocked his head to the side and listened as she told him about Brownie Nutkin's visit. When she was finished, he bobbed his head and flipped his tail, then with a flutter of wings he flew away through the night.

Grace left the window open for his return.

She went to the computer and opened a Web browser. She first stopped at the forum she maintained, *Granny's Site of Faerie Folk*. She hated the new-agey type of crowd it sometimes drew, but she had not found a better way to attract the right type of person. She scanned through the posts to see if anyone new had mentioned wanting to host Folk in their home.

Some people stumbled onto the Board and began following the old ways as a lark, then logged on to talk about the amazing "coincidences," like washed dishes or folded laundry. Others knew the Folk were real and paid more than lip service to their deeds.

One new post was from a woman in New York City who wished she could have brownies or sprites in her apartment. That was barely large enough for one brownie family and not enough room for all the Folk of Briarwood House. Grace shook her head. There were too few homes. Most of the other Fair Folk had retreated, but housefolk needed homes. Too many of them were refugees in a world that had little room for magic. Still, she would ask the auntie in the NYC district to send her Robin Redbreast to investigate. Maybe she could place at least one of the families staying with her.

Her network of aunties had taken the place of the village wise women whose province the hearth and home had been for thousands of years. Most of them were successful career women, a few were stay-at-home-moms, but they had all proven their dedication to keeping the Folk safe in the world. They provided the contact point for the goodwives to make certain that each was maintaining a healthy habitat for the housefolk. Grace had taken the titles from folklore, because it gave the housefolk something they understood, but in truth the aunties' and goodwives' roles were more akin to a park warden watching the habitat of a spotted owl.

The Folk's habitat had shrunken steadily since the industrial age began. Not for mystical reasons, but simply because housefolk were poisoned with the rats or run over in the street with squirrels. As humans made the houses air- and water-tight, the housefolk could not leave the homes they lived in, so families could not marry and dwindled, then died. The population had dropped precipitously over the last century. Though Grace's efforts had slowed the number of senseless deaths, it seemed as if every other robin brought news of a housefolk killed simply by trying to live in the modern world.

A flurry of wings called her away from the computer. Robin Redbreast stood in the window, his body taut with anxiety. He trilled and danced from one leg to the next. Grace stiffened as he spoke of danger.

A bogeyman.

This was worse than the abusive man she had feared. She wanted to grab her scrying bowl and call the Faerie Queen, but that was a child's fear speaking. Keeping the housefolk safe was her job.

She got a bowl of cream from the kitchen and carried it into the living room. Old clear grain fir paneling lined the walls. Her grandfather had built the house using wood from the property and the warmth of his touch was still visible in the details.

Mallory eyed the bowl of cream when she set it on the brick hearth, but he knew it was not for him. Grace stirred up the coals of the fire with a brass poker—she'd had to sell the iron tools her parents had kept by the fireplace. Iron and faeries didn't mix.

The embers glowed red and sparked into the air. She opened a box on the mantel and pulled out four chestnuts.

Grace rolled the chestnuts between her palms and stared at the fire. "Brownie, hobgoblin, sprite, and gnome. Folk of Woodthrush House attend me." She tossed the chestnuts into the flames.

She settled in one of the wingback chairs facing the fireplace and waited. A chestnut cracked and she heard the gentle rustling of autumn leaves. She did not turn her head, but saw the brownies of her house sidle into the room and sample the cream. Each nut-brown face, wrinkled as a dried apple, bobbed to her and she nodded back. Mama Seedkin had her nursing infant with her. She had come as a refugee to Wood-thrush House a fortnight ago, heavy with pregnancy and the only brownie to escape the demolition of her family's homestead. Grace had not seen her since she had given birth. The baby's face was as wrinkled as his mother's; he sputtered when she held the bowl of cream to his lips for a symbolic taste.

Out of the corner of her eye she saw Brownie Thistlekin, the head of the family who truly be-longed to Woodthrush House, slip in and take his place among the refugees. Brownie Nutkin clung to him like a burr. Granny Winesap, as irritable an old lady as faerie had ever produced, came close behind, fussing over the young brownie as if she were his real granny.

Another chestnut popped like a gunshot, and the sparks flew up the chimney. The embers stirred themselves, glowing red in the flames. Three twisted hawthorn figures, with eyes of glowing coal, stepped out of the fire, one after the other.

The cream hissed when the eldest of the three hobgoblins raised the bowl to his lips to taste. He passed it to the other two before settling on the hearth.

The next two chestnuts popped one after the other. In their echo, she heard a patter of feet and smelled new-cut grass. The sprites ran sideways down her walls and stood like gossamer spiderwebs defying gravity. The gnomes tumbled in through the open window, tracking dirt and clippings across the floor. Their round, plump faces were upturned with curiosity.

She waited for them to sample the cream.

"Blessings on you, my dear Folk." It broke her heart to see so many crowded into one home, but she loved them all. "I have distressing news. Will you pay heed?"

They murmured assent, their voices no louder than crickets.

"Robin Redbreast has the tale."

The company cleared a circle in their midst. The bird flew into the center and cocked his head, eyes bright with knowledge. He began to dance. His voice trilled and chirped, telling the tale. In the pattern of his wings and the flip of his tail, he painted Briarwood House.

Robin Redbreast seeks the Folk of Briarwood House. He seeks, he searches, he hop, hop, hops through the attic. In the nooks, in the crannies of the house, he looks. The Folk of Briarwood House are hiding in the nooks and the crannies of the house.

Why do they hide? They hide from the hound. The hound, terrible and fierce, hunts them. It hunts, it hunts. Hunting, it crushes them. The hound, terrible and fierce, hunts the Folk and they hide.

Who is the Hound's master? The Folk of Briarwood House hide their faces. Terrible, terrible. The bogeyman rises. He sets snares for the Folk. They go still as stone. The bogeyman strikes the goodwife and sets snares for the Folk.

They hide. They hide. They hide from the darkness.

Robin Redbreast ended his dance and the Folk in Grace's home shuddered and whispered to each other. It had been years since a bogeyman last came into the mortal world. The Faerie Queen had driven them out of her realm before Grace's great-grandparents had been born, but some still lurked in the lands of the Unseelie Court. The rebel fae who made up the court kept the bogeymen as gruesome pets.

She let the Folk collect themselves. Their voices buzzed in conversation, the youngest demanding to know what a bogeyman was; the elders trying to comfort the ones old enough to understand.

A bogeyman meant death for the Folk. He would suck the light and life from hearth and home. He would hunt down each of the Folk in the home before killing the goodwife. Then he would slip into the skin of another unwary mortal man and seek a new hearth and home.

When Grace drew breath to speak, the Folk all hushed. "I need your help to aid Folk whose hearth and home are in jeopardy. Will you?"

Brownie Thistlekin stood and bowed. "Granny, you need not ask us. We are yours."

"Wait now." Granny Winesap thumped her broom on the floor. "I'd like as any for that spleeny flap-mouthed haggard to know what-for from us, but we ain't any sort of match for a bogeyman."

"I grant you that, Granny Winesap." Grace leaned forward, feeling like the Faerie Queen on her throne. "The bogeyman is too massy for such as we to deal with. He needs hard steel to put him down and cold iron to lock him tight." Neither of which her Folk could handle without life-threatening burns. "You are but new come to our home. We use the same things which drive you from hearth and home to drive bogeymen out—the dying beliefs, the mortal eyes which see only what they will, not that which is true."

"How do we do that, Granny?" Brownie Nutkin asked.

The child was so eager it pained her. But she had promised his mother she would look after him and Grace would not chance Brownie Nutkin near a bo-geyman. "Well . . . as the eldest male brownie of your house, I need you to stay here on guard. You need to be ready for your mama and sister."

"And what of the rest of us?" Granny Winesap asked.

"We put on a play. Mortals don't hear a hobgoblin crack, they hear a gunshot. And when they hear a gunshot, what do mortals do?"

The Folk stared at her, rapt. The newer refugees glanced around to see if they could get a hint from the folk who had lived with her longest. The ways of mortals were strange to them.

But Grace knew what it meant to be mortal; that was why the Faerie Queen had taken her as an infant and raised her. Grace had only been returned to her parents so she could serve as a liaison between the mortal world and faerie. She knew the ways and means of the human courts now—the courts of law—and she used those to keep her Folk safe. "They call the police who will come with their hard steel and cold iron. They will put the bogeyman down for us."

The dawn air had chilled Grace's skin when she began her jog, but now her velour jogging suit seemed over-warm. She turned another corner in the subdivision, watching the trees as she went. She wore a small hip bag which banged against her with every step. Anxiety had been her companion since the meeting with the housefolk last night. She reached for the silent iPod she wore as part of the uniform of joggers. Grace had left it off so she could focus while she waited for the housefolk to move into place, but the idea of distraction tempted her.

Robin Redbreast flew in front of her and circled, chirping. The housefolk were in position. Grace sighed and turned her path toward Briarwood House.

The house stood behind its trees as if it were disdainful of the subdivision which had grown up around it. A long oak-lined drive separated Briarwood House from the street. Grace jogged down the sidewalk at the edge of the property. She could not set foot on the soil of Briarwood House without alerting the bogeyman of her presence. The time for that had not yet come.

In an elm, Robin Redbreast waited for her.

Grace paused next to his tree and pretended to stretch, until rustling told her that Mallory had arrived. Mama Nutkin rode upon the cat, her wrinkled face bleached to the color of bone with grief.

"My condolences, Mama Nutkin, on your loss."

"Eh, he was a good one, he was. My family has always appreciated you for sending him here." She rubbed her long nose, sniffing. "He was a good one."

"Your son is also good. He was most adamant that he was not a child and should have been allowed to come." Grace smiled at the memory of Brownie Nutkin's protests. "I have left him in the care of Mama Seedkin while we tend to business here."

The wrinkles climbed into a smile. "I bless thee for looking out for him. He'll get a hiding when he comes home for the trouble he gave to you."

Grace shook her head as she slipped into the formal speech of her childhood as a changeling in the Faerie Queen's court. "The trouble comes not from him."

Mama Nutkin lost her smile. "That I know."

"The Folk of Woodthrush House are here to aid you. The laws which prevent you from acting against a guest of your goodwife do not hinder us."

"'Tis no guest! A bogeyman is in our hearth and home."

"I know this, too well."

"My boy, he don't know a bogeyman from any other angry man. But that bogey, he kept going on about how he'd track us all down, long as we were in the house. And my boy, he got it fixed in his head that we had to get out of the house." She shook her head, ears flapping. "I raised him better than to abandon hearth and home, but losing his da shook him up fierce-like."

"I hope that after this morning's work, your hearth and home will be safe." Grace glanced once more at the house. Its facade presented a blind innocence to the street. "When you hear a hobgoblin's crack, I pray you, lock the goodwife in the attic."

"Play a prank on the goodwife? But she ain't never done nothing to the Folk. Always been wonderful, she has."

"I am certain of it. We want to keep the goodwife safe while we drive the bogeyman out of your hearth and home."

"Well then, Granny, we will do as you say."

"Then all will be well." Grace pulled a small note from her hip pack and held it down so Mama Nutkin could take it. "Will you give this to the goodwife when you have her safe and sound?"

Mama Nutkin's eyes grew as large as copper pennies. "Give it in the broad light of day? But how without showing myself?"

"You may have to do just that. We need her to understand what it is she brought into her home. If she does not take care, the bogeyman could return and all our effort would be for naught."

"Aye. I'll do as you say. It won't take long."

"With luck, the bogeyman will be gone before the hour has passed." She rubbed Mallory on the head. "Return her safely." The cat blinked once in agreement and sauntered into the tall grass. "Mallory."

He looked over his shoulder at her.

"Remember the hound." As if to say that he feared nothing, he yawned, then melted into the bushes, carrying Mama Nutkin with him.

Robin Redbreast cocked his head, bright eyes shining, asking her if it were time.

Grace waited until she thought they must be back and then signaled him. He took wing toward the house and circled it once, flying low so he passed the ground floor windows.

A gunshot shattered the dawn stillness.

Though she had expected the hobgoblins' explosion, Grace flinched as the sound split the morning. She pulled her cellphone from her pocket and dialed 911. As she waited for the operator, her breath felt fevered.

When the tinny voice answered the phone, Grace's rehearsed response leaped from her throat. "Hello? I was jogging, and just heard a gunshot coming from a house."

"Where are you?"

Grace gave the address hurriedly. Indistinct voices yelled in the house. It sounded like a man and a woman engaged in bitter argument, a sample of her sprites' mimicry. "I can hear yelling inside."

Lights in the other homes flashed on and people came to stand on their front porches.

And then a real scream, full-throated as only a human could voice.

"A woman just screamed." The hobgoblins must have shown themselves to the goodwife, as they chased her to the attic for safety.

"Officers are en route, ma'am."

She hung up the phone. Straining, she tried to hear past the housefolk's glamour to the true noises in the house.

A man in a business suit approached her hesitantly. His tie was still undone. "What's going on?"

"I don't know. I was jogging and heard a gunshot."

"That fellow Ella has been seeing . . ." He trailed off as if realizing that Grace would not know who anyone was. Another scream pulled his attention to the house. "Someone should do something."

"I called the police." It would be bad if a mortal went into the house now, while the Folk were still out. "They're on their way."

Her words seemed to make him relax, as if he were grateful for a reason to stay out of it. Around them, a small crowd of neighbors gathered.

Another gunshot blasted through the morning air and Grace's heart leaped to her throat. They had only planned one.

Through an open window, she saw a man's shape hurry past. A moment later, something shattered against a wall in the house. The woman screamed again. More dishes crashed; the woman was weeping now. Her sobs echoed weirdly in the morning air, bouncing off the houses and seeming to come from all around them.

Grace thought the sounds were brownies and sprites, but she was no longer certain. They had a plan, but that extra gunshot changed everything. Grace glanced at the horizon.

Another shot shattered a window of the house. The crowd screamed and scattered. Grace stayed rooted to the spot, panic filling her stomach; something had gone wrong.

She scanned for Robin Redbreast or Mallory, but neither was in sight. The sun had not yet risen, which meant the bogeyman was still in his element. It didn't matter. She had to get him out of the house, even if the police weren't here yet.

Grace stepped onto the soil of Briarwood House for the first time, knowing the bogey would feel her presence as the foster daughter of the Faerie Queen. Ignoring the cries behind her, she sprinted across the lawn to the front door.

Two short steps took her up onto the porch and then she pushed the door open.

The front hall was a chaos of shattered crockery. A dining room lay to the right, a front parlor to the left. And in front of Grace, the goodwife clutched her ankle at the bottom of a broad staircase to the second floor. A bruise was blooming under her right eye. The collar of her shirt had been ripped, exposing her shoulder. No blood though. Good.

At the top of the stairs, a man filled the hall. His head nearly brushed the overhead light, and his shoulders crowded the walls. His eyes were so sunken in his skull as to seem almost invisible. The light careened off his face, as if it could not touch him, leaving shadows where there should have been none.

The bogeyman saw Grace and recognition dawned. He smirked. "Couldn't wait, Faerie Queen's brat?"

The goodwife lifted her head to stare. Grace grabbed her arm and hauled her to her feet. Worse things waited her than a sprained ankle if they stayed.

The bogeyman lifted a gloved hand and showed her a pistol. Even with the leather, the iron must have burned with cold. "This world makes such interesting things."

Outside, sirens finally sounded.

Grace pulled the goodwife, limping toward the front door. Behind them, the bogeyman started down the stairs. The house shuddered under his weight.

Brownies flickered in and out of sight as they raced around her.

In a fluid arc, the bogeyman leaped down the stairs to land in front of them. He twisted with unnatural speed and pointed the pistol at Grace. "I had thought to use this on the House vermin, but the iron will work just as well on you."

A frying pan bounced off his head. The bogeyman staggered as the steel slipped past his defenses to raise a welt on his mortal flesh.

Brownie Thistlekin stood on the dining room table. He held another skillet poised to throw, his hands in oven mitts to protect him from the cold iron.

Grace pushed past the bogeyman and threw the front door open. "Coming out!" She brought the goodwife across the threshold of the house into the dawn.

Four police cars sat on the lawn with police officers pointing their guns at the house. They held their fire as Grace led the goodwife down the steps. In the house, a beast snarled in rage.

Grace dragged the goodwife to the ground and shouted again. "He has a gun!"

The bogeyman appeared in the doorway, shielding his face from the sun. His hands were by his sides. The police shouted. He stopped.

She wanted him to threaten her. She wanted the conflict to continue so he would be stopped, so the cold steel would end his threat for all time. She rolled onto her back and met his gaze. Switching to the old language of fae, so the mortals would not understand her taunt, she said, "You've disappointed your masters."

He howled at her and raised the pistol.

The morning echoed with shots fired. The bogeyman jerked back as his knee flashed red. Grace saw the twin realities of mortal and faerie sight—in one, the man fell to the ground and the police swarmed around him, shouting.

In the other, the bogeyman burned as the iron passed through the mortal body and into the faerie flesh. She lay back on the ground and pressed her hands to her face for a moment. Rousing herself, she turned to the goodwife. Her face was white as milk.

It was hard for Grace to guess human ages; every adult bore the clear signs of mortality etched on their face. The fine lines on the goodwife's face seemed as obvious as canyons, but her hair was a dense shadow of black even in the morning sun. The goodwife's face was drawn so tightly over her bones that it seemed as if they would poke through. Her eyes started from her head like one who had been doused with clover juice, seeing the world for the first time.

Which, no doubt, she had. Brownie Thistlekin had volunteered to do it, if it needed doing. "Are you all right?"

The goodwife still stared at Grace with open shock on her face. The clover juice must be showing her the touches of fae that clung to Grace. That, and the note Grace had sent in, should tell the goodwife who she was.

"I— Did you?"

Before Grace could answer her, Robin Redbreast flew out of the attic; he twirled and spiraled in the air.

Mallory is coming. Be prepared.

Grace swallowed; the Hound. Her cat streaked around the corner, a line of jet black. Mallory ran with his belly low to the ground. His paws reached out to grab the earth and hurl it past him. His eyes were wide and his ears flat against his head, listening to the sound of the beast behind him.

The bogeyman's hound rounded the corner. Heavy muscles rippled under its fur. Its great black feet ate the earth, each stride reaching hungrily for the cat.

Grace got to her feet to draw the Hound away from the goodwife. She ran into its path, giving Mallory time to get free. It howled and reared up with dark jaws snapping at her. She fell under its weight. The earth rolled her back and forth as gnomes shifted the soil beneath her. Teeth hissed past, biting the grass.

A gunshot rang out and the beast's body thudded against her.

Beneath the grass, a gnome's pudgy hand reached up and patted her shoulder, questioning. "I'm fine," she whispered.

The hand withdrew with a sigh.

Someone pulled the hound's body off her. An officer knelt at her side.

"Just lie still, ma'am." He pressed a cloth against the bite in Grace's arm.

She gasped at the burning pain, and let herself begin shaking. In the midst of panic, she had not felt the Hound bite her. She sat up, wanting to get away from the bloodstained grass. The stink of the hound clung to her like smoke.

Robin Redbreast danced on the lawn, puffing his feathers and telling his tale. His red breast shone like a shield of blood as he strutted and pranced.

Beyond him, the police had covered the man-shape on the porch with a coat. One of them held the goodwife by the arm, steering her away from the body. The goodwife spoke to the officer escorting her and their path changed, coming to Grace.

"Dr. Hamel?" The woman's voice was hesitant

and sounded broken. "I—My name is Ella Dennison. You—" she stopped.

Of course she couldn't finish her sentence, it sounded insane in the modern world. "Yes." Grace lowered her voice. "After we finish with the police, I'd like to help you understand what happened this morning."

It had to be soon, while the events were still fresh in her mind. Waiting too long would give her ways to believe that it hadn't happened, that the hobgoblins were her imagination. In Grace's years of bringing goodwives into the fold, she had found that she had to introduce them to the Folk while their worlds were upside down. When everything seemed chaotic, one more new element fit right in and gave each woman something to hang onto as they stitched their lives back together.

Ella laughed, breathlessly. "That would be good. Understanding would be good."

Ella stood in the front hall, brow furrowed as if trying to spot someone in the shadows. Grace glanced back to Brownie Thistlekin, but he was gone. She turned back to Ella. "May I offer you some tea?"

"Yes, thank you." Ella's fragility seemed even more pronounced in the house than it had out on the lawn in front of Briarwood House.

Grace showed her to the den and saw her settled in one of the wingback chairs by the fire.

Two mugs of tea waited for her on the kitchen island. Brownie Thistlekin took care of her as though she was his own child. She grabbed the cups of tea and carried them in to Ella.

With its leaded glass windows and fireplace, the room welcomed her into its fold. The light from the fire cast Ella's face into sharp planes of fatigue.

She jumped as Grace entered the room, then smiled at the sight of the cups. "Thank you. How is your arm?"

"It's fine. A benefit to living with faerie folk." She set a mug on the small end table between the chairs. "I hope you like chamomile. I find it's good for calming my nerves."

"Faeries? That's . . . I don't understand."

The events of today must already have begun to slip from Ella's mind. Brownies seemed impossible to those who first met them. Grace sat in the other wingback chair. "Are you all right?"

Ella shuddered, as if the bogeyman had just touched her. "What happened this morning?"

"You had a bogeyman in your home."

"Ron? He was difficult, but until today—"

"He beat you, didn't he?"

Ella froze. The only sign of life in her was a vein in her neck, throbbing with tension. She seemed barely to breathe. Her gaze flicked to the fire. "Yes."

Grace let her stare at the flames, waiting as she had with the other wild things in her home.

"Is it . . . It wasn't human, was it?"

"No. Bogeymen eat the souls of men and wear their forms like a mask. The man whose body the police took away has been dead for some time."

"Oh my God."

Grace sipped her chamomile to give Ella time to think. "Where did you meet him?"

"A bar. After work, with some friends . . . Did I meet the man or the," her voice slowed as she tried out the new term, "the bogeyman?"

"Probably the bogey. They have a history of abusing women."

"I didn't know what I'd invited home."

"That's the bogeyman's trick."

"Will he come back?"

Grace shook her head. "Not there. We've made wardings for you that will keep out anything you don't invite in."

"My mother always told me to trust the Folk." Ella grimaced. "I thought I was humoring her."

"I'm sorry we had to frighten you."

Ella blushed. "I think that's the first time I've ever really screamed."

"It's one thing to hear tales of the Folk; it's another when you see your first hobgoblin. Three might have been laying it on a bit thick, but witnesses needed to hear you scream. I'm sorry."

"No, it's fine. The brownies explained when they were trying to get me into the attic. Brownies! I can't believe it." She tilted her head. "Did you scream when you saw your first one?"

Grace hesitated. "I was a changeling child. The Faerie Queen took me when I was fourteen months old and raised me till I was thirteen." She laughed.

"I did scream the first time my birth mother used a vacuum."

"That must have been hard on you."

"To say the least. I had never used anything from the industrial age. So some things were easier and some things were harder."

"I meant, not knowing your parents." Ella tilted her head. "Weren't you lonely?"

"Not until I came home." Grace put her mug down on the table. "But I invited you here to explain the Folk. Do you feel up to meeting another brownie?"

Ella went as still as a doe in the forest. "I assume you don't mean a little girl selling cookies . . . ?"

They all made the same jokes at this point. "No. But I do have some Thin Mints in the freezer, if that would help."

With a laugh, some of Ella's stiffness softened. "Is that what I met?"

"Who. And yes. You met Mama Nutkin, I believe. Her son is the one that warned us about the bogeyman." In the far corner, Brownie Thistlekin sidled into the room. He nodded once to let her know he was ready. "Brownies, indeed all of the housefolk, are naturally shy creatures. So even in a house full of them like mine, I rarely see one, but I hear them. The thumps and bumps and creaks of an old house are usually related to one of the Folk. Most people hear the heartbeat of their own homes without realizing it, but can go their whole life without seeing one of the Folk."

"Like me," Ella whispered.

"It's not unusual." With a nod, Grace indicated the corner behind Ella. "If you turn slowly, Brownie Thistlekin is standing over there."

Ella turned so slowly that Grace wanted to tell her she did not have to be *that* careful. Brownie Thistlekin held very still, waiting for the moment when Ella saw him. He had done this before for Grace, and was the only one of the Folk in her house willing to show himself to a mortal without dire need.

As Ella ogled at him, Grace said, "Never thank a brownie; you'll hurt their feelings and make them think they are not welcome."

"How does that—"

"It makes them think that the relationship is at an end. Friends trade favors with one another all the time. To thank means that you want nothing more from them. Like a servant. Leave a bowl of cream out if they do something you appreciate."

Ella nodded, understanding softening her face. "I'll have to leave out a trough of cream when I get home."

Grace suppressed a sigh of relief. Ella had all the makings of a fine goodwife.

She caught a hint of movement in the edge of her vision. Brownie Nutkin stood at the edge of the room. He was studying Ella and turning his broomstick over in his hands. The wee lad bit his lower lip. He took a step forward. Then another. On his toes, he edged into Ella's line of sight.

Grace whispered, "Ella . . . allow me to introduce

you to one of your own housefolk. This is Brownie Nutkin."

He gave her a short bow. "How do, goodwife?"

Ella let her breath out slowly. "How do, Brownie Nutkin."

There was no way to explain to Ella exactly how brave Nutkin was being, to come out in the open like this. Grace pressed her hand against her mouth. She was so proud of him.

"It seems I owe you cream and more." Ella's brow crinkled and Grace could see her working out how to show gratitude to someone without thanking them. "If . . . if there is ever anything you need from me, don't be afraid to let me know."

"Dost thou mean that?"

"I do."

"And the nasty man is gone?"

Ella's breath caught audibly in her throat. "And never coming back."

Brownie Nutkin straightened his shoulders and stood to his full knee-height. He turned to Grace. "Then, Granny, we'uns don't need a new hearth and home."

"For that, I am glad."

"I do wish . . ." Nutkin hesitated and blushed. Asking for something outright was rude, and Grace could guess that he was imagining his mother's instructions. "Will you take me home?"

Ella nodded. "I would be glad to."

Grace smiled at the goodwife. "Then let's make

your first lesson, how to safety-proof a car for the Folk."

Maybe someday she could teach the folk to integrate fully into the mortal world again. But for now, one more habitat had been saved.

THE SONG OF THE WIND

Paul Crilley

The trees used to sing to me, a private song of autumn winds and gray chill. Ancient branches swaying in a stately dance, dying leaves whispering intimate words that spoke directly to my soul.

No longer, though.

When autumn comes around, I leave my home and walk. Brianna thinks she understands why I do this, but she does not, and I haven't the heart to tell her. I wander far through the cold rain. I climb the hills in my path and perch on the highest peaks, the land spread out below me in a wave of browns and greens, straining to hear the voices that once spoke to the very depth of my being, that once inspired me to trap fleeting emotions on a prison of paper with bars of ink.

I never hear them though, and I know I never will. Not unless I leave Brianna, something I will not do.

For that was when the wind stopped singing to me: when I met Brianna and we fell in love. She is a fickle mistress, the wind, my muse, and she demands a faithful lover.

Most of the year I don't even mind. But when the wind starts driving up the hills, ruffling the manes and tails of the highland ponies, I know I must leave for a few weeks lest I bring resentment to bear on someone who does not deserve it.

I take my lyre with me, which for most of the year is wrapped in silk and wool and placed carefully in a small chest. When I climb the hills I place it on my knees and close my eyes, feeling the wind vibrate the strings to a thrumming song, and think back to the time when I was a bard, traveling from village to village, playing and reciting for an appreciative audience.

I would remember those days and weep silently to myself, begging the wind to take pity on me and sing her song.

She never does.

Dusk falls gradually around me, blending in quietly with the rocky crags. I look up and see dark clouds scudding briskly past the lighter grey, feel the wind refreshing against my face.

I close my eyes and breathe in deeply, cold air filling my lungs. I feel suspended in such moments. My body does not exist. My mind flies with the wind, soaring in the twilight breeze over mountains and forests, rippling lakes and roaring oceans. I am one with the wind. I feel I can accompany it anywhere.

When I reluctantly open my eyes again, a girl is standing before me. I do not see her at first, dressed as she is in a grey shift that blends in with the rock and sky around us. She is staring at me intently with eyes black and cold, her mouth turned down into what is almost a pout of displeasure.

"It is dangerous for one of your kind to be so far out," she says, and although her voice is barely above a whisper, I hear her clearly.

"The same can be said for you," I say. I gesture at her flimsy dress. "Are you not cold?" I ask. "You can have my jerkin if you like."

She frowns at me. "No," she says after a moment. "No, I am fine. Though it is kind of you to offer."

"A fire, then? You are welcome to share. You should not be alone at night. I assure you, you have nothing to fear from me."

"I know, Cuan the Bard. You are a goodly man."

"How—"

"I think I will offer you a gift," says the girl suddenly. "Your greatest wish. What you have always wanted. Will you accept?"

"I do not understand," I say, confused. "What do you offer me? I deserve nothing. I have shown you only common kindness."

"Not so common, I fear. I offer you your greatest wish, Cuan. Your talent. That which thrives on aloneness and contemplation, but shrivels and dies in happiness and love."

I gaze at her, realization dawning. "My poems . . . "

"Yes. I can give you the urgency back, the desire

to allow your thoughts to take you where they will without being pulled back by the sanity of your love. That need you once had, that urge to write everything down or go mad with the denial." She stares at me, and smiles. "I can give it back to you."

She leans forward and touches my heart. Then she turns around and disappears over the rocks.

It is as if she was never there.

The day is colder today, winter making her presence felt. I climb to the summit of the next hill, the way forward made difficult by the uneven rocks. I try not to think of my encounter from last night. I woke up realizing what had happened, aware that I was a very lucky man. Not many talk to a denizen of Faerie and get off so lightly. Men are known to disappear for seven decades or more, and come back looking not a day older, only to crumble to dust as the ages suddenly catch up with them.

I cannot even remember what we talked of. It is like a mist has descended over my memory, leaving only vague pictures and half-remembered feelings.

I reach the summit and look down. Forests dwindle away to the north. I will have to turn west now, to keep with the hills and mountains.

A brown leaf, caught in the eddies of an ill-tempered wind, flies past my head. I reach out and catch it. It crackles in my hand, falling into brittle parts. I release them, watch as they are recaptured and led away into the gray sky. The wind grows stronger.

And I hear her song.

Cold shivers run all over my body. I lift my head, letting her caress my hair, my skin. I open my arms to her embrace as she grows stronger, her voice louder. Leaves are whipped from the trees down below and tossed into the blustery grey sky. The wind soars through my body as if I am not there, borne from distant lands. Joy rises within me. A feeling of excitement starts as a small ball in my stomach and spreads throughout the rest of my being. I feel a sudden happiness with life, a contentedness, presented to me by the briskness of an autumn day. I am complete, two halves of my soul reconciled for the first time ever.

And I remember what the faerie said to me last night.

I run all the way to the next village, my mind afire with ideas and compositions, experiments with sound and verse that would never have occurred to me before. I forget more in those hours of running than I have ever thought of in my whole life up till that point. I feel like I am going mad with frustration, with the desire to have paper and quill in my hands and put down the thoughts that are searing my mind with their brilliance.

I take out a room and with the last of my coins purchase quill and ink, and an obscenely small amount of parchment: it is not required often in this tiny village.

I sit on the floor and write down ideas and

concepts, thoughts and feelings, in handwriting almost too small to read.

I awake, my head throbbing. I try to sit up, but my arms will not support me. I collapse heavily to the floor and retch. I try to remember what happened last night, why I am feeling so ill. My last recollection is of touching the quill to paper and making the first ink stroke.

I roll to my side and gently push myself up. A sight of devastation greets me.

Paper is strewn everywhere, covered in illegible writing. I pick up a piece. I have written on the paper, then when it ran out, I have simply written over the top again, over and over until all beneath is unreadable. The walls are covered with scratched and angular writings, the knife I used still embedded deep in the wood. I try to read the words, but none of it makes any sense to me. A nonsense of drunken thoughts and unreadable writing.

Fear wells within me, a feeling that does not quite mask the hollowness that permeates my being. I get slowly to my feet, drained and weak as a newborn babe.

What has happened to me?

And then I realize. My gift.

My curse.

I wait as the dusk folds around me like a damp cloak. The wind bites me, no longer invigorating, but draining. It travels beneath my skin, filling my bones with a leaden numbness that makes it difficult to move.

I am on that same hill again, surrounded by the rocks and the crags. I could not move another muscle if my life depended on it. The rush to get here before the day was over took everything left out of me.

I have been cursed. I realize that now. How foolish was I to accept a gift from the fey? Just because I treated her with kindness, I thought I would be treated likewise. My naivete has ruined me.

She comes, forming out of the darkness like a ghost in the mist. She tilts her head at me quizzically.

"I know you, yes?"

"You do," I reply weakly.

"From where?"

How fickle they are! "You gave me . . . a gift. You touched my heart."

"Oh, yes!" The faerie clapped her hands. "You have returned to thank me."

"I have returned to ask you to take it back. I am drained. I wrote everything that was in me, verses and sonnets, one on top of the last, so that I can read none. It is as if a part of my being, my essence has left me. I feel empty. As if my soul has been riven from my body."

"The flame that burns bright, dies quickly," says the faerie. "It is part of the bargain."

"I made no bargain!" I double over in a coughing fit, my anger useless and fleeting. "What . . . what are you?" I asked weakly.

"I am Leanan-Sidhe," said the faerie. "To some their muse; to some their death."

"You are evil."

"Not I. I belong to the Seelie Court. We are . . . benign."

"You have emptied me!"

"I gave you my gift, and that is not something I do lightly. You have created more in this one night than you would have done in your entire life, but such brilliance claims a price."

"I did not ask for this gift."

"You asked the wind to speak to you again. I am the wind. I am inspiration." The fey reaches out and stroked my cheek. "We were lovers once, you and I. We were joined as one, till you deserted me, deserted your muse. I have simply answered your pleas, Cuan the bard."

"So I die."

The faerie shrugs. "I do not know much about you human people. You lead such short lives anyway, how can you even notice?"

Tears flow down my face at the unfairness of it all. The uncaring obliviousness of this creature that has ruined me.

The faerie peers at me, a look of confusion on her face. "What did you expect?" she asks.

"I just wanted to write while I was happy, in love."

The faerie backs away into the darkness. "Goodbye, Cuan the bard."

The darkness swallows her up. I sit on the rock, shivering, my teeth chattering, too weak to move.

"I just wanted to write again," I whisper.

I return home. It takes me days, maybe weeks more than it should. All the way I fight. Fight the thoughts that soar through my mind, the descriptions of autumn trees sighing in the wind, the poems that lay themselves before me, fully formed, waiting only for me to acknowledge their presence. I develop a fever. For days I am delirious, though still I manage to fight off the things racing through my mind, the demons waiting to destroy me. I don't think I eat. I only drink when I stumble into rivers and fall face first into the icy water. I have to hold off. I won't give in without seeing Brianna, to apologize for ruining everything. Why couldn't I have been happy with what I had? Why didn't I leave well enough alone?

The shock on Brianna's face when she sees me is enough to make me weep. I fall into her arms and hold her tightly. A curious mixture is happiness and sadness. For this is what I feel. I look into her eyes, her beautiful green eyes. I reach up and touch her face.

"I love you," I say. "And I have lost you."

She looks down at me, confusion and pain evident. She strokes my skin. I feel peace at her touch.

"I am dying, my love. My soul has burned high and devoured itself. I have been cursed by faerie."

I hug her tight to myself let my tears flow.

*   *   *

I hold off for as long as I can, but I know it will be days at most. I explain everything to her, of my past and my writing. I give her my bound papers, all the things I have ever written, that I kept hidden in my chest.

She tells me she is with child.

Oh, my love, how I have betrayed you!

Dawn, watery and gray. I stand outside and breathe in the fresh, cold air. It rained last night. Wet leaves dance through the air, taunting me. The wind yanks my hair with cold fingers, as if trying to pull me away. I turn and go inside. Brianna is still asleep, curled beneath three blankets in the darkened bedroom. I go to the chest and unlock it. I lift out my small lyre and lay it carefully on her abdomen, where the life we created together grows.

I fetch a piece of parchment, quill and ink. I sit in a chair at the foot of the bed and stare at her smooth face, her milk-white skin. The voices scream in my mind, sensing their imminent release, clamoring to be free, to destroy me. I fight them off, force them to wait as I put them into some kind of order, as *I* decide how they will be let out.

I title my poem, my last gift to my first love.
Brianna.

The wind blows through her long hair as she stands on top of the hill just behind their house. She reads the poem again, even though she will never forget the words as long as she lives.

She carefully tears the parchment into tiny pieces, then opens her hand.

The fragments, the last bits of Cuan's life, are snatched away from her as if by a jealous child, flicked and tossed into the grey sky. She tries to see them as they fly away, but they are invisible against the sky.

She stands there, at the crest of the hill, for a long time afterward. She is listening to the song of the wind, feeling its caress upon her face.

It sounds like Cuan's voice.

FIRST BALL . . . LAST CALL

Rob Thurman

When the world ended, the very first thought I had was of my first dance. I didn't even like dancing—damn, how embarrassing would that be? Yet there it was. That was the memory I flashed back to. That's where some part of me considered my life starting. A dance. Or maybe it wasn't the dance. Maybe it was the girl. I'd loved her, not that I remembered her name now. But at the time I thought I loved her. I *knew* I lusted after her. But isn't that how love goes? Her skin was dusky and warm, her eyes fields of lavender, her black hair pulled up and then falling, a solemn black sea around her bare shoulders.

Okay, yeah, it was definitely the girl.

The world ended and I was still thinking with the brain between my legs instead of the one in my head. The cock ruled the roost. At least I admitted it. I doubt my partner would. He was all about the manners and shit that hadn't mattered before and damn sure didn't matter now. I cut him some slack though, because he could shoot straight, ride for hours on end without bitching too much, could cook over a camp-fire without turning a rabbit into charcoal, and, bottom line, at the end of the world, you made do with what you had.

It had been ten years ago—when it had happened. The sky turned gray, the sun a sullen distant red, and the entire world shook. I looked back now and saw that shaking for what it was: death throes. The world had died that day and since then we were nothing more than scavengers on a corpse.

They had done it . . . destroyed it all as if it was a toy they'd tired of, didn't much care about any more. Broken and tossed under the bed to not be thought of again.

Maybe it was partly our fault. We'd forgotten they existed more or less. We weren't watching for them, weren't prepared. They were nothing more than stories, legends, nonsense tales to tell little ones to put them to sleep. Long ago when we knew they actually existed, saw them, made trades that never turned out quite right, I think we learned their bite was worse than their bark, no matter how innocent they could make themselves seem. We'd learned that playing games with them was the quickest way to get into trouble. So we forgot about them—the reality of them. We *made* ourselves forget and I think even the stories themselves would've disappeared in time.

But we didn't have time. Without us any more, they played with themselves, and not in that good way you're thinking. Well, not in the good way *I* was thinking. While we forgot them, they continued to play their lethal games: one side against another, alliances constantly shifting, greed for power growing, greed for gold, jewels, fruits of the earth, greed for the air itself. For the stark differences they claimed, good versus evil, righteous versus unholy; in the end they were all the same. Vicious, feral creatures who finally turned paradise into hell. There were only two good things about that. The first was that they managed to kill nearly all of themselves in the process. The second was we got to kill the ones that were left. Revenge wouldn't bring back the world, but it was better than nothing. It was a damn sight better than sitting around waiting to die. We spent the final days wiping out the last of those freaks one by one. It was a hobby. Everyone needed one. Even now. Especially now.

"At the last outpost, the guy slinging the brew said two more riders went crazy and killed themselves. Third crew to eat their guns this month." I shrugged. "Can't figure why they're in such a hurry to get where we're going anyway. Gutless maggots. Yellow-bellied chicken shits through and through."

Scotch took off his cowboy hat, showing the yellow-blonde hair he sawed short every few weeks with his knife, and smacked me hard with it. "Seven, if you do not stop speaking that way, I will end you. I've told you a thousand times it makes me question my *own* sanity." Our mounts bumped shoulders without complaint with the motion.

I grinned. "That's why I do it." We weren't from around here, far from it, but we went where the work took us. This past year that had been Arizona, Nevada, Mexico—up and down, round and round. Those bastards could hide like nobody's business. They were getting smarter, and tracking them was getting harder. If I could entertain myself by talking like a gen-u-ine cowboy and drive my partner nuts in the bargain, well, hell, that's what I was going to do.

He grumbled, but put his hat back on. It wasn't to soak up the sweat. It wasn't hot. It was never hot any more. Never warm. It was always winter now, but the rays of the sun, small and bloody as it had become, would sear flesh the same as that cook-fire and rabbit I'd been thinking of earlier, especially if you were fair-skinned. I wasn't. My skin was dark enough that the sun didn't bother me much. My hair was darker still and I kept its twisted strands tied back in a long tail. It was easier than combing it every day or cutting it once a month. There wasn't a lot of time for personal hygiene on the hunt, whether it was here on the western trail or up north in the cities. If you had water and soap, you were lucky. If you wanted to feel warm water again, you'd have to heat it yourself.

When the Earth had stopped, nearly everything else had stopped with it. I didn't know how or what they did. Some hideous last magic, the kind of magic that if you had seen would've no doubt burned the eyes from your face, peeled the skin from your flesh, and driven you to a gibbering madness that would infect everyone you then cast your blind screaming gaze on.

I shook my head. That was the best part of pretending to be a cowboy. Not having to think thoughts like those. No matter how it had happened, what grisly magic was unleashed, nothing worked. Cars didn't run. Houses didn't heat. Lights stayed dark and forever would. I didn't much care about the cars, although they would've made the chases shorter. But a warm bath to soak away months of dust and the ache of the trail, I'd have given Scotch's right arm for that. His left too, if that's what it took.

I patted Pie's neck and wiped a damp hand on my pants. At least the guns still worked. I'd cut one of the son of a bitch's throats if I had to—and I had, but just the touch of them made your flesh revolt. Unnatural. Unclean. Murderers of the world. We passed what had once been a cactus. It should've died in ten years of cold but it hadn't. It had twisted and warped, turned black and wept a slime that slowly ate through the ground around it with a sizzling stench.

I looked away. We were in Hell. I'd never believed in Hell, but that's where we were. Clearing my throat, I asked my partner, "You remember your first dance? With a girl?" I grinned lazily as the mounts plodded on. "Maybe I'm jumping the gun. Maybe it was a right purty sheep, flowers in her wool?"

Scotch scowled. His face wasn't made for it. It didn't stop him from trying, but with a straight nose, clean jaw-line, eyes the same color the sky had once been, a scowl just didn't take. It made him look noble and probably prettier than the girl he'd danced with. Which I promptly told him. It was a better insult than the sheep one.

The scowl disappeared and he laughed. I didn't hear him do that much. I didn't do it much myself, not and mean it. These days who did? "I will never know why I didn't kill you ages ago," he snorted.

"Because you're not good enough," I said smugly. "You were never able to take me down." It wasn't as if we hadn't gone at it over the long years. Boys will be boys and all that crap. "Not even in racing. Your nag never saw anything but the ass-end of Pie." Pie, hearing his name, lifted his head and rolled an eye back at me. I gave his dark neck another pat. Despite the grime of the trail, his coat gleamed as black as a ripe blackberry. Not that there were blackberries now, only the memory of the sweetness of a sun-warmed one bursting on your tongue.

"Nag? Shall we see about that?" Scotch caught me off guard as his mount took off like . . . how'd they say it? Oh, yeah, like his head was on fire and his tail was catchin'.

Or more like the unreal slide of ice and snow in the beauty of a frozen waterfall falling down a mountain. His coat was as white as Pie's was black, or it had been. He hadn't fared as well against the dirt and grime as Pie had, but I remembered what he'd looked like before we pulled this assignment and ended up in this nightmare mess of a desert. He'd been winter incarnate. But now he was a dirty bat-out-of-hell that I sent Pie after with one loud yee-haw.

"I heard that, you bastard," Scotch's irritated words trailed behind him. I corrected my earlier thought. Everyone needed two hobbies. Dispatching murderers *and* irritating their partners.

Unfortunately, he wasn't the only one that heard. Someone had been waiting for us and our race was over seconds after it had begun. Scotch was galloping his horse past a rusty-red outcropping of rock when the monster took him down. The cat leaped over and tackled him out of the saddle and to the ground in a movement so fast and fluid I barely saw it. Pinning Scotch to the ground, it saw me coming and lifted its head to unleash a growl that put the rumble of thunder to shame.

But it hadn't seen me coming after all. It had heard me. It had no eyes, not ones it could use to see. Skin was seamed shut in ugly ribbons of red flesh where eyes should've been. Its ears were larger than they should've been, as were its widely splayed nostrils that sampled the air while spraying pink tinged mucus. It wasn't a monster, no matter how it looked. It was just another victim.

I hurt for it, something that should've been a glory of nature, hurt to my core. And while I knew it had to eat, same as we all did, I couldn't let it eat my partner. I hit it clean-center with a shot between those two absent eyes. I almost felt guilty, but it was fortunate to be out of this world and hopefully on to a better one. Then again, it might just be dead and there was nothing more—nothing clean and pure. The dark magic could've destroyed that too, but if that were true, I still thought it was better off. I vaulted off Pie and helped roll the big cat, heavy as I was at least, off Scotch. My partner had puncture marks in his upper chest with a small amount of blood soaking through his faded green shirt, but other than that and having the wind knocked out of him, he seemed all right.

He coughed and wheezed, pulling in air, as I pulled him up to a sitting position. "I . . . still . . . won," he panted.

"Yeah, if the race lasted four seconds and the finish line was being eaten by a big-ass desert cat, you won. What do you want for a prize? Pie can give you a big sloppy kiss. He likes the blonde mares," I drawled.

"Braying . . . ass," he hissed and glared.

"Nah, he's not so much for those." I waited a minute then when he could curse me without running out of air and his eyes rolling back in his head, I heaved him up to his feet. "You all right? You want to go ahead and make camp? We've been on this one son of a bitch for a week now. Another day won't hurt."

He shook his head. "No. It's not bad, and I'm tired of this one. He's run too far, too long. I want him dead, Seven. He's already killed two huntsmen. Let's make certain he doesn't kill any more."

"You got it," I affirmed. He was right. They'd killed the world; I didn't want to see one of them kill a single fucking thing else and certainly not us . . . the ones who couldn't put things right, but could make them pay. Vengeance was all we had, and it only made me want it even more.

Once up, swaying, but up, he looked at the dead cat, maimed—*changed*, then shoved fingers into his hair. "Why? Why didn't they stay legends and fables where they belonged? Why did they have to be real? Why did they do this? Why would they destroy everything? Just . . . *why*?"

No one would ever know, and thinking about it would only make you as crazy as the riders that were the talk of the outpost, the ones who'd eaten their guns. They'd probably thought *why* one time too many.

I shook my head silently, for once not having a smart-ass comment. I urged him toward his mount then helped him back up in the saddle. Once there he sat straight, and if he was in pain, he hid it well. From the beginning, after all the confusion, the mourning, the despair, when we'd finally found a mission, coordinated, been partnered up, and sent to avenge what we couldn't save, I'd told myself I'd make do with what I was paired with. Turned out Scotch was the best partner I could've hoped for. He'd never let me down. Not once. Now I did know what to say. I asked, "Did I ever call you a wuss? Wimp? Pussy?"

He took his hat I handed him and settled it into

place. "Only every other day and in about a hundred more imaginative ways."

My lips quirked as I smacked his mount on the flank. "Good. Don't want you forgetting that."

Then we were back on the trail. Ignoring his rolled eyes, I studied the ground from my saddle for sign of our quarry's passing. I spotted them easily. It wasn't as if the one we were after was trying to cover his tracks any longer. He was probably too far gone for that. Two huntsmen had almost ridden him into the ground before he killed them. He'd be exhausted and desperate. Desperate wasn't good, not with two kills under his belt, but exhausted was, and we'd use it.

After another couple of miles, Pie lifted his head and blew softly through his nostrils. He knew better than to warn our prey. "He smells water," I said softly. "There must be a spring up ahead. That's where the bastard's going. He must've run out of water." And monsters or not, they needed water the same as any other creature.

We picked up the pace to a slow gallop. We passed a horse ridden to death, its tongue as dry and lifeless as the sand it lolled across. Another victim. Maybe that made me pick up the pace a little, pulling ahead of Scotch. Or maybe it was that I was so damn tired of them. Slaughterers, nightmares made flesh, *evil* . . . evil in a way that even I had never known the meaning of. I'd put down so many of them, but at that moment I wanted this one dead more than all the others put together. He'd killed two of our comrades, rode an innocent animal to an agonizing death, ruined all that I could see and ever would see. Even the stars at night were blinking out one by one. For all that, this one meant more than all the others put together. I wanted it. I needed it.

When you want it, it sharpens you, makes you better.

When you *need* it, it makes you sloppy.

I was sloppy.

Pie and I crested a gentle swell and I saw the water. It was a putrid shade of green, glimmering in a red-rimmed basin, with stunted, oddly twisted shrubs clustered here and there around it. I heard slurping and saw a tree with silvery leprous bark and long blade shaped leaves. The tree had grown in the painfully sharp shape of a bow bent beyond endurance until its leaves trailed in the water, drinking with a passionate thirst. What I didn't see was the son of a bitch with the gun.

Not until it was too late.

I felt the bullet hit me in the chest. They say it feels like being kicked by a mule. Yeah, that's what *they* say. It didn't. It was a hundred times worse. There was the free-fall as I was thrown from the saddle and the hard thump as I hit the ground. All I could see then was sky. I longed for the forever-gone blue or the black of night with the thousand and one stars . . . not the random handful that remained these days, but gray was all there was. The gray of nothing. The gray of indifference. The gray that would slowly eat this world's remains and move on to eat the whole of reality for all I knew.

I heard Pie lie down next to me with a grunt, blocking me from further fire. It'd be nice to say I'd known Pie since he was a frisky colt, but Pie had known me when I'd been the shaky legged new-born. He'd no doubt thought I was a nuisance the same as I'd once thought about Scotch. I hope he'd changed his mind like I'd changed mine.

Scotch's rifle fired, the shots so quick that the sound blended into one massive crack. I heard a scream; I was glad of that. I wanted to hear that mur-dering freak shriek until his throat bled, that and more, and much more—so much more, but I settled for the scream and then a second one followed by a splash. I managed to turn my head towards the spring and saw Pie's lambent gold eyes staring into mine. The cat's-eye pupils dilated. "Hungry," he muttered, the words pushed harshly through the long throat. "Eat. Now. *Hungry*."

"Go," I said, words slow and painful. "Feast as you deserve, honored one."

He stared at me a moment longer then dipped his head. The kelpie rose to his hooves and cantered into the water. He buried his teeth, sharp and curved, in the flesh of the dead human lying on the opposite bank. There was a flash of tangled beard, gaping mouth, and an eyeball pulped by a bullet from Scotch's rifle before the body was dragged into the water. I wouldn't have thought it was that deep, but kelpies are versatile and Pie and the body both dis-appeared under the boiling surface. In a moment or two the water calmed until a geyser, far redder with blood than poisonous green, gushed upward. Then it fell, splashing back heavily, and beneath the water Pie fed. He'd more than earned it. The desert was hard on him. He dripped water wherever he walked. That was how kelpies were born—in water. They spent their lives leaving it wherever they went, which was good for Scotch and me when springs were few and far between. We had our own water source. But Pie had been meant for lochs and rivers—the desert pushed him to the far reaches of his endurance. He needed this meal.

"Blind fool. Suicidal half-wit. Careless. Idiotic beyond all measure of the word." Scotch was kneeling beside me. "How did you last in the courts, much less the Unseelie Court, with strategy such as that?" He used his human-made knife to cut my shirt open with one subtle slice. We had no blades of our own. Once we'd come from Under-the-Hill to the human's Earth—the Earth that was now, all our dwarven and elvish-forged blades had disintegrated. Our rainbow-chased armor turned to dust and blew away. The magic that had made them had been undone by a human magic grimmer and blacker than we could ever comprehend.

"I relied on my unfathomably handsome face." I tried for a grin, but didn't make the shadow of a smile. "He was a human. A grubbing-in-the-mud human. A worthless adversary."

"Excepting these worthless adversaries destroyed their world and ours," he exhaled. "Ego and vanity, always the downfall of the Dark Court." He pulled off his gloves and probed the bullet wound in my upper chest with his bare fingers. They felt warm against the icy chill of my skin. He already knew. From the appearance of the wound, he would. I'd seen the same wounds before and the pain—it was far worse than it should've been. I didn't need to see the mercury tainted veins pulsing and striating outward, my black blood flowing far more freely than a normal bullet or blade would cause.

I said it for him. "It's silver. There is nothing you can do, Ialach. The Wild Hunt will go on without me and I know I am the luckier for it." Being a cowboy wasn't as distracting now as it had been. Taunting my comrade with those stupid peasant words now would've been cruel. I was cruel—had been cruel. I was Unseelie, born and bred to malice. Yet when I saw true malice when the humans killed their mother, our mother, I knew the Dark Courts knew nothing of genuine cruelty. Nothing but pretenders to the throne were we. I'd saved what remained of my old self for the humans and I'd done things to the ones we'd caught—terrible yet justly deserved things—that kept some of the hungry shadows in me alive.

Ialach deserved none of that, though. If I were to die, I'd die speaking as I'd spoken for most of my life. Better he have memories of our past lives than the one we lived now. "You will not die," he said between clenched teeth. "You bastard. You will *not*."

"No?" I felt the stirring of the dark amusement of old. The Seelie were so determined, so noble, so fearless, yes, in the face of death itself. So very Ialach.

Still, I liked to think I had corrupted him, if only a little, these past ten years. Then more waves of pain came and I shut up, intent on biting off my lower lip before humiliating myself by screaming.

"No," he said, the determination as palpable as my pain. "When the sun sets for the final time I do not want to be alone. Even your constant ear-shattering imitation of speech is better than that."

I focused on him to see the pretense of humor creasing the sun-creased skin around his eyes. Actual humor from a nose-in-the-air, death before dishonor, shimmering robes, white horses, constantly with the never-ending . . . the never-Oberon's shriveled worthless balls-ending ethereal-singing High Court Fey. I had taught him something after all. Or he had taught me something—that you can be enemies so long that you are actually closer than friends. He taught me that word as well. There was no word for friend in the Dark Court—ally, comrade-in-arms, former ally (otherwise known as "sorry-is-that-my-dagger-in-your-back")—but not friend. I grinned, tasting my own blood, and asked, "Can you make sure I die with my boots on, pardner?"

Let him remember this moment with a laugh or a groan or, best of all, annoyance, but let it be this moment . . . not my death. And I was going to die. I had no doubt of that. If we had our magic left to us, I might have had a chance, but we did not. When the world died, we had felt the shake and death rattle of it in Under-the-Hill. Our home might be a step to one side of the humans' reality, but it was also a reflection of the Earth itself. Reflections are the first to go. Our home began to die as well. Those legends and fables returned to our memories as the truth they were. Many of us managed to remember the way and galloped our steeds to the world of man to see what was wrong. What could be done?

Everything and nothing.

The human race's unnatural magic obliterated ours. What we'd once had, we had no more. Our weapons and armor faded away. Any charms, spells, or pure destructive streams of magic were gone. We were no more than humans with pointed ears and a severe allergy to silver. It was pathetic. We discovered we couldn't go home again—not that it mattered. Time Under-the-Hill passed as a river compared to a stone on the bank that was earth. If we had had the magic left to re-open the door, we would have found nothing. Not death, but nothing at all. Earth had died, but Under-the-Hill was only the memory of a gravestone. Those of us that had left had barely escaped in time. Under-the-Hill had washed away, we knew, for no one there had ever followed us out.

I closed my eyes, clenched dirt and sand in my fists as the silver-agony spasmed through my body.

Fairy tales . . . I had been thinking of fables and legends. Humans remembered us better than we remembered them. Iron and silver: some of them recalled our weaknesses. When we joined together, Light and Dark, to vent our fury on those that would be the Grim Reaper of us all, and unleashed the first

Wild Hunt in a thousand of their years, tens of thousands of ours, a few of them knew how to fight back. A bullet was a bullet, but a silver one was a bullet made of the deadliest of poisons.

When they had slain the world, they had perhaps slain all of existence, as well—what else would blow out the stars like candle flames? Somehow they had torn a gaping wound in reality itself. They might not know themselves how or what they'd done, but they'd done it all the same. Their magic had exceeded their grasp. I'd have thought they'd have lain down and gone with it when they realized their fate. But no. Stupid and predatory to the end.

They had learned magic of their own. It took me forever to puzzle out what an automobile . . . a car . . . was supposed to do, but when I did, that was magic I would've liked to have seen on the move. Their magic was greater than ours had ever been: cities I couldn't have imagined if I had tried and a surplus of weapons that, despite our heritage, even we of the Unseelie Court found to be obscene. With our swords gone, we'd learned to use the least offensive of them: guns.

Then there were the ones called nuclear bombs. Little suns. They had possessed thousands upon thousands of those, a human had told me after I sliced off his ear. When the end came, they had none . . . that information had come with the removal of his other ear. I'd removed his nose as well . . . wasn't that one of their sayings? Cut off thy nose to spite thy own face? And wasn't that precisely what they had done? Thousands of small venomous suns erupting all at once . . . in one last battle . . . one last pitting of ego against ego.

Knowledge, and a lack thereof, against reality: the sun, the moon, the stars, the earth beneath our feet, the air in our lungs. Everything that had been, everything that was, and everything that wouldn't be again.

And here we were.

For now. I didn't know how long it would take the earth to rot away, the last star to disappear, the sun to set and not rise again, but the Hunt would remain . . . at least until there was no one left to punish. And as much as Ialach would deny it, the Hunt would survive without me.

"Why do you call yourself Seven? There has never been a time you have not called yourself that and these years we have ridden together you would never tell me why."

I slitted my eyes. "I am dying," I pushed the words through the pain, "and you would like a bedtime story?"

"It would be only fair, as you were the one to name me." Ialach shrugged as he placed the point of his knife against my chest and sliced me open much as a goose for a banquet. Or a pig for a barbeque with all the fixings. The slippery words of the Fey— water over a pebbled stream—and the harsh ones of humans were mixed up now. "And I thought it might distract you," he added, but those words were distant. Far away.

I sucked in a breath and decided breathing was distinctly overrated. I didn't think I'd closed my eyes again, but the darkness came all the same as I felt fingers slide past my skin and into my chest. Then those things like feeling and pain went away and I lived in the memories. I had named Ialach Scotch. But it hadn't begun as Scotch.

It had started as Buttercup.

Seelie and Unseelie had been enemies before anyone knew when, but that didn't mean we didn't all know each other, duel with each other, insult each other, screw each other. The Courts were small; time was long. What else was there to do? Ialach happened to be the only unlucky Seelie bastard to be born with yellow hair. All the others naturally had windswept silver-white veils to rival the feathers of the purest white dove. The dove was a notoriously stupid bird, which seemed appropriate to us black-haired Unseelie. I was the first to pounce on the difference. There were flowers that were the same color as the buttercups outside in the human world, with an equally embarrassing name that grew Under-the-Hill—in the High Court at least, needless to say. In the Dark Court we had black roses that wept tears of blood and scarlet lilies that ate butterflies. Yes . . . ate butterflies. We were truly beyond pretentious.

From the moment I spotted Ialach, he became Buttercup to the entire Dark Court. That was the cause of our first duel. It was a tie, but as I swore up and down, it was only because I could not stop laughing every time I addressed him as Lord Buttercup.

When we had come here and discovered what the humans had wrought, I'd stumbled across a sweet in one of their shops. Butterscotch, it had been called, and it was similar to the color of Ialach's then much shorter hair. As a peace offering between new partners, I called him Butterscotch instead of Buttercup and tried to kill him for only the first week or two. Eventually we discovered something from the time we last walked with humans: *uisge beatha*. The water of life. Scotch whiskey. Scotch had seized upon several bottles and drank nothing but that or water from then on. Taking the name for his own. After three years, I gave in and stopped telling anyone and everyone in the outposts we passed the truth of it. Once you decide not to kill your partner, you have his back. Not in the Courts, but here. Always here. And then he goes and stabs you in the chest. Where had I gone wrong?

I woke up to a night sky. Hazily I counted ten lonely stars. Ten out of the one time thousands that spread across the darkness. Not long now. No, not long. I coughed against a dry throat and asked hoarsely, "Are my boots on?"

"No." Scotch's voice was beside me. I turned my head to see him squatting by a small fire to add another chunk of dried manure. "Just in case you were weak and useless enough to die, I wanted you to wander what lies beyond eternity in your socks cursing my name. My *real* name."

I was lying on a sleeping bag, covered with two blankets, but I could see my toes. I wiggled them.

Nothing but socks was right, the bastard. Not that I didn't like socks. That was one thing humans had done right. Thick, warm socks beat striding black marble floors in silk hose and knee-high boots . . . oh, damn, and a crimson-lined cloak that was bespelled to drop blood-tipped black thorns in my path. I really had been a fucking douchebag. I didn't know what a fucking douchebag was, but a human had spat it at me before I gutted him. I took that to mean it was a fair enough insult.

"And why aren't I dead? With the silver and then you helpfully stabbing me in the chest, I expected something less in the living realm."

"I didn't stab you in the chest. I cannot believe all the Seelie that you bested in duels. Swatting pixies should've been beyond you. You whine like a satyr who's lost his nymphs and his cock." He sat beside me, stirring a can of beans. Another human invention, less appreciated than the socks. "I didn't stab you. I cut only as deep as needed to remove the bullet." He had his gloves off and I could see the silverburns on his fingers where he had plucked it out of me. "Unfortunately it wasn't deep enough to discover if you in fact have a heart. Now none will ever know." He ate a bite of beans. "Then I stitched you up with a few of Pie's tail hairs."

I was alive. Shit. That was damn near unheard of. Human speech, bad habits—easy to slide back into when you can throw all that grand leave-your-partner-with-a-good-memory fairy princess crap out the window. "They've tried taking silver bullets out before. They go too deep. Nobody lives. The poison of the metal spreads too fast."

"Guess I'm a helluva sight damn faster than any other sumbitch 'round these parts." Scotch grinned.

I laughed, groaned and held my chest, and laughed again. Ten years to bring a Seelie down to my level or at least half way between. It was worth the wait. "Hungry?" Scotch spooned up some more beans, putting the spoon in front of my mouth. I growled that I wasn't an infant and reached for the spoon. I managed to get at least one third of the spoonful in my mouth, the rest on my chin and blanket.

"So," Scotch said as I mopped my face with the blanket, "I'm still waiting on that story. Why are you called Seven?"

I had threatened to kill and had killed one or two who had been foolish enough to say my birth name aloud in the Dark Court. I had been known as nothing but Seven since I could heft a sword, but if I owed anyone, it was my partner. Wasn't that a bitch?

"It's short for seventeen," I gave in and grumbled. "When I was born my father was drunk. Well, he was always drunk, but he was drooling drunk this time. When he stood at my mother's birthing bed to name me, he became, they told me," I winced and it wasn't because of a bullet wound, "caught up in the moment. He declared I'd be called Prince of Shadows, He Who Rides Among the Storm Clouds and Will Forge the Blackest and Mightiest of Swords to Strike Down the White Army, Spilling Their Blood as a River . . . by then he sobered up some and remembered my mother had slept with his three brothers, his archenemy, and I think Titania. Mom always liked to mix it up. That's when he added Born of a Whore Who Would Rut With Any Barnyard Boar That Would Have Her. And then he passed out or I wouldn't be Seven. I'd be Twenty or Thirty. Seven is short for seventeen which is short for seventeen syllables of Elvish. He thought I was a cretin because I couldn't memorize my name until I was fifty." Which to give me credit was about a human child of four. "There. That's your story. Happy now?"

He leaned back against the rock wall we were camped again, beans forgotten. His smile was as wicked as any Unseelie could hope for. "Actually, I think I am the most happy that I have ever been in my life. Let me bask in it for a moment." Tilting his head back, he looked up at the ten stars and for once wasn't, as we always did, counting them—the sand trickling down the hourglass. This time he was seeing them simply as stars. I could see by the softening of the stubborn jaw. He might not be a portrait of joy and rainbow farting bunnies, but he wasn't grim. For a moment I could see home in him, see the magic lost.

Looking back down, he leaned over to search in his saddlebags to hand me a bottle of his precious scotch and lift one of his own.

I was shaky, but not so much I couldn't clink my bottle against his with the peal of a bell. It sounded the same as the ones they rang at most of the outposts—a habit the Fey who ran them had picked up from the humans.

Last call.

Not yet perhaps, but soon. Close enough to be draining your glass and ordering that last round. There was no one I'd rather drink that last round with than a Seelie Fey. Who could possibly have known?

"You were the worst of the best," I said and meant it for the compliment it was.

"And you were the best of the worst," he offered solemnly in the same spirit.

Maybe Scotch was as fast with a knife as he said or maybe there was a tiny speck of magic left in us after all. A magic that came from finding out what a millennia of balls, duels, conniving, spying, wars, taking the throne, losing the throne, all over and over again had failed to teach us: there was no Light Fey, no Dark Fey.

There was only the end.

BEAUTY

Jenifer Ruth

It's funny. Most of my kind can't see the wonder in this new human world. They're blind to anything that they don't control. So many of the lazy bastards would rather sit and hide in their hills and cut themselves off from the mortal realm than explore something ever-changing. They feel that a world that they created is much more wonderful than anything a human could dream.

Maybe it's because I need these fleeting creatures in order to survive that I enjoy the world they made so much. That's probably it. I and the other Sidhe who still roam the open roads are all the creatures who feed from the mortals or are closely tied to them. Like pets or small children, we can marvel at their ingenuity. We are amazed when they show us something we didn't expect.

The massive city sprawling around me is a perfect example.

Life, bright and noisy, fills the desert valley. Lights pulse and sparkle in a thousand different dancing patterns, bright enough to rival the stars in the sky. Music pounds on every street corner, the bass beating in time with the rhythm of the human heart.

But while luck and human inventiveness rules this land, magic is its undeclared king. Hidden realms of illusion melt together with the mortal's technological wonders. Mankind created the city, but the presence of the Sidhe adds that extra sparkle to it.

As with New York and Hollywood, Las Vegas sits as a crown jewel in the land of the Sidhe, at least for those of us who know how to appreciate it.

Though all fae creatures remain in the world of fantasy as far as the humans are concerned, times have changed for both mortals and for us. The plague of man has spread to nearly every corner of the earth. The untouched field and wood have become a memory buried under suburbia. These days it doesn't matter what court a Sidhe was from originally. Underhill or overhill is all that matters. If you stayed underground, you might as well not exist. Living topside is the only way to go.

So Las Vegas is a haven for the flashy and the dark creatures who shun hiding in the mounds, a feeding ground for Seelie and Unseelie alike.

And tonight, I'm one of them. Normally, I don't troll the streets looking for prey. But I need a new meal, since I just drained my last one. L.A. tends to be a better, more fertile hunting ground for my kind, but Vegas would have to do in a pinch. I should've known better than to let my last donor take up the offer to headline here, being as weak as he was. But I've always been too considerate and giving to my donors, especially when their short little lives were nearing the end. After all, I promised them a full draught of fame in return for their soul.

A Sidhe always keeps her word.

So now I, one of the divine Leanan Sidhe, have to resort to walking the streets and searching for a proper repast.

Luckily in this town, I'm not the type that the average tourist would spare a second glance, making it easier to hunt. I'm careful not to draw the wrong kind of attention. My black slacks and white silk top are of nice quality but not overly done. My long red hair can glow in certain lighting and my delicately carved features are known to inspire great works, but gorgeous women are a dime a dozen in a town where plastic surgeons advertised on billboards. So while I might not be fifty pounds overweight and wearing some wretched, skin-tight knock-off dress bought at one of the venders parked on the sidewalk like most of the tourist crowd, I don't exactly stand out.

If the average vacationer does notice me, it's not for my looks. The way I scan the streets, eyes constantly sweeping, might draw a gaze and a raised brow. I don't pause to gawk at the sights. One bad Elvis impersonator is very much like the next and none have the vital energy of the original. I've seen it all before and I don't have the time to waste. I don't blink as men and women in bright colored vests flick cards sporting half-naked women in my face. My step doesn't falter as young men with carefully gelled hair offer me free dance club tickets in hopes that I'll attract paying male customers. What would I want with any of that garbage?

These average mortals don't rate my attention.

Another woman, so beautiful and golden that she practically glows, skips past me with a herd of frat boys baying at her heels. Unlike me, she doesn't try to blend. She doesn't need to. Her laughter rings out like the chime of so many bells on a lonely night. She tosses her head, shaking out her sunny mane, and two more men join the chase.

The humans can't see past the glamour that hides her less than human features. They don't notice the over-sized, red-tinted, wild eyes. They can't tell that her teeth gleam more brightly than they should, or that they are slightly pointed. They don't notice the hungry desperation in her gaze when she looks over her shoulders at her growing group of fans.

As they follow her, the all too mortal men have no idea that some of them may never find their way back again. The ones who do will never be the same.

I give this twenty-first century will o' wisp a nod of acknowledgement as she dances by. It looks like I'm not the only one out hunting tonight. Luckily, we each have our own types of prey to hunt and they rarely overlap. Not that there isn't plenty to choose from around here in this never-ending flow of humanity.

What happens in Vegas stays in Vegas, and some-times the visitors never have the chance to leave.

I pick up the pace. I'm not nocturnal or anything; it's just in this city, the best hunting is in the early hours of the night. If I want to find a new meal, I need to start seriously searching.

I stop for a second as a flash of green at the corner of my eye grabs my attention. I smile and wave at the little leprechaun hiding outside a casino entrance. I hadn't seen one of his kind on the Strip before. Being a bit on the literal side, they tend to stick to Rainbow Boulevard. If the humans had any idea about what was buried at the end of that street, they'd have ripped the area apart. You put that many little people at the end of the only rainbow in a town built on greed and the treasure almost hoarded itself.

The little man glares at me, mouthing a curse that I don't bother trying to translate. I guess he doesn't want attention drawn to himself, probably a pick-pocket waiting for some minor jackpot winner to come out of the casino. Or maybe he's avoiding the spriggin standing guard at the door. That particular casino was run by a member of the Unseelie court, one that didn't want to be locked away beneath the ground. If the leprechaun thought he'd put some-thing over on that owner, he'd be lucky if he didn't end up splattered by a red cap or worse.

The Italian mob might be famous for its violent casino antics, but they had nothing on the Unseelie.

Whatever. I have better things to do than waste

my time in a pissing contest with the vertically challenged. I can see a group of humans gathering at the corner. Heavy metal blares from that direction.

Maybe I found my meal.

I weave my way through the crowd, not an easy feat as packed in as they were. Still, if the person drawing this much attention is as good as he seems from the size of the crowd, my next meal ticket is a sure thing. Of course, humans aren't always the best judges of talent.

My anticipation is short-lived. The canned music isn't nearly savory enough to signal a feast for me and the so-called artist is more of a showman than a true connoisseur. To the beat of his speakers, he slaps and sprays paint on the canvas stretched on the ground at his feet. Slowly, a picture of some mundane talk show host appears out of the mess, to the thunder of the crowd's applause. It's an interesting gimmick, something the tourists must love. Monetarily, it's a winning gamble, sell the painting and get some donations thrown in the hat at the same time. But I wouldn't call it art. I know creatures that can fart better paintings.

And my opinion is the only one that matters. Of course, that doesn't stop me from reaching out and draining what little bit of creative energy I can from the scruffy man.

Who am I to pass up a quick snack?

I manage to push my way back out of the crowd without getting too disheveled. I pause to straighten all the wrinkles from my clothes and fluff my hair.

Looking around, I don't see any prospects, so I move on down the street. As I make my way, I'm seeing more and more people with giant drinks shaped like famous landmarks literally strapped around their necks. It might not be my thing, but inebriated prey was easy prey. So, I guess, the more the merrier.

As I cross an alley, I feel a tug of magic. Someone has cast a strong glamour over the area next to the large green dumpster.

I can't help but peek, curiosity getting the better of me. A beautiful woman, who resembles me though with much more flash, is pressing a man against the wall. His hand is up her skirt and he's groaning as her mouth travels down his throat. She senses my presence, tossing her hair back and smirking at me. Her eyes glitter and glow though there is no light in the alley. The human, deep in his own passions, never sees the nails on her left hand growing into claws, even as she wiggles those elongating fingers at me.

One quick slash and he doesn't even have time to scream. The Baobhan Sidhe follows him to the ground, drinking the blood gushing from his neck. Not a single drop escapes her hunger.

I feel jealous at the ease of her feeding. She doesn't have to be picky. Any human will do for this vampire. Male or female, young or old, skilled or not, it doesn't matter as long as the person falls for her beauty and can be lured away from the pack. Of course, she can't keep her prey around for years or even decades like I can, especially if I'm careful to space out my feedings. She has to hunt every night without end.

Still, at times like these when my energy is low and I haven't found a donor, I envy her. Being picky doesn't always pay.

I shake my head and start walking again. I don't want to draw attention to the Baobhan Sidhe, not when she hasn't had time to hide the body yet. It wouldn't do any of us good if the human police were called. We Sidhe exist in the shadows and live well that way. We would all suffer if the humans believed in our existence again. It was one thing when there were fewer of us, and less humans as well. Now we are everywhere, our numbers growing despite having to live without a mound. As long as the humans continue to relegate us to children's stories, the easier it is to be the hunters and not the hunted.

I mean, would a group of kelpies be able to stand in front of the giant fountains that were the mainstay of the casino across the street if people believed in them? Sure, they're disguised as a group of not so attractive, hairy men, laughing and flirting with women as they passed. A beautiful horse standing there would've been horribly obvious. But with little effort, they are able to separate lone tourists and drag them into the water. Several minutes later, they reappear, lean against the railing, and start flirting again. No muss, no fuss, and no one the wiser. No human could imagine the number of people who disappear in such a public place without a trace.

That human disbelief is our greatest weapon.

I stand across the street and watch the kelpies for a while. With the fountain going through its hourly show, no one will wonder what I'm looking at. I'm just another out-of-towner taking in the free entertainment and the glory of water dancing to the musical stylings of Frank Sinatra. With people stopping and focusing on the gushing water, the kelpies make quick work out of at least three women as I watch. With such rich pickings, they won't have to hunt again this week, maybe even this month.

As the music fades, the lights dim, and the water falls, I turn back to my own quest.

Surely someone with untapped talent is around here somewhere. I mean, this city is huge and it's considered one of the showbiz capitals of the world. I've even heard it called a musicians' Mecca. Maybe I'll have to resort to chatting up another headliner. I hope not. I hate making due with slim pickings. Once the person is already established as an artist, they aren't as tasty or as filling. But I can survive a few months, even a year on one if I have to.

A trickle of strings, a melodious turn of chords flows its way to me. My lips curl at the corners and I close my eyes to absorb the pleasure of the music trickling over my senses. Yes, this is what I'm looking for. I can practically taste the sweet nectar floating on the breeze. A pure, artistic soul beckons.

The man I find sitting cross-legged on the sidewalk, an open guitar case in front of him, isn't classically handsome. He isn't at all the type of guy that would attract the attention of someone who looks like me. He's young and a little rough around the edges. His brown hair is shaggy, falling into his face and covering his eyes. But he's got good bone structure and is in good shape. Still it isn't his looks that lured me to him. Like an uncut diamond, his persona can be polished to a gleaming splendor at a later date.

It's his music that compels me, his art that draws me near. I stand to the side, swaying along with the rhythm of his song. I ignore the other humans that hurry past him without so much as a pause or a tossed coin, never bothering to even glance his way. What did they know about art? It takes someone of my kind to shove greatness in their faces before humans ever notice it. The strongest of the Leanan Sidhe run the music industry, control the art world, and dominate acting, all from behind the scenes. There, we show mankind their own marvels while feeding on the souls that produce the wonder.

I open my eyes and smile at the man, reaching into my pocket for the thick wad of bills I'd taken from my last artist after he died. It wasn't like he'd need it now anyway and considering the amount of coke he was snorting at the end, no one would miss it.

I toss the bundle into this man's case, grinning at the heavy thud it makes against the thinly padded leather.

His eyes widen at the amount, a jarring sound ringing from his instrument as his fingers miss a few key strings. But I don't mind the discordant noise. I have his full attention now.

He pauses, a question gleaming in his eyes. He clears his throat and pats his guitar. "Is there something you want to hear? If I know it, I'll play it." He flashes me a shy grin. "If I don't, I'll play it anyway."

And let the games begin. I grin back, letting him see I appreciate his attempt at humor. "I'd like to hear something you wrote, if you don't mind."

Sucking in a deep breath, he nods, fumbling for a moment as his fingers glide over the frets. I know the sound of my voice shakes him. That *is* the point. Sweet and melodious, my voice was created to both tempt and inspire the true lyricist. I am the muse that will lead a human to fame and glory while eating his soul a drop at a time. I am Leanan Sidhe.

As music is this man's calling, its ultimate corruption is mine.

A presence in the shadows draws my attention from my next donor. A trow lingers in the shadows, watching with its own hunger gleaming in his squinty orbs. My musician must have great untapped ability if he is enchanting enough to draw this ugly creature out of its trowie and deep into the human-packed city. Trows, solitary and shy creatures similar to trolls, don't do crowds. Only the most skilled musician can lure them from their underground homes.

I feel a stab of pride at the creature's presence, wanting to pat my new pet on his head to show my approval of his musical strength. At the same time, I can't allow this other creature to challenge me for my prey. Having my human trapped underground playing wedding music for the next few decades would be an incredible waste of talent.

Not to mention, just listening to the talented musician play was making me hungry.

I glare at the ugly, hunched little creature. I waste a bit of my remaining magical power in a short pulse, showing the trow that I meant business. I am Sidhe and the trow was a lesser being, almost lower in importance than the humans. If he thinks he can take my musician without a fight, I am more than ready to prove him wrong. The trow might be physically stronger than me, but my magic could rip him to shreds before he could make his first move.

He simply needs to be reminded of that fact.

The creature growls as he feels the weight of my magic but slinks away, head bowed between its disproportioned shoulders. In moments, the shadows swallow him and not even his stench remains.

The musician doesn't notice the exchange, concentrating on performing a delicate set of chords that flows into a lovely melody. It shocks me to see that no one else notices the beauty laid out before them. How can humans be so blind to their own greatness, their own splendor? How could they survive if it wasn't for my kind guiding them from behind the scenes?

"That's amazing." My voice drips with compelling magic as I move a step closer. It's nearly time to pounce. A little more attention and he will be mine. "What do you call it?"

The man swallows and licks his lips. He doesn't

meet my gaze as he shrugs. "I don't know. It just came to me."

I smile. Of course it did. He is in the presence of a muse. I've helped lesser talents than he to achieve masterpieces that will be remembered for eons. "Does it have lyrics to go with it?"

He closes his eyes and shakes his head. His shoulders stoop a bit as he speaks. "No. I'm not good with words."

I take the opportunity to kneel down beside him, reaching out to touch his guitar. I run my fingers over the battered, but obviously well-loved, wood. I allow my expression to show only wonder and appreciation, not the desperate hunger that lurks just beneath my skin. "I doubt that. With time and the proper muse, I bet you could write a song that would grip a person's heart and squeeze every drop of emotion from them. You have the potential to reach the hearts and minds of millions."

He laughed, his nervous fingers plucking strings at random. "No way. I don't have that kind of talent. If you think I do, you obviously don't know me."

"I know enough." I sat down completely, leaning close enough for him to feel the heat from my body but not close enough to touch. I watch people walking by, ignoring what will one day inspire them. I bump him with my shoulder, finally getting him to look at me. "What's your name?"

"Kyle," he whispers. He ducks his head, eyeing the ground again, but he doesn't move away.

My shoulder still touching his, I take a moment to

draw in a bit of his energy, enough to get a taste of his soul so I can find him whenever I want. I will let him believe he still has his freedom, that he comes to me by his own choice, but he is mine now. Yes, this is the one I was looking for. I reach into my pocket to pull out one of my cards, already heavily charmed to bring me whatever I desire. I hold it out to him, waiting for him to accept my offer and activate the magic. "Well, Kyle, have you ever wanted to be famous?"

He takes the paper, glancing down at it as the charm binds him to me. He grimaces, but not from the magic. I can feel the hope and anticipation vibrating in him, at war with his mortal sense of despair. He's so afraid to believe. "This is Vegas, lady. Everyone wants either fame or fortune."

This *is* a town that gives rise to dreams as easily as it crushes them beneath its neon-clad feet. "Well, I can give you both fame and fortune if you trust me." I tap at the card, adding a bit more compulsion to the magic. "Take your time. Look me up. You'll find I'm the real deal. I've worked with many artists like you. I know when I find someone who will be great. I also know how to help them meet their ultimate potential."

I push even more magic at him, feeding that part of him that he draws his inspiration from. So much promise there, waiting to be tapped. I feel giddy with anticipation and struggle to contain it. All in good time. "With my help, you can be great." I climb to my feet, dusting off my slacks.

His hand trembles a little as he clutches my card.

He's so cute sitting there trying to act as though being discovered happened to him every day. He's struggling to act cool. He doesn't want me to know for certain that he'll be calling me, probably before the next sun sets.

But he will. They always do. And I give each and every one of them exactly what I say I will. I show the world the beauty they create. I help the mortals discover what they are capable of. I make them famous. Their names will be remembered long after they are gone, their music still savored even after their deaths. I assist my artists in gifting the world with beauty, a beauty that helps all of mankind to forget for a moment how fleeting their lives truly are.

And I feed from it. I may pay for my food, in my own way, but don't make any mistakes. Don't imagine that I'm some kind of guardian angel or selfless saint. I am one of the monsters, one of those creatures that humans still fear even as they claim they don't believe such evil exists.

The Sidhe are not kind, not generous and giving. We are glorious. We are horrid. We are magnanimous. We are petty. We are astonishing. We are resentful. We are strong. We are envious. And in one way or another, those of us who still live in the mortal world have to eat to survive.

And I eat beauty.

PENNYROYAL

Kerrie Hughes

I was afraid and angry as I lay face down in the grass with blood filling my mouth. Two jerks had jumped me from behind and I bit my own tongue when I hit the ground. One of them was searching my backpack while the other held me down by sitting on my back. He had one hand on my head to keep me from seeing him. I decided not to move.

"What's she got?" the one on my back said.

"Just clothes, a wooden flute thing, and girl stuff."

"No money?"

"Check her pockets."

Rough hands went through my jean pockets and hoodie.

"I'm not finding anything." He leaned forward. "Where's your money, little girl?"

I mumbled but ended up coughing blood instead.

"Let her talk, dude."

He took his hand off my head and I felt something ram into him and knock him off my back. He let out a *whumpf* of air and started to call for help.

"Son of a bitch!"

Grrrrrrrr!

I scrambled up and saw a large black dog sitting on one guy; the other was backing away slowly. The dog leapt off the first guy and ran at the second, chasing him across the grass. First Guy got to his feet and ran in the opposite direction. I looked around but didn't see the dog's owner. Even though I was still a little dizzy, I thought I should hurry up and get to safety. I rolled up my sleeping bag, put my pack on, and headed toward street-lights.

London was proving to be more dangerous than I had planned. I had only been away from the Seelie lands for three days, and I was already rethinking my plan to run away to the city in order to avoid the upcoming hostage ceremony.

My name is Mistress Galadria Pennyroyal of the Seelie Clan. I am the fifth daughter of Lord and Lady Pennyroyal, and I will be exchanged, scratch that, was to be exchanged in a ceremony a week from today. A daughter of the Seelie given for a daughter of the Unseelie as a contract to continue the Peace. Now I'm just some dumb fey girl masquerading as human, who exchanged a life of privilege for a bloody mouth and nowhere safe to sleep.

A wet nose on my hand interrupted my pity party. It was the black dog. I had stopped walking and had dropped my sleeping bag on the sidewalk and was staring off into a cemetery. The dog sat back on his haunches and looked up at me. He resembled a black German shepherd but had one gray ear.

I pushed my sleeping bag up against the fence and sat on it; the dog lay down next to me. I reached over and let him smell my hand, then scratched him on the head.

"So you are my savior tonight."

The dog, of course, said nothing.

"You can call me Gala; what name should I call you?"

He put his head down but kept his eyes on me.

"I'll just call you Dog for now. I'm too tired to think and I still need to find a place to sleep."

Dog got up and looked toward the cemetery.

"Good idea. The dead can't hurt me, and if you sleep next to me I won't be too scared."

We got up and went in. I found a caretaker shack, which was locked. Fortunately, there was a garden hose we could both drink from and I washed the blood out of my mouth. We located a soft but dry patch of grass behind a nearby mausoleum and I got in my bag. Dog lay down on top of the bag next to me; I probably fell asleep immediately.

The next day I woke up to the sound of church bells. I really wanted to get more sleep but I didn't think I could stay here.

"What's for breakfast, Dog?"

He cocked his head and looked at me.

"I guess we'll have the candy bar."

I offered to share it with him but he sniffed it and declined. Then I shook out the sleeping bag, rolled it up, and went over to the shack to get some water. I took off my hoodie and tee shirt, leaving me in a bra. I was sixteen, but as a fey girl I looked like a ten-year-old human child. I guessed I couldn't get a job in a bar or busk for my supper in Piccadilly Square, another kink in my plans.

My hair was stark white and my eyes were purple. I had considered dyeing my hair to blend in with the humans but discovered that some of the human children would bleach their hair white, so I just cut my hair and pulled it back in a ponytail. I pretended I had purple contacts if anyone asked about my eyes.

I washed my filthy hair with a little shampoo I still had and used the lather to clean my face. I debated stripping down and washing the rest of my body. Dog would be standing nearby and if anyone saw me they would just see a naked girl whose skin was more peach colored than a sallow pink like most Britons. I hated how sticky and disgusting I felt.

"Okay, Dog, be a gentleman and turn around."

I quickly peeled off my jeans and underwear and washed the rest of me. The water was cold but it felt good. I dried off with my T-shirt and pulled my last clean shirt, socks, and underwear out of my backpack and put them on. I combed out my hair and looked at my dirty clothes.

I thought that life with freedom from responsibility would be wonderful. I would make money by playing my flute and wander from town to town, meeting interesting people, and seeing the world. Instead I met thieves, rapists, and an endless parade of homeless people who were half crazy and often addicted to herbal intoxicants. It wasn't paradise for those without homes and no one to love them; it was a sewer with rats. If you were lucky a dog might take pity on you. I looked over at Dog, who was still looking the other way.

"This is ridiculous. I feel like a fool. You know what, Dog? I'm going to have to go home."

He turned around and woofed in what I would swear was agreement.

"Do you want to come with me?"

Another woof and a hearty wag of the tail.

I laughed and threw my dirty clothes into a nearby garbage bin full of old flowers. I had to put the muddy jeans back on. I then tied my hoodie around my waist, but decided to leave my sleeping bag at the door of the shack. Maybe someone like me would see it and need some warmth.

"I think you need a better name." I said, as I put my pack on and tightened the straps. "I'm going to call you Galahad, after my favorite knight."

He made a small noise that sounded like a harrumph and cocked his head.

"Galadria and Galahad, sounds a little dorky, does it not?"

He snorted and walked over to me, did a head-butt to my hip, and trotted away.

I followed him out of the graveyard and then took

the lead. We were headed to the oldest oak tree in London.

Methuselah's Oak was located in Hampton Court Park. The Royal Botanical Society estimated its age as 750 years, and has protected it from being cut down. Ancient oak trees are portals in and out of the fey world. This oak was a wide, gnarled giant that looked like it was split down the middle with an expanse of grass parting the two sides. A fey only needed to walk between and utter a short cantrip to travel to an identical tree on the Otherside.

Galahad and I walked up to the tree and I put my hands on the trunk. Instantly I felt homesick.

"Are you sure you want to come with me?"

He nudged my hand with his nose and licked it. I took that as doggy agreement and I led him into the middle of the tree. Then I knelt down and wrapped my arms around him, closed my eyes, and said the necessary words. I felt a warm shiver run through us and then opened my eyes.

The fey world looks very similar to the human world. Our buildings have our own style, but the landscape is basically the same as it was a century ago when Merlin created this pocket of safety.

"What do you think, Galahad?"

He looked around and then looked back at me.

"Well, I suppose we should head for my parents' home. It's a few hours from here and I've got that much time to craft an apology or a really good lie."

*   *   *

We walked for a while down a dirt road, cut across some fields, and got water from a brook. Galahad caught a fish and ate it. Apples and plums were plentiful. They tasted sweeter and juicier than I remembered. Perhaps it was the naturally beautiful state of my own world that made me think the human world would be just as lovely. I knew very little about our larger cities though and it made me wonder if they too had homeless and ill people living on the streets.

I talked to Galahad along the way and voiced my fear that the Unseelie Court would be a lonely place where everyone would shun me. He said nothing more than a small woof or chuff as we moved along.

"I don't know what's going to happen to me, Galahad, but I promise that at the very least, if the Unseelie Court is too dangerous, I will have my older sister Gisele take care of you."

He barked and ran a circle around me. I laughed for the first time in over a month.

Just before we merged onto another road I stopped behind a stone wall to relieve myself. Once I emerged I looked around but didn't see Galahad anywhere. Instead I saw a pixie sitting on an old stump nearby.

"Excuse me. Have you seen a black dog?"

The pixie pointed toward a field of tall corn and the remains of an old brick farmstead.

"He ran that way chasing a jackrabbit," he replied in a small voice.

"Thanks." I answered with a respectful bob of my head. "Galahad!" I called out.

I got no response so I walked across the road and called again; still no response. The old home looked completely abandoned with the roof caving in. I hoped he hadn't gone inside. I went around the house and called out again. I heard a footstep and turned around, then someone grabbed me and put a foul-smelling rag over my face.

I had a pounding headache and winced as I tried to turn my head. It was dark outside and it took me a moment to remember talking to a pixie and then being grabbed. I decided to be as quiet as possible until I figured out where I was. I seemed to be on the ground with my hands and feet tied and a rag around my mouth. I blinked a few times and adjusted to night vision. I could see a small campfire nearby and two forms sitting near it. They were talking.

"He should have returned by now," said the first.

"Mmm. Even with the dark he had plenty of time to get there and back twice," came the answer.

They definitely sounded like either brownies or redcap. Most likely redcaps, since brownies stayed clear of treachery while redcaps reveled in chaos.

"She's small. Maybe we should carry her to Harwick's house."

"If he doesn't come back soon with Weed and his cart, we'll need to slit her throat and take off."

"Aye, that."

I swallowed hard and tested my bonds. They were well tied. Then a whisper brushed my ear.

"Stay still and quiet."

My heart jumped in fear, but whoever it was sliced the bonds on my wrists and put a dagger in my hand. Then I heard an odd sound, like the folding of spellwork, and a large form sailed over me and into the bigger of the two redcaps. Just like what Dog, I mean Galahad, had done in London.

Both redcaps squealed in fright as Galahad wrestled one to the ground. I worked quickly to get my gag off and my ankle ropes cut. I heard a scream and a crack, then fierce growling. I approached the fire with the knife in my hand and saw one redcap dead on the ground, his throat ripped out. The other one was facing down Galahad with a knife of his own, a bigger, more vicious looking knife. Neither looked at me, and the redcap charged at Galahad, who leapt forward to meet the attack. The redcap rolled on the ground under him and out of reach, then somersaulted backward and landed on the dog's back. Galahad twisted and rolled but the redcap sunk a knife in his chest and I gasped.

The redcap got up in a flash and came running toward me. I gripped the hilt of my dagger and dodged off to the side as he met me. He tumbled forward and I threw myself to where I knew he would be when he rolled up to leap again. My dagger sunk into his gut and I swiftly decked him across the nose with my freehand. He screamed in pain; the nose of a redcap is large and sensitive like the bullocks of a boy, and the sound was strangely satisfying. I grabbed his wrist and pulled my dagger out of his gut, then sliced his throat along the jugular. I was panting and shaking as I did the deed.

"By the stars, Gala, you are better at offense than defense."

I plucked the knife from the redcap's fist and took a look at the other guy. His knife was on the ground. I picked up that one too and went over to where Galahad was lying on the ground.

Galahad was dressed in black leathers, a black shirt, and long coat. His black hair was wild looking, with a streak of white on one side. He smiled with a big wolfy grin despite the obvious pain he was in. I dropped the knives and went down on my knees next to him. I moved the hand that covered the wound in his chest aside.

"Should I call you Dog, Galahad, or do you go by another name?" I asked as I examined the wound under his shirt.

"You may know me as Black Shuck, but you can call me what you like."

I knew the name Black Shuck. Sir Black Shuck, Knight of the Unseelie Clan. Courtier to Queen Tatiana; was it possible the Queen knew I was gone?

He winced when I probed the flesh a bit, "I have healing skills. Please take a breath and then let it out."

He did as he was asked. "I do not hear the rattle of a punctured lung. How do you feel?"

"Tired."

"What about the pain? Is it burning, throbbing or stinging? "

"Burning."

"I need a minute. Stay there and breathe deeply; try to relax." He did as he was told and I looked around the area. I located a spiderweb, an oak leaf, and fresh feverfew. The redcaps had a flask of whiskey that smelled fairly decent. I went back to Sir Black and knelt down.

"Okay, hold still."

I laid my cheek on his bared chest, just touching the wound, took a deep breath, and hummed as I breathed out. I felt blood bubble up to my cheek. Then I sat up and poured whiskey on the leaf, then spread the spiderweb on it, placing it web side down on the wound. I put my cheek back on the wound, and hummed again. He sighed in relief. I poured some more whiskey on the feverfew before handing it to him.

"Put this in your cheek and chew it slowly, but don't swallow it."

Again, he did as he was told and I closed up his shirt and my hand over it, then took a deep breath and hummed a short cantrip.

"That feels amazingly good."

"Can you get up?"

He nodded and I helped him get to his feet.

"Can you walk?"

He moved around a bit.

"I can."

"Would you rather do it in dog form?"

"I don't feel strong enough to shift. This will have to do."

I gave him back his dagger, and put one of the redcap's knives in my hood, the whiskey in my pocket, and the other knife through a belt loop. I checked the stars and looked around.

"What did they want with me?"

"The pixie confessed to being part of a slaver ring just before I broke his neck."

"Eew."

"Eew? You just cut the throat of a redcap."

"You ripped out the throat of the other one first."

We looked at each other and then I laughed nervously. He put his hand on my shoulder and then hugged me.

"It's good to be alive. Don't waste another thought on them."

I let him hug me for a minute and then broke away.

"Do you have any idea where we are?"

"Yes. Down this road is a bridge. If we cut across the field past it there's an inn not too far away."

We walked the road quickly and in silence. The full moon had been a blessing, but if someone were looking for us it would also be a curse. Once we passed the bridge and started across the field, we stopped and I checked his wound.

"Can I spit this out now?"

"Yes. How do you feel?"

"A little dizzy, a little pain, but otherwise fine."

"The feverfew can take away most pain. Want some of the whiskey?"

"No, let's get to the inn first."

He led us across the field and to the dirt road. It was a bit cold and he stumbled a little, probably dehydrated and tired, so I put my arm around his and walked closer.

"Can I ask you why you ran away?"

I thought for a moment. It was a question I had given a lot of thought to when I was sleeping on the ground, meeting people who wanted to steal my meager belongings and skipping showers. I really hated skipping showers.

"Gala?"

"It's a hard question."

"You don't have to tell me."

"No, I want to tell you. It all kind of started when my dad accepted the request for one of his daughters to be a royal hostage. I was excited at first, but then my Uncle Felix came over to discuss it with Father and Mother. He was saying how I would be the most suitable. I was a bad choice for Seelie marriage because I'm not a proper lady."

"What did your parents say?"

"They agreed."

"I see."

We walked in silence for a few minutes.

"I think I could have put up with that, except my sisters were telling me how I'd have to live with crazy deformed people and sadists. Then they said I would be expected to marry into my foster family someday."

"I can see why you wouldn't want to marry a sadist, or someone crazy for that matter."

"I know the Unseelie are not all crazy, just like the Seelie are not all beautiful. It's just that I've never wanted to marry anyone. I want to apprentice with a master healer and become one someday."

"A noble profession."

"Not if my foster family won't permit me."

"I see the problem."

"My turn to ask a question."

"Yes?"

"Were you sent to find me?"

"I was."

"By my family?"

"By your foster family, actually."

I stopped in my tracks and he faced me.

"Why would they want to find me? They don't even know me."

"The request upon your family was no mistake. The queen knows all her subjects and takes an interest in the royal families of Seelie. You were sought out because our best seer saw that you would be a great asset to our clan."

I thought for a minute. "But it was the choice of my father as to whom he would send as hostage."

"Yes, and we thought it would be you, but once you ran the request would fall on one of your sisters. That is not in the queen's plans."

"Then why not just ask for me?"

"The seer sees what he sees. He foresaw that you would need to run away, decide to come home, and be ready for your legacy."

"Isn't a legacy nullified if I know about it?"

"Apparently not in this case."

"What else do you know?"

"Nothing I can share."

"You were more fun as a dog," I said as I started to walk again. He laughed and caught up to me.

"I hear that quite a bit."

The inn was in sight and we slowed a little. I almost didn't want to stop walking, but his wound would need tending and we were exhausted.

One week later

My parents had been more relieved than angry, especially when Sir Black Shuck of the Unseelie Court made it clear that Queen Tatiana would be expecting me well rested at the exchange ceremony. Now I stood in line outside the throne room to be given by my queen to the Unseelie queen in exchange for one of their children as a peace hostage. I was dressed in purple to match my eyes and had orchids woven into my hair.

My father escorted me to the throne of Queen Mab where we both bowed and her chancellor announced us.

"Lord Percival Pennyroyal and his daughter Galadria."

He then took me from my father and led me to the Unseelie queen, where I was greeted by Sir Black Shuck. He gave me his arm and I smiled. He looked very nice: still all in black but in fancy court leathers and wearing a peace tied sword.

I curtsied to the queen and she nodded to me.

"Welcome, Galadria, I place you with the Lady Oleander, our best healer to be fostered until you come of age. Do you accept your fate as I decree it?"

"I do."

"Then, sir knight, please escort our new hostage to her foster home and entrust her with the royal gift."

"My thanks, Queen Tatiana; I can only hope to be of service."

And with that, Sir Black led me out of the courtroom and to a very lovely woman with long grey hair twisted back into a braid. She wore the robes of a royal healer and I nearly skipped to meet her.

"Lady Oleander, this is Galadria Pennyroyal."

She smiled at me and I bowed. I nearly stuttered my greeting. " I, I am very pleased to meet you."

"I have a gift for you."

She nodded to someone beside her and a page brought out a white Cu Sith, a treasured fey dog of the royal court. He was beautiful. I looked at Lady Oleander and then at Black.

"He's mine?"

"Indeed he is."

I dropped to my knees and the dog came forward and licked my face.

I was never gladder to be me.

UNLOCKED GATE

Dean Wesley Smith

Cindy Kemp would have sworn on her dead uncle's favorite Chevy, even bet that she wouldn't go shopping for an entire week, that the color green couldn't be drained from anything. Especially beer.

Okay, she would have been wrong, so it was damn lucky no one thought to bet her before all the green draining started.

"Incoming!" she shouted over the nasty beat of someone doing ugly things to a Neil Diamond song, not that she liked Neil Diamond.

She slid the glass of green beer down the polished oak bar like a puck in a shuffleboard game. Ben and Wolf-boy, two regulars sitting at the bar, quickly got their beers out of the way as the new one slid past. She held the pose of an expert beer-slider, her hand high over her head, her wrist twisted slightly to the left, as the glass with the perfect head of green foam stopped exactly in front of the goofy-looking guy with thick hair and a long nose.

Not a drop spilled.

Man, she was good!

The customers crowded against the bar applauded. Wolf-boy gave her his famous wolf-whistle, which even turned heads on the dance floor. Every time he did that, she expected bottles on the back bar to shatter like in a bad television commercial.

She bowed and then winked at the other bartender, Judy, who just shook her head, her long red hair flapping around in a ponytail behind her back.

The guy with the long nose gave her a beaming smile that made Cindy's stomach queasy and his nose seem even longer, if that was possible. The guy's father must have been a cobbler.

She turned quickly to the well and began work on a drink using crème de menthe and rum for the trashy blonde woman beside him. The bar went through gallons of the smelly green crème de menthe once a year. The rest of the time the bottle just sat on the back bar growing mold, as if anyone would even notice with the green color.

God, she loved St. Patrick's Day in Chicago. It was still early in the evening, yet Peter's Place was jamming. The music hugged her like her best winter coat, its bass beat rattling the bottles. The music was the party; all she did was push things along with tons of green beer and ugly green drinks.

With the music so loud, she could barely hear drink orders unless she bent forward, giving the guys at the bar the perfect hint of the tops of her breasts. She figured it never hurt to tease a little, toss out a little bait just to see who might take the hook. Of course, if someone like the guy with the long nose took the bait, she would toss him back. She had her standards after all, even though she was damned horny and had been for weeks now.

St. Patrick's Day brought more than just the regulars out to play, especially since Peter's Place was so close to the University of Chicago and tucked in the middle of a street of shops that stretched for blocks. Students jammed the long bar three deep, covering just about every foot of Peter's Place's hardwood floors. Some of the regulars had gotten in early and claimed the dozen stools. Everyone else stood, drinking, eating peanuts, and shouting over the music.

Huge barrels of salted-in-the-shell peanuts were scattered around the room. She had a hunch that some of the poorer students used a glass of beer and a few bowls of peanuts for dinner more often than not. Peter, the owner, didn't seem to care or notice. The salty peanuts kept the floor a white dusty color and people drinking. On New Year's Eve, right at the tick of midnight, everyone threw peanuts. So far no one had been seriously hurt. She just kept thanking the workforce gods that her job didn't include sweeping the place.

She pulled her blouse away from her chest a couple of quick times, letting cooler air inside her shirt. The fans hanging down from the tall ceiling tried their best to keep the air moving, but she had no doubt that by midnight, she would be sweating like after a good workout. The music already had a good thirty people on the small dance floor in the right corner, which wasn't helping the heating factor either, especially the way some of them were jumping around.

She glanced over at the goofy guy with the nose. There was just something about that nose that kept her staring at it. Maybe it promised other large body parts. She tried to imagine a wild night with that nose and the idea just made her laugh. If there was ever an argument for plastic surgery, the poor guy had it sticking to the front of his face. He should offer to do ads for a plastic surgeon. The before and after pictures would be enough to convince anyone.

Again she fanned her blouse open and closed a few times. Maybe she shouldn't have worn silk tonight. She had bought the green blouse two days before in the thrift shop off the Loop. The rich from the Lake Shore area gave away some of the best designer clothes, and she wasn't above buying them at a tiny fraction of the price. Even though she was a working student, that didn't mean she couldn't dress in the style. It just took a little more creativity and patience in the thrift stores.

Tonight, she had on a sexy green skirt with the light-green silk blouse, unbuttoned two buttons down, and a dark green silk tie that she kept loose and tossed over her shoulder when dealing with dirty glasses. The green shamrock post earrings and the green ribbon holding her long brown hair in place added a put-together touch to the outfit.

She was "hot green" and she knew it.

She finished the crème de menthe drink that smelled like Listerine and glanced at the guy with the nose. He had turned and was talking to the blonde who had ordered the drink.

The woman had no sense of taste in clothing. She wore a thin green cotton blouse tucked into Levi's two sizes too small. Rolls of fat flopped over the tops of her jeans, straining the poor blouse, pulling it tight against her tits, which sagged some and needed to have a bra covering them.

Cindy almost felt sorry for the blouse. On the right woman, with the right stuff under it, the blouse would look nice.

Mr. Long Nose was sure interested in what that poor blouse was straining to hold in. He stared at the blonde's chest like her eyes were there. Cindy sat the drink down in front of the blonde and waited for Mr. Long Nose to turn away from the peep show long enough to pay for it.

If he bought two more of those drinks for that blonde, he was going to be very sorry later. Crème de menthe tasted like mouthwash going down. Cindy couldn't imagine what it tasted like coming back up, but she knew for a fact it smelled horrid. She had seen a few too many women in the bathroom realize just how bad that green stuff really was for them. Every St. Patrick's Day she thanked the workforce gods that her job didn't include cleaning up the bathrooms either.

In front of Cindy, a large guy with a football jersey shoved his way through the crowd and slammed his half-full glass on the bar between Wolf-boy and Ben. Wolf-boy and Ben were math majors who loved to drink. And they often kept her entertained with fast one-liners and catty looks at others.

Now, both looked at him over their glasses, giving Jock-Boy the annoyed look the two had perfected for jerks at the bar. But the big jock wasn't into noticing anything but himself.

"How come I didn't get a green beer?" he shouted over the music.

"You're too tall," Wolf-boy said, just loud enough for Cindy to barely hear.

"Too stupid," Ben said.

Jock-Boy ignored them and held up his glass for her to see.

It was full of regular-colored beer, or something that looked like it. Whatever it was, it hadn't come from any of their taps, since every keg they had on line had been filled with green food coloring.

No doubt the guy was pulling some sort of scam on her to get a free beer, but it didn't matter. Nothing was going to ruin her good mood tonight. It was St. Patrick's Day and if she was lucky, she would cut out a prime candidate out of the crowd and get laid before breakfast.

Jock-Boy sat the glass down again and said, "Well?"

"Don't touch that!" Wolf-boy said, leaning away

from the yellow beer in mock horror, like it might blow up.

Ben leaned the other way, also showing mock horror. "It's been . . . recycled."

She laughed and then pretending to be very careful, took Jock-Boy's glass between two fingers like she was holding a dead frog and poured out whatever was in there. She got him a clean glass and pulled him a green beer, again making sure the head was perfect on the top.

She placed the beer in front of him. Before he could pick it up and turn away, the green vanished like it had never been there.

"Not funny!" the guy shouted over the loud music at her.

Both Wolf-boy and Ben were now very seriously studying the golden-filled glass, clearly as stunned as she was feeling.

Jock-Boy hadn't touched it. No one had but her. Something must be going wrong with the food coloring Peter had put in the kegs.

She glanced down at Judy, but her partner behind the bar was busy at the second well and hadn't noticed anything going wrong. Typical. The woman could ignore a fight, a fire in a garbage can, and two women slapping each other at the bar all at the same time. And had.

Suddenly, the green beer Wolf-Boy had been sipping on lost its green. Then Ben's did the same.

"Okay, now that's something!" Wolf-Boy said, bending down and studying up close his glass.

Ben looked almost afraid of his beer. Maybe this would be what they both needed to slow down the drinking. Two math majors who were so damned smart that they were bored with school, so they drank and ate peanuts and kept her entertained every night.

Maybe this was a joke they were pulling? They could do such a thing. Maybe they had set up Jock-Boy. That was possible, too.

"Nice trick, guys," she said, smiling at the three of them.

All of them looked at her with far better poker faces than any three college boys could ever have.

Oh, shit, they hadn't done it.

Suddenly, the green vanished from the crème de menthe the blonde was drinking, leaving an ugly white liquid in her glass.

Okay, this was going beyond funny, beyond a trick. She didn't like this and she had no idea what was happening. She hated not being in control and knowing what was happening.

Color just didn't drain out of drinks like that. Either someone was playing a really great prank or she had just stepped into an old Twilight Zone episode. If Burgess Meredith walked up to the bar, she was going to run for the back door, right down the top of the bar if she had to. She had watched far too many of those old episodes while dating Danny, a Star Trek geek majoring in physics.

If he hadn't been so damn good in bed and so damn good-looking, she would have left him after about the thirtieth episode in a row of The Twilight Zone, followed by the tenth time she had had to watch Men in Black, the first movie, not the second one. But not even the good sex had been enough for her to stay after the night he came to bed wearing pointed ears, a blue shirt, and no pants, muttering about his need to pon farr, or prom fart, or something like that.

That had been two months ago, and now she asked every man she met if he was a Trekkie before ever thinking of jumping into bed with him. Sometimes even great sex wasn't worth pointed ears.

Cindy made herself take a deep breath and just stop, taking stock of all the regular colored drinks in front of her. Even the jerk in the football shirt wasn't doing anything but staring.

Suddenly, the blonde's green blouse turned clear, as if the light green color had been sucked out through the edge of her sleeve. Her blouse was now completely see-through. Mr. Long Nose almost dropped his glass of now golden beer as he stared at the blonde's tits.

The blonde, who clearly already had one-too-many crème de menthes, didn't seem to even notice, but Cindy and everyone else along the bar sure did. Now it was clear the woman needed to lose a lot more than twenty pounds. Through the clear shirt, you could now see her butt crack and thong underwear.

Shit, those things had to hurt, especially sitting on a bar stool for hours.

Cindy shuddered and turned away as fast as she could, but she knew that image was going to haunt her. A butt crack ghost, more frightening than any real ghost.

Out of the corner of her eye, she caught a glimpse of something on top of the bar, moving back toward her well.

Mist.

An odd-shaped cloud of green mist moved over the golden beers and then past her well, sucking the green out of all the limes in her fruit tray.

She rubbed her eyes and the green mist seemed to vanish.

"I think I need a drink," she said.

"I need a green beer, with no tricks," Jock-Boy shouted.

She grabbed another glass and poured him a green beer, not caring that it really didn't have a good head on it.

It was simply too damn early in the night to lose it. She wasn't even tired yet. Hot, yes. But tired, no. So this couldn't be happening.

But it was.

Along the bar on the other side of her well, the customers' beers and drinks started losing their green color. And a guy wearing a green hat with a big "O" on it suddenly found himself with a pure white hat on his head.

Damn, this would be funny if it wasn't so damn scary.

She could feel her heart pounding like a dozen

muggers were coming after her trying to get her cell phone and purse.

She stepped back away from the bar, hoping that her wonderful green outfit kept its color. She had never been one to wear white, except as an accent to some bright color or another. And she had paid thirty bucks for the green silk blouse and the color fit with two of her other outfits, so she sure didn't want it ruined.

"Squeeze the pimple," she said to herself softly. "Squeeze the pimple."

She relaxed.

It always worked, cleared her head. She had taken almost two years of self-defense classes and another year of martial arts training, and the one thing her instructor had taught her was that fear never helped in any situation. If she started feeling afraid, staring feeling her heart race, she needed to drain that fear out of mind like draining a big old whitehead pimple.

From that moment on, every time Cindy had felt afraid, she just muttered "Squeeze the pimple" and the fear just went away.

"It's the drainin' of the green!" one short woman shouted over the music, her eyes wide. She dropped her golden-colored beer and the glass shattered on the floor. Beer and salt and peanut shells always made for a nice mess for the bouncers to clean up.

Cindy stared at the woman as the poor thing, clearly two drinks beyond reason, backed away from the bar with a horror-movie look on her face.

Now Cindy was sure she was in a Twilight Zone episode. Or a really nifty hidden camera show.

That had to be it.

She made sure her hair was out of her face, that her blouse was adjusted, her tie down and in place, and looked around for the hidden cameras. There were none that she could see, but that didn't mean they weren't there.

Again, out of the corner of her eye, Cindy caught a glimpse of some "thing" that was green on the bar. This time it looked like more than just a cloud. It had a human shape. A green mist-filled human shape.

And was very short.

And that short, green-mist thing was going from person-to-person along the bar, draining the green from everything.

Suddenly, as if coming out of thin air, an old guy with a white beard and balding head appeared near the bar in front of Green Mist Man. He had on a long gray trench coat that made him look like a flasher. He carried a staff-like stick in one hand and moved through the crowd like it didn't exist.

"Let's go," the old guy said to Green Mist Man.

None of the other patrons around the old guy seemed to notice anything different. They were either holding up their drinks, or pointing to something that had been green and was now a pale color.

Cindy stared at the old guy as the music changed to a punked-up version of "Greensleeves" that actually had a danceable beat. Every year the DJ played that song and every year now she had hated it. At the moment, she was too weirded-out to even think about hating it.

The old guy ignored her and the music and all the people around him and kept his attention on Green Mist Man standing on the bar.

Cindy moved over closer to the old guy in the trench coat, ignoring the complaints of the customers. She needed to hear what he was saying over the loud music.

Cindy stared at his eyes. They were a deep blue, and seemed to show an intellect and intensity she didn't see much in the college guys she dated. He would have made a great Gandalf if he were about six inches taller, tossed out the ugly trench coat for a white robe, and let his beard grow just a little longer.

"No arguments," the old guy said, again to Green Mist Man on the bar. "You've already caused enough problems here."

The Green Mist Man seemed to shrug, but the mist was swirling so much, Cindy wasn't sure if it was a shrug or a "get screwed" sign.

"Yeah, I know you just got started," the old guy said, seemingly having a conversation with a cloud of the color that had been drained from drinks. "But this is where it stops. You know you don't belong here, no matter what today is."

The old man grabbed at the Green Mist Man, clearly making contact with what looked like a misty arm about two feet above the bar. He then turned and started for the door.

She had to be seeing things, but now, after all

this, she had to know for sure. She grabbed the black police baton that she kept behind the bar for emergencies. It could knock a guy coming over the bar at her out cold before he had time to even duck. So far, she or any of the other bartenders hadn't had reason or need to use it, but she felt better with it in her hand.

She quickly moved down the bar to where Judy stood talking to a customer, ignoring completely the strangeness going on around her as Judy could do so well.

"Cover for me. I'll be right back."

Cindy ducked under the lowered bar entrance at the cocktail station, not giving Judy any time to answer. Somehow, Cindy managed to stay with the old man through the crowd. From what she could tell, the old guy seemed to be dragging Green Mist Man along, talking with him all the way.

Clearly the old guy was nuts and she was buying into his weird hallucination.

Normally she wasn't the type to follow nutty old men who carried a big stick and looked like flashers. She liked her men young, driven, and well dressed. But before tonight, nothing had ever happened to the color green in her bar. It seemed like it was going to be a night of firsts.

Cindy managed to get out the door right behind the old guy. She nodded to the bouncer, and then followed the old man in the trench coat and little Green Mist Man up the street like she was a peeping tom sneaking along behind two lovers.

"You're not going to tell me how you got in, are you?" the old man said, keeping up the conversation with his misty companion.

There was a pause, and then the old guy laughed, sort of a crackling-of-brittle-paper sound. "I figured as much."

It was like listening to one side of a really stupid phone conversation.

As the old man walked down the sidewalk and past the alley that went in behind the bar, Cindy stopped, about to turn back to have the bouncer report the old guy to the cops. Suddenly two things happened at once.

First, the air started to shimmer just inside the mouth of the alley. The old man stopped, then shoved the little Green Mist Man at the hole with a shout of, "Don't come back!"

Then, from the other direction, two guys just appeared out of the air over the street about ten feet behind the old man, stumbling for a second as if they didn't expect a step down.

There wasn't a step in the middle of the street.

And those two couldn't have come out of thin air.

"You're losing it," she muttered to herself.

Could she still be at home dreaming? Maybe it was from serving the food coloring. She had read that dye could cause people to see strange things. Or maybe she was just going nuts from not enough sex in the month since she and Twilight Zone Boy had broken up.

Both men sort of staggered toward the old guy

who had his back turned to them. They both carried bats, but they sure didn't look like baseball players. Something about them looked off, like they had been sleeping in a dumpster the night before. Their clothes were soiled, their ugly plaid shirts not tucked in, their shoes untied and caked in a thick mud. They squished when they walked and Cindy couldn't tell if they were squishing or if the mud was.

She forced herself to take a good look at them, even though everything about them revolted her. One guy had a leg that was turned directly away from his body to the right. The other had two left hands.

One had an ear-looking thing glued to the middle of his forehead with a dangling earring made of beads hanging down over his nose. It looked like a women's ear.

"Now that's gross," she said out loud.

Even from twenty steps away, they smelled like a dumpster behind a fish place in August. Suddenly before Cindy could even guess what they intended to do, they raised their bats and stepped toward the old man.

They clearly meant to hit him hard on the side of the head and back.

"Hey!" Cindy shouted. "Watch out!"

Her voice echoed down the street and she saw the bouncers turn toward her. They were too far away to really help, so she started toward the very one-sided fight.

The old guy spun and managed to get his long

staff up to ward off one blow, but the other blow landed solidly on his shoulder. She didn't like the sound of that at all.

She had no idea what she would do against two weird guys with bats except maybe distract them, but she just couldn't let them beat up an old guy.

"Squeeze the pimple," she muttered as she ran. "Squeeze it hard!"

The old guy was on his knees, his hands and arms trying to cover his head. His big stick rattled on the pavement and rolled away from him.

She reached the two and planted the baton against the side of the guy with the third ear stuck in the middle of his forehead. He staggered away, but the other smelly guy hit the old man once more before the two of them turned away as she swung at them.

They half-ran, half-staggered back into the street. A moment later they vanished into thin air like they had never been there.

The shimmering that was still in the air at the mouth of the alley vanished as well as the old man slumped to the ground.

This St Patrick's Day was sure not turning out to be as much fun as she had hoped, and a whole lot weirder than she ever imagined possible.

Cindy shouted to the bouncer to call for help as she knelt beside the old guy, trying to not get his blood on her skirt. Bright green skirts just didn't come along very often.

"Hold on, mister," Cindy said. "Help's on the way."

The old guy focused his gaze on Cindy. "You're the bartender who was following me."

Cindy could tell the old guy was in intense pain.

"Don't talk."

She flipped her green tie over her shoulder and eased closer to him as he fought to focus on her. He had a broken arm and shoulder, and who knew what kind of internal injuries. It was amazing he was talking at all, considering how much blood he was losing from a cut on the side of his head.

"Did you see the shimmering in the alley?" the old guy demanded, staring up at Cindy. The guy had a gaze that could stop a speeding train and Cindy knew she had to answer him.

"Yeah, I saw it."

"And I knew you were watching me in the bar through my shield. You have a natural power, young woman. Someday you will make a good candidate."

"For what?" she asked.

"The Knight Watchmen, of course," he said, closing his eyes in pain.

"Rest. You need to save your strength." Cindy glanced up as the bouncer signaled her that help was on the way. A half dozen people were standing around in the street and on the sidewalk, watching and whispering.

The old guy chuckled. "You'd think after five hundred years, I'd learn to watch my back a little better."

Cindy ignored the five hundred years comment, now knowing for sure that the guy had escaped from a special home somewhere.

"They came out of nowhere at you," Cindy said, wishing like hell that the help that was coming would hurry up.

"Actually, they didn't," the old guy said, then coughed again, this time spitting up blood on his white beard.

That couldn't be good. Cindy knew that much from watching movies.

"I should have seen them coming," the old guy went on. "Just getting too old for this."

"Easy," Cindy said. "Just hang on."

"We got him, kid," a man said, shoving Cindy aside.

Cindy fell backward onto her butt on the curb of the sidewalk, then got up quickly and brushed off her skirt. She was about to say something to the man, but then realized there was two of them.

Cindy just stared at the two who had shoved her aside. They were not medics. They both carried long wooden staffs and both were also wearing long trench coats. One was older than the other, but for some reason, she couldn't really see them clearly. Maybe they had all belonged to the same convention of flashers.

She took a deep breath and focused on the night and the street around her. The air felt intense, crisp. For some reason the smells of the night air were sharper. Something about helping someone made everything feel more intense, almost like the sex had been with Twilight Zone Boy.

"He's going to make it," one man said, glancing around as he kneeled over the old guy.

Cindy just kept staring at the two guys in trench coats. She could see energy in and around both of the men, and strange carvings on the big sticks that were constantly in motion. Both men seemed to almost glow like soft lights.

"Glad to hear that," Cindy said.

"You can see us?"

She pointed up the street at the crowd. "I think most everyone saw what happened."

Slowly like an out-of-focus camera viewfinder coming into focus, the two of them came clear.

One of the guys was about her age and really cute. Far too cute to be wearing a stupid trench coat.

The other looked very old, only with no white beard like the dead guy. He looked like the type who would flash a person on a street corner and then just laugh.

The cute guy stared at Cindy and smiled. "Seems we have a future recruit."

Cindy didn't let his smile flutter her heart for more than a second, maybe two, even though it was an amazingly lust-filled smile. Or at least that was what she wanted it to be at that moment.

He stood and offered her his hand. His touch sent electric shivers through her entire body and her knees felt like they might not hold.

God, he was good-looking, glowing like he had a lot of light coming through his skin. He was taller than she by a few inches and had thick, wide shoulders. His thick, brown hair was just the kind she liked to run her fingers through. She started to raise her hands to do just that, then stopped herself. His facial features all worked together, nothing too long or too short. And his smile reached his wonderful green eyes that seemed to see right through her.

If someone last week would have asked her to describe her perfect man, she would have described the guy in front of her.

Oh, no, he couldn't be gay, could he? Maybe if she jumped him right here in the street, she would find out.

She shook her head yet again and the intense feeling eased just a little. She had to get herself under control. The old guy getting beat up shouldn't be shaking her up this much.

"Squeeze the pimple," she said, softly.

"Excuse me?" the guy said, touching his face near his nose.

"Nothing," she said. She took a deep breath and forced herself to think. The fantastically good-looking guy in the trench coat just stared at her.

She had to say something, get to know this guy. But what could she say? After a long moment the need to say something overwhelmed her and she said the first thing that came to her mind.

"I'm not going to be a flasher."

Oh, God, how lame was that?

Both men laughed and the older one said, "I think with your body, the world will be sad about that."

The young guy's laugh was as good as his looks, and again she thought about just jumping his golden-glowing body right there in front of the crowd around the old guy, who still hadn't come to yet. Now that might make the paper.

And no doubt it would make the Internet as well. Not the way she wanted to be famous. Damn, she had been horny before, but never like this. What the hell was going on?

A siren in the distance broke that thought.

Get it together. Ignore the fact that he smelled like freshly baked rolls, that his skin glowed like a perfect suntan, that his laugh was infectious, and his green eyes showed he was smart, damn smart.

Ignore all that.

He was wearing a trench coat, for God's sake.

What other bad habits does he have?

Actually, she more than anything wanted to see exactly what was under that trench coat, but managed to not say that out loud as well.

"I've got to get back to work," Cindy managed to finally say. "Sorry about your friend there."

"First," the cute guy said, "could you tell us what happened?"

"She saved my life, that's what," the old guy said, opening his eyes.

"Glad to see you coming around," she said.

"Thanks to you," he said. "I was getting a leprechaun out of the bar, one of the members of the Seelie Court I think, and she somehow saw us and followed me out here. I got attacked from behind by a couple of boggars pretending to be zombies, clearly run by the Unseelie Court, and she beat them away from me before they could kill me."

Both of the other men in trench coats nodded, very serious looks on their faces.

The good-looking one sighed. "That means the war might be breaking out again."

"Maybe, or just a couple of rogues," the old man said.

Cindy stared at them. It wasn't a convention of flashers. It was a convention of nutcases.

The sirens were getting louder. Help was almost here.

The guy helped the old man to his feet while the good-looking guy handed him back his staff.

"Hey," Cindy said. "Aren't you disturbing a crime scene?"

They all laughed, which made the old guy cough.

She was getting damned tired of them just laughing at everything she said. If she wanted to do stand-up, she'd go down the street to the local comedy club. There, the audience wouldn't be flashers. Or at least not all of them.

"I'll take care of our friend and the crowd," the cute guy said to the other.

"Thank you, young woman," the old guy said as the other guy helped him toward a spinning hole in the air that had just opened. "I owe you."

Then the old guy and the other guy were gone, leaving Cindy standing beside the cute guy. Her heart fluttered with both excitement and panic.

"So what was all that?" she asked, hoping her voice sounded as firm as she wanted it to sound.

"We belong to a group of men and women called

the Knight Watchmen. We protect humanity from all the fairies, trolls, and other creatures that live in dimensions among humans. We are like the policemen of the Unseen World. You just sort of got into a skirmish between two of the ruling courts."

"Yeah," she said, shaking her head. "And I'm Alice and I've fallen through a rabbit hole."

He laughed and extended his hand. "My name is Sean. Sean Ballard. I'm from Seattle originally, but that was a while back now. You wouldn't believe me just how long ago."

Cindy almost didn't take his hand, then she remembered how nice his touch felt. "Cindy Kemp. Student and bartender from Chicago, now living in the Twilight Zone."

Again electricity seemed to flow through their touch, and he seemed to light up again with that golden-tan glow.

Maybe she should start calling herself "Electric Girl" because of the way she kept lighting up Cute-Flasher Boy.

He actually held her hand a little longer than he should have. She didn't mind one damned bit. A very large part of her wanted to not be angry at being played for a fool, but instead to just learn everything about this wonderful hunk. But somehow her anger won the fight and she pulled her hand away.

"So really, what is going on?"

"Did you see the Men in Black movie?" he asked.

"Far too many times, I'm afraid," she said.

"We're the magical version of the guys from that movie. We chase fairies and elves and trolls and bogies and try to keep peace between the two Seelie courts. And we try to keep them all honoring the great treaty that keeps them out of the human world. The organization has been around a long, long time."

"Cute," Cindy said. The feeling of wanting to jump his bones vanished like toilet paper flushing down the drain. "So next you're going to do a flashie-thing to me and I won't remember any of this."

"Yeah, I'm afraid so," he said, looking slightly sad. "But you have natural magic power like I did. The Knight Watchmen have noticed you now. When your power comes in full, you will be recruited and we can meet again."

She stared at him. The crazy things he was saying made as much sense as anything for what she had seen, but she still wasn't going to believe it.

"Come on," he said, gently taking her by the arm and turning her toward the bar. The police sirens were getting close, real close.

"One more question," she asked as they walked the short distance back toward the crowd, letting the electricity flash between them. She wanted to jump him so bad, she almost couldn't control herself. And he smelled so much like fresh-baked bread, she wanted to just lick his skin. "Why do you smell so good?"

He smiled. "All good magic smells wonderful. Bad magic, like those boggars pretending to be zombies, smells awful."

She shook her head and again the voice cleared. "Smelly magic," she muttered to herself. "Great, what's next?"

"For now, nothing I'm afraid. But maybe in the future we'll meet again. I can hope. And maybe, if you are strong enough, you'll remember me."

Her heart actually skipped a beat and her breath got short.

Then he raised that stupid long stick of his and banged it into the ground and everything went white.

"So what happened out there?" Judy, the other bartender, asked as Cindy ducked back under the gate and headed back for her station behind the bar.

"Just the first fight of the night," Cindy said, putting the black baton back where it belonged under the bar. "They all ran off before the cops got there."

Suddenly Judy leaned toward Cindy, sniffing. "Wow, what have you been eating?"

Cindy glanced at Judy who had followed her down the bar, sniffing. Had her partner behind the bar lost her last brain cell? "Nothing, why?"

"You smell like freshly baked bread."

In front of her both Ben and Wolf-boy nodded.

"You do!" Ben shouted over the noise and music filling the bar.

Everyone had lost it and she needed to get back to work.

"It's a new perfume," she shouted back at them. "Called Magic."

She had no idea why she said that. But when she

did, for just a moment, the most handsome man she could ever imagine appeared in her mind, laughing.

Damn, she was so horny, she might have to call Twilight Zone Boy if she didn't find someone tonight.

But the party for St. Patrick's Day was just getting started. She just might meet someone yet. Anything would be better than watching that stupid Men in Black movie one more time.

MUSHROOM CLOUDS AND FAIRY RINGS

J. A. Pitts

Molly woke repeating some of the words the Hound Master used when one of the young pups got a little too nippy. She stretched, raised her head off the toadstool she'd been sleeping against, and looked to see who was knocking at her door.

Only there wasn't a door. She was sleeping in a ring of toadstools, The knocking wasn't the Matron of Switches to remind her she was late for breakfast with the fairy princesses. Nope, the mushroom clouds that dotted the skyline were most definitely not on the agenda, as far as she recalled. As she watched, two more bloomed close at hand, and the world shook with a pair of great, fiery thumps.

Molly wasn't scared, despite the booming and cracking that had woken her up. She'd had plenty of years practicing to be brave. She was the terror of all the little princess fairies who roamed the White

Queen's palace. But Molly wasn't a fairy. She'd been snatched at birth, swapped for a doppelganger, and her parents, with seven other children, were none the wiser.

Once Molly realized she was growing to be bigger than the rest of the wee ones she played with, things began to unravel for the Matron of Switches, the ornery old brownie who was responsible for keeping order amongst the nursery brood.

Twice Molly had to be bespelled to stop her temper, and once, though it was only whispered about, it was reported that the White Queen herself had come down to the nursery to quiet young Molly and set her to right. Molly still had the mark where the White Queen had touched her with the ice wand she waved around. The scar kept her temper in check most days and reminded her just how angry the White Queen had been.

She looked down at her pack. Inside was the seedling she was to swap for another child. The half empty bottle of moonshine she'd snitched from those nine-pin crazy dwarves set nestled against her hip as secure as could be.

Mushrooms were not new to her, nor toadstools, though they had a whole different magic to them. These mushrooms that dotted the horizon were made of fire and ash, she could tell even from here. A nasty wind blew around her as well. The trees and bushes erupted into flames, but she stood unscathed in her fairy ring.

"I'm not sure what the big'uns have gotten

themselves up to," she said to no one particular. "But there is no way I'm taking responsibility for this with the Matron of Switches."

All the young'uns in the nursery feared the Matron of Switches. She loved nothing better than to march one of the fairy princesses out into the garden and laugh at her tears as she picked their own switch for one transgression or another.

It wasn't until Molly was big that the other fey began to find an advantage to her height and strength. That was the winter when wolves broke into the garden where the princesses were having their tea party. Molly picked up a garden hoe and set about the young wolflings, sending them scattering back across the hedge with their tails between their legs.

That time the Matron of Switches did something far worse than switching young Molly. She kissed her on the forehead and sent her to her room with an extra plate of sugar cookies. Molly had been so undone that she'd almost wished to be switched. At least then, she'd have known where the tears were from.

Soon after, the White Queen saw fit to send Molly on a trip to her birth world. It was here she saw others like her, tall and gangly, all arms and legs, with nary a glittery wing, nor a pointed ear. Here her plain round ears and lack of wings didn't set her apart. And with that knowledge grew a sense of purpose. The White Queen explained to Molly that the Matron of Switches had suggested she be allowed to visit the world she'd been born to. It was a very big responsibility, but as Molly was a big girl (compared to the fairies, at least), she could probably handle it.

Molly set about learning the things the fairies wanted her to learn. She preferred to run with the dwarves down in the kitchens or wrestle with the gnomes out in the garden . . . as long as she was cleaned up and at tea at the proper time, all was forgiven.

When it looked like the fires were going to keep burning a while, Molly began to look longingly at the moonshine. She loved the way the dew of the mountain made her all warm and tingly as it worked its way through her belly. The long sleep it gave her would probably last long enough for the firestorm that swept the mountain to burn itself out. She nudged the little seedling in her pack and whispered, "Maybe we should take another little nip, sleep a bitty bit, and see if the big'uns get their house in order while we're in dreamland." Not like the fey would notice the time going by. Twice before, she'd been gone to the land of the big'uns for days and nights, only to return to Summerland the same day and in plenty of time for afternoon tea.

So Molly settled down in her little nest of leaves and took another long sip of mountain whiskey. She watched the sky above her flash with gold and red as the clouds were swept away and the black of night fell on the world.

"I'll just swap you for a big'un after I've had a bit more nap," she whispered to the seedling. "They'll all be busy what with the burning and all."

The next time Molly woke she noticed two things right away. First, she was a mite taller than she'd been when she went to sleep. Second, the fiery storm that had swept over the mountain was long gone, and all sorts of green and growing things were smashed right up against the circle of toadstools she slept in. Her feet were right on the edge of the ring, and her hair, where it had grown over into the edge of the circle, had turned white as ash.

She stood, making sure her satchel was handy, and noticed that all her clothes were too tight and the satchel was a lot tinier than she remembered it.

There in the bottom, with her seedling, were her dainty white gloves for tea parties with the fairy princesses and the good, stout knife the Hound Master had snuck into her pack the first time the White Queen had sent her forth into the land of her forefathers. She took out the knife and tucked it into the band of her too-tight britches. Her top was so small, her belly showed, and her shoes had burst off her feet while she slept.

"I must look a sight," she told the seedling. "But I reckon it's time to go fetch one of those big'uns like the White Queen demanded."

She looked around, tucked the moonshine in her satchel for safekeeping, and stepped outside the ring.

She forgot just what being in that ring did for her. As soon as she'd stepped over the toadstools, her head began to throb from all the durn moonshine.

"Well, little bit," she mewled to the seedling. "Let

that be a lesson to you. Too much moonshine makes your head throb and your eyes blurry."

After a minute where she thought her insides were going to crawl out through the back of her eyes, she was able to take a second step and look around the riotous world of greenery.

"Nothing for it but to begin," she said pushing through the underbrush. "Ain't no girl-child gonna fall from the sky."

Soon enough she came upon an old road that was cracked and overgrown. She remembered these pathways from her last trip here. Highways, the big'uns had called them. They'd sure let things go, she thought. No pride in keeping a tidy place.

She walked for near an hour before she saw her second surprise. There among the weeds and brambles was a row of rusted-out carriages filled with the bleached bones of the dead.

The fey knew about the dead. The Black Queen liked to send them against the White Queen's armies from time to time—shambling corpses that blundered over tea parties and had no respect for doilies or placemats.

These were not shambling, however. They lay as quiet as mice, jumbled and tossed about in the insides of their carriages. Some of the glass was intact, but in general, the good green of the world had begun to overtake them and hide them from pleasant folk.

The first real hill she was able to climb let her get a good look at one of the villages the big'uns liked to gather in. While the fey had cute little cottages or in the case of the White Queen, an enormous castle, the big'uns had tall thin towers that reached up to the sky.

Only now they were broken as well: shattered spires and rusted skeletons of fortresses that scraped the sky. It made her sad, the way the big'uns had let their villages go to seed. Sure enough, the roads were overgrown with wild things, vines and twisty prickers like blackberries and worse.

Everywhere there was the pale white of bones amongst the deep green of the forest that had invaded the villages and scoured the world.

"You know what I think," Molly said to the seedling. "I'm thinking the big'uns done broke this old world. I can't never go back to the tea parties and cotillions if I don't swap you for a right goodly girl child."

Molly walked while the sky was shiny and bright, and kept walking after the skies overhead were filled with twinkling lights.

She lay down in a clearing, not far from an old house used by the big'uns before they'd all gone and killed each other. With the seedling lying on her chest—which had grown a might more lumpy than the last time she recalled waking up, she discussed their options.

By the time sleep took her she'd resolved herself to start the morning right, have a bit of tea and one of the three cakes she'd brought with her, and do a little witching to help her find her way.

As the sun rose the following morning, streaking the sky with violet and lavender, Molly walked to the middle of a wide swath of clover and settled her little pack onto the ground in front of her. From inside, she took out a blanket covered in pink hearts and yellow moons. Once this was spread, she set two places. In the center she placed the teapot the Princess of Pansies had given her for her last birthday party. They really didn't know when anyone's birthday was, since time in the Summerland didn't actually flow like a river. It was more of a suggestion; at least, that's what the Master of Hounds had explained to her when she'd asked. She liked the old man, who was a human like her, one of the big'uns that had been taken at birth. He'd worked through a lot of years; growing old with the fey took a long, long time.

Once she'd poured her tea and plucked one of the sweet cakes from her satchel, she set the seedling on the far side of the blanket in front of her teacup and poured a dram into the saucer. This way, the seedling could have a bit of a soak in the hot, sweet concoction.

Having drunk her fill and nibbled the edges of the cake, Molly pulled the knife from her waistband and held the tip against her thumb, just enough for the sharp point to draw a single bead of blood. She leaned over the dregs of tea in her cup, allowed the one drop of blood to fall down amongst the leaves, and swished the cup three times widdershins. Then she tipped it upside down, letting the final drips fill the saucer. While the tea drained, she packed everything back into her satchel.

Sitting cross-legged on the clover, she picked up the teacup and turned it over, studying the leaves that had congealed in the bottom of the cup. "I see," she said aloud so the seedling could hear her and not be afraid. "There are no people anywhere I can find." She looked across the great rolling hill up to a block of broken towers. "But people lived there once upon a time. There may be something in that direction"— she pointed away from the rising sun—"that's like people, only just."

She tapped the tea leaves out onto the ground and stashed the teacup back into her satchel. As the seedling had begun to grow just a little, she decided to braid it in her hair so she wouldn't lose the wispy thing, and allow her a chance to see the sights.

They walked for the better part of three days, by turns galumphing across the open spaces and creeping through the broken bones of the world. They slept by turns in carriages (empty of old bones), carousels, and lopsided buildings with their insides turned out and their outsides flopped around like old slippers.

"I grow weary of all these broken palaces and gaping skulls," she said on the fourth day. The mountains were starting to fall behind her, and the vast plains opened before. "Buttercup told me once there was a magical city on the edge of a very large lake," she said confidently. "There, if you were a very brave princess, you could meet a surly wizard or maybe a brave soldier who would do your bidding if you smiled daintily enough."

She touched the long curl that fell down from behind her left ear, with the seedling woven in amongst the locks. "Do you fancy meeting a handsome waif to steal your heart?"

But, as always, the seedling did not join in the conversation, and Molly grew tired of the very quietness of the world.

"I wish we could just go home," Molly said one day as the sun set over a field of rusting carriages. "I'll deny it, if you repeat it," she said to the seedling. "But I even miss the Mistress of Switches."

On a cloudy day deep in the countryside, after three days of rain that spluttered like a fire and stung Molly's exposed skin, they happened upon the metal man.

She assumed he was a man, for he was dressed for war. The thickness of his limbs and the weapons arrayed along his arms and legs spoke of great battles yet to be fought.

"Hello, warrior," she said to the stoic sentinel.

He did not respond, just stood poised for action.

"I bet you would like some tea," Molly said after watching the metal man for a solid hour. "The Mistress of Switches says even the most recalcitrant child will mellow with a nice cuppa."

She set the tea, blanket, cups—three this time— and plates, of course. The first cake she'd nibbled to nothingness, so she broke the rose petals from the second one and allowed a bit of crumbs to dust each of the three plates.

The tea was hot and sweet, straight from the pot, but the warrior did not sit with her. She felt wary of touching him, so thinking back to the way the Master of Hounds handled the new pups, she took her best gloves from her satchel and put them on. Then she took up the warrior's teacup and held it to his angular head.

"I'm sure you'll like this. Fairy tea is much better than the draught of stinging rain and sunshine you've been living on these many years."

She poured the tea from the cup, where it ran, thick and viscous, into the cracked face of the warrior. Not at all like the good, hot tea she'd poured from the pot, but fairy tea suited the tastes of the imbiber.

The warrior seemed to like the tea, for he did not complain. After she'd had a second cup of her own, she poured four more cups into the gullet of the metal man. Then she sprinkled a few of the crumbs from her nibbles into the open face, and set about packing her things.

"That is all I can do for you," she said to the metal man. "I dearly hoped to hear your tale, but I fear I am not to your liking." She took out the jackknife, cut a long curl from her very own hair, and laid it in the open palm of the metal man. "If you ever decide to waken, and find yourself in need of company, this should help you find me."

Then she blew him a kiss and slung the satchel over her shoulder. She'd gone no more than seventy-three steps, not that she was counting, when she heard a scratchy, creaking noise from behind. She did not turn, but smiled, whispering to the seedling to be quiet and brave. Then she walked toward the next village in search for a wee bairn to take home to the White Queen.

For three days the metal man followed Molly and the seedling. At first the metal man spoke to her in a language of the forge, full of clatter and clanking and steam. Each day, Molly would stop for her tea, and the metal man would stand just beyond her sight, but she could hear him, panting and wheezing like a bellows. She would pour a third cup and let it sit while she curled up for a nap. When she awoke, the tea was gone, and the cup returned to its saucer with nary a crack or nick in the fine porcelain.

Once, during her morning constitutional, Molly thought she heard a raspy sort of singing, but decided it was more likely the wind.

On the fourth night since her last tea party, the metal man came staggering into her camp site. She'd set a tidy little fire to keep the dark at bay, and was considering another draught of tea, when she saw him.

"Welcome, Mr. Man," she said standing quickly. "So you have decided to join us on our journey?"

The metal man took another step forward so the flickering light of the fire painted him in roils of red and orange.

"I do not understand," the metal man said, his voice like a stiff wire brush over the bottom of an exceedingly sooty pot.

"What vexes you?" Molly asked, turning so the seedling could see their visitor.

"Each afternoon you sit at tea, and each afternoon I come and drink what you leave me," he said. "You must know I have taken the tea and the occasional crumb that you have offered for me."

Molly nodded once, trying to keep the smile from her lips.

"I crave the tea," he said mournfully. "And my capacitors yearn for your company."

Molly felt herself blush. Not many had ever requested her company. "Shall I pour tea, then?" she asked, stepping toward her satchel. "Would you like that?"

"Yes, please," the metal man said stepping closer. "I would know if that is what wakened me from my long sleep."

Molly smiled as she set the blanket on the ground. Perhaps it was my kiss, she thought quietly, lest the seedling grow jealous. Even a kiss blown upon the wind can have a mighty effect.

Once the tea was set, and the second cake nibbled a bit more, the metal man was able to move about more freely, and his voice had mellowed to a timbre suitable for a gentleman.

"I was a man once," he told Molly as she packed away the magical teapot. "I had a family and everything, before the world came to an end."

"Why did you decide to destroy the world?" Molly asked. "Were you tired of it?"

The metal man shook his angular head and wept

tears of clear oil. "Hubris," he said, the shame obvious. "We had made wonderful discoveries, like the ability to copy ourselves into robots." He turned once, his six arms extended and his weapons sheathed. "We were no longer confined to the fragile shells we once were. We'd conquered death."

Molly sighed as she leaned back with her toes pointed to the fire. "And yet, you have all died, it seems."

"Alas," the metal man said, kneeling by the fire. "I fear you are correct."

"What were you about before I woke you?" Molly asked.

"I was seeking another," he said quietly. "Someone else to have a conversation with."

"And here I found you." Molly said, smiling. "And we may converse as long as our hearts allow."

"I would like that," the metal man said. "And I will watch you while you sleep. Keep the wild things from your camp."

"There are wild things?" Molly asked, yawning. "I have seen no one at all until I met you. That is, beyond the bony dead."

The metal man, Sir Reginald, Molly dubbed him, knew of a place, many days from here, where he'd had a signal once upon a time.

"It could be a bunker," he said.

"Like a castle?" Molly asked.

"Yes," Sir Reginald said. "Like a castle where the good folk hid while the world burned."

"I would like to find this place," Molly said. "I

grow weary of this lush greenery and the sparkling sunsets."

"Is that so?" Sir Reginald asked.

"Perhaps not as much as I had thought," she admitted. "Now that I have you here for conversation."

The whole wide world woke one morning to the sound of Sir Reginald whooping and cavorting like men-at-arms when they've had too much of the hard cider on festival nights. The clanking was what woke Molly, and she sat up so fast, she nearly sent the seedling flying into the underbrush. She'd only just thought to reach out and catch her as her hair went flying around in all directions. She tightened the braid that held the seedling, stood up and straightened her shirt before clearing her throat at Sir Reginald.

"I've found it," he said solemnly. "I've found the signal once again, thanks to you and your divination."

"The tea guides, and the blood follows," she quoted the White Queen. "We only have to be open to the way."

Sir Reginald bowed to her and a crooked smile touched his metal-plated face. "You are a wonder, that's for sure."

They had a spot of morning tea, where Molly drew out the serving and the eating to the point that even Sir Reginald, who was a novice in the way of tea parties, grew restive.

"Why do we tarry?" he asked after Molly had had her third cuppa and picked the tiny seeds off a sliver

of cake. "Did you not understand I have found a signal to a bunker, er . . . castle, where there may be
people?"

Molly looked sideways at the metal man, who'd
grown less stiff since he'd been sharing her cake and
tea. "You grow tired of my company?" she asked.
"Are you so quick to abandon our grand adventure?"

The metal man sat back at that, a thoughtful glint
in his bejeweled eyes.

"Do you not wish to return to your tea parties and
the princesses?" he asked quietly. "Have you not re-
galed me with tales of the Master of Hounds, the
Mistress of Switches, and the scullery maids and
their scandalous ways?"

"You know I have, sir knight. And I told you those
tales in confidence." She paled at the thought of
those stories getting back to the palace of the White
Queen. She'd not sit again for the welts and blisters
she would receive for such impertinence.

"We must complete your mission," Sir Reginald
offered.

"Of course," Molly said, standing and tossing
aside the last of her tea. She hastily bundled the pot,
cakes, plates and blanket back into her satchel. She
spun around four times, and stopped facing the
metal man. "I have flung off my melancholy and am
ready to face the unknown."

"You are a peculiar young woman," the metal
man said. "More comely than a rose, as witty as a jay,
and as innocent as freshly fallen snow."

Molly cocked her head to the side and looked at him. "Do you jest, Sir Reginald?"

He bowed once again. "You are the fairest lass I have seen in a thousand sunrises."

Molly blushed, but straightened. "Let us off, then, you sly one. I would bet a thousand sunrises have passed without you seeing a soul alive, until I came along."

Sir Reginald sniggered.

Soon the merry band was climbing down a steep ravine, chasing the signal that the metal man could hear.

"Tell me of it," Molly asked as they rested part way down the ragged cliff face. "Do they sing to you, these old ones? Or do you hear the voices of other metal men such as yourself, full of clicks and clacks such as you sang to me when we first met?"

"They call for aid," he said solemnly. "For rescue and succor. I do not know if they live, but I have hope for the first time in an eon."

"Then that is good enough for our adventure," Molly said brushing dust from her britches.

They climbed for the rest of the day, only pausing when the sun dipped below the edge of the mountains to the west. They made camp along a deep ledge where they could have a small fire and sleep without fear of rolling to their deaths in the midst of the night.

The next morning they climbed again, a sense of urgency suddenly overcoming Molly. The metal man, Sir Reginald, had grown quiet and would not speak of the signal any longer other than to say, "It is very old, and very sad."

At the bottom of the great cliff wall, they turned northward and walked amongst the jumbled stones and thick brush.

"We are close," Sir Reginald said on the second day after they'd reached the bottom. He held out his cup for a second helping of tea. His hand had grown softer, rounder in the intervening days. Between the whispered kisses that Molly blew to him each night, and the power of the tea, the metal man transformed.

By the third night, they happened upon a vault door: a great gear pushed into the side of the rock face.

"Here is their final resting place," he said. "They are inside."

Molly hefted her satchel up higher on her shoulder and stood as tall as she could. Time to be brave, she told herself. This is the moment of truth.

She took the gloves from her satchel and put them on. When Sir Reginald looked at her, she wiggled her fingers at him and smiled. "The Mistress of Switches always says to present your best when meeting new folk."

"Sound advice," Sir Reginald said.

"Here," Molly said, bending and plucking a small red flower from the ground at their feet. "Place this in your hair."

She stood on her tip-toes and wove the red flower into Sir Reginald's wavy, golden hair. The metal of his complexion had faded to a softer texture and his angular head flowed with golden locks.

"I believe," he said as she stepped back to admire her work, "that the tea may have some magical powers I had not expected."

"As the Mistress of Switches reminds us, we must be who we truly are when we sup with another and share our table."

"I see," Sir Reginald said. "Shall we see if any others remain to satisfy your quest?"

Sir Reginald strode forward, touching a sequence of keys on the great door. After a moment, the whole world shook as the great cog rolled to the side, revealing a long passage into darkness. After a minute, pale light began to shimmer in the tunnel, and Molly poked her head inside.

The cavern was filled with great, long couches, each covered in glass. "Like the tales of Sleeping Beauty," Molly said to Sir Reginald as they examined the sleeping forms within.

They were children, from the smallest infant to children old enough for skipping and knitting, tea parties, and grand adventures.

"So many," Molly said as she walked deeper into the cavern. "Do you wonder where all their mommies and daddies have gone away to?"

Sir Reginald turned to a bank of glittering and glowing machines. With a swipe of his hand over what appeared to be a large crystal ball, he was able to learn the fate of these many children.

"There are no parents," he said quietly. "No one to raise them once they wake."

Molly was horrified at first, clasping the seedling in her fist and spinning in a slow circle. When the tiny light of the day hove into view a second time, she paused and looked back at Sir Reginald.

"Can you wake them? One at a time?"

"Yes, I believe so," he answered her, his voice full of questions.

"Then we shall do as I was asked," she said with confidence. "The White Queen asked that I return a girl child to her in exchange for this seedling. A fair trade that would serve both her whims and the whims of the fickle fates."

She leaned over one of the sleeping couches and brushed the frost from the glass. Inside slept a girl of about six summers, her fiery red hair falling around her pale face, a splash of freckles coloring her cheeks.

"We will start with this one," she said, turning to Sir Reginald. "I will take her to the White Queen. The Mistress of Switches can show her how a child should behave and we can let the seedlings have this world. They would grow here, and make it a place for themselves."

"That is a fine idea," Sir Reginald said, tears in his amber eyes. "There are many children here. Will your Mistress of Switches accept them all?"

"If she will not, the Master of Hounds will accept a few," she said with a growing sense of right. "And the scullery maids all lament their childlessness. It is obvious by their actions and the way they skulk about with the men-at-arms."

"And how do we get there from here?"

"Easy-peasy," Molly said. She took out her jack-knife and strode out of the cave. Sir Reginald followed quickly, as if afraid to be left alone.

"Here, watch."

She took the knife and scoured a circle in the thick grass. Once she'd done this, she took out the teapot and dribbled a bit of the sweet nectar into the circle, allowing the brown liquid to fill the cuts she'd made into the earth.

Finally she sat and sang a quiet song about moonbeams.

Sir Reginald gasped as a ring of toadstools sprouted before his eyes.

"Here is our way home," Molly said rising.

"And the seedling?" he asked her.

Molly reached up and took down her long braid. For a moment, she struggled with the knot, but the seedling seemed to leap from her hands and onto the ground. In a heartbeat, a young girl stood before them, eyes like seashells and hair as fine as corn silk.

"You have grown, sister," the seedling said with a lilting laugh. "The Mistress will not recognize you all big the way you are."

Molly spun on her knees, as the seedling ran toward the woods. "Bring me a sister," the seedling called as she disappeared into the shadow of the wood.

"Well, isn't that a fine how-do-you-do?" Molly asked, standing.

Sir Reginald had stood too close to Molly. Her head came nearly to Sir Reginald's chin. She was too close to him, and he to her. For a moment, she thought to step back, to catch her breath, but a wave of dizziness nearly overwhelmed her and Sir Reginald caught her. She lifted her eyes to his and as the world succumbed to a fiery sunset, she found her lips pressed against Sir Reginald's.

The Mistress of Switches had not mentioned this in her tea lessons, Molly thought. Once they had parted, she picked up her satchel and took Sir Reginald's hand. "Let us get this child to the queen," she said. "Won't the princesses be surprised when we bring this lot home?"

HUNTING THE UNICORN

Jane Lindskold

Black moon against a white sky. The scent of dried rosebuds fills the air. It is a lovely night for a unicorn hunt.

From the Unseelie Court, the champion rides forth. She is the daughter of a bodach and an urisk, but unlike either of these, she is lovely as a night sky lit only with stars and the glow of the palest of crescent moons.

Her hair falls long and silken, its hue the shining reddish brown of polished chestnuts. Her dark eyes are large, shaped with a piquant slant, framed with thick lashes. Her lips are full, yearning for kisses they have never felt.

This beauty's name is Blackrose. She is clad in close-fitting leather armor, supple as the sealskin from which it was crafted, embossed with arcane runes of protection. Her riding boots come to just below her knee, showing off shapely calves and surprisingly dainty feet. A cloak of moss green shadows is draped about her shoulders, fastened with a brooch of tiger's eye.

She is hung about with weapons: a bow of rowan wood and a quiver of birch arrows, a long sword whose blade is silvered steel, and a hunting knife with a hilt of ivory and a blade of pearl. To her saddle is strapped a heavy ax, its honed head protected in a leather case.

Her mount is a kelpie, currently in the shape of a shaggy dark-brown pony with a wicked eye. This is cheating, because the hunting of the unicorn is supposed to be a contest between the two champions alone and unassisted.

If the kelpie has a name, he's not telling.

Upon Blackrose's slender upper arm is an ruby-colored armband not only shaped like a twisting, curling dragon, but which is, in fact, a twisting, curling dragon, small but ferocious, capable of breathing fire or spitting acid. Its name is Flamewing.

More cheating, but since when did the members of the Unseelie Court not cheat or lie or trick when such would be to their advantage?

From the Seelie Court, the champion rides forth. He is the son of an enchantress who loved a hero of the Rade. From his mother he is gifted with a talent for sorcery, from his father an ample allowance of luck. From both he has been granted beauty.

*   *   *

They called their child Sunset, because he was born in the twilight years. When he grew into manhood, his name became Sundeath for reasons no one could explain, yet no one questioned. Sundeath's features are noble yet strong, chiseled from oak, not pine. His hair is the brilliant gold of the sun at midday, but his eyes hold the dark purple of late summer iris or the violets that nestle almost forgotten in the grass. His shoulders are broad and his figure strong, yet granted the willow's gift of bending. His lips hold a smile, but there is something wistful about it, as if they long for a sweetness they have yet to find.

He is clad in a tunic the tawny golden-brown of a mountain lion's coat. Beneath it he wears tight-fitting trousers a few shades darker. His riding boots are of matte black leather, his belt and cuffs of the same material. The cloak that falls from his shoulders is made from leaves enchanted into silk, myriad sizes and shapes fitting into each other with miraculous skill.

His long hair—it has not been cut since Sundeath was declared a man—is braided tight, interwoven with a filet of silver, dewdropped with sparkling gems.

He carries no weapons but a hunting knife, sheathed at his belt. From behind his saddle hangs a coil of rope. On the other side is cased a fine meshed net. Both rope and net are woven from the same remarkable materials: a father's love, sunlight on water, the breeze ruffling a kitten's fur—all strong, all gentle, all nearly impossible to touch. Sundeath crafted these himself, for he is a sorcerer of some note.

He rides upon a stallion named Zephyr. Zephyr possesses a high crested neck, liquid eye, and flaring nostril. His coat is dapple grey, his flowing mane and tail pale silver. His trappings—even his shoes— are gilded. Otherwise, there is nothing extraordinary about this steed, unless it is that he is of a breed that is closer kin to flame and storm than to any earthly horse.

In the hands of Sundeath as he rides beneath the black moon is a small harp of gold, set with gems. Each of seven strings is enchanted to play some desire if so invoked. His work again, the result of many long hours delving into the mysteries of the heart and soul. Mysteries that, especially when related to love, are very strange to Sundeath indeed, for although he has been given much love— children are rare in the Seelie Court—and given back love in return, the magnificence of passion has been hidden from him so that someday he might be a champion.

Blackrose knelt in the moist duff, checking tracks that an eye less sharp would certainly have missed. The tracks had been made by a small cloven hoof and were similar to those of a deer, but with more delicate lobes.

A human tracker viewing these marks would have been puzzled, for they were far enough apart to indicate a relatively long stride, yet the tracks were not as deeply pressed into the soil as those of a deer of the appropriate size would be.

But Blackrose was of the Unseelie Court, intensely trained over many long years for this very hunt. Rising, she dusted off the palms of her long-fingered hands. Then she motioned the kelpie, who had been off to one side idly eating centipedes, to her. Untwining Flamewing the dragon from her arm, she showed it the trail.

"Find and follow," Blackrose commanded as she swung herself into the kelpie's saddle.

When Flamewing had the scent, Blackrose dug her heels into the kelpie's flanks.

"A good pace, but not too great," she commanded as the horse-like beast broke into a gait somewhere between a trot and a canter. "We have the trail, but even Flamewing may lose it. Unicorns are wise and clever, else what delight would there be in the hunt?"

"The queen and king might disagree," replied the kelpie in a voice like slow water. "You may care about songs to be sung, honors to be won, but they care for little but the creature's horn. Poisonings have been rising in the court. The waters run foul. The unicorn's horn offers remedy for this and more."

Blackrose could not disagree. She knew her goals and those of the monarchs of the Unseelie Court differed somewhat. Parented by a bodach and an urisk, she was not of noble lineage. But taken from her parents—who were paid well in gems and land— Blackrose had been reared within the Unseelie Court. Her tutors had been the finest, the curriculum demanding. Nothing was stinted on her gear or attire. Yet never had she been permitted to forget that although she might be fair of face and form, sharp of wit and swift of hand, to her titles and honors would only be granted if she proved herself a worthy champion who won for the Unseelie Court what it desired.

When the seers came before the monarchs, bearing with them an orb of polished quartz that showed within its smoky depths that the way into the unicorn's land was opening, Blackrose was prepared.

She had long ago chosen her equipment, testing herself against creatures far more fearsome than a slender semi-equine whose only weapon was a single horn. She had slain fachan and nucklelavee, and even a dragon—a much larger version of the little reptile who now fluttered ruby-bright to guide her along the unicorn's trail.

Blackrose's time had come and nothing, certainly not her rival from the Seelie Court, would keep her from her goal.

Ruby-scales flashed ahead. Blackrose drove the kelpie in the dragon's wake, along the unicorn's trail. With any luck the unicorn would be found and slain before her rival even located the spoor.

Then to her ears came the sound of sweet music.

Although the Seelie Court boasted seven times seventy princes and fair damsels by the score, although the arts of wooing and courtship were as treasured as those of music, poetry, and the chase, still between those fair lords and yet more fair ladies very few children were born.

Many a loving heart brooded over being denied what was given in plentitude to even rabbits in the fields and minnows in the streams. The wise said that infertility was the price for a long life. They told all they should be content with what gifts they had been granted. Most repeated quite loudly that they were indeed content.

Yet when a child was born the level of rejoicing gave lie to these claims of contentment. So it was when Sunset was born. Celebrations and dances were held and he was spoiled to an extent that would have ruined a less hardy soul.

Those days of infant indulgence passed quickly enough. As with most of his kind, Sunset grew swiftly, his childhood lasting hardly any longer than that of the human youth he might have resembled if any of human born could be so fair.

Even after he had gained the semblance of a young man, Sundeath knew well he was but a child. Enchantments and conjurations that were easily done by those who were in outward seeming his peers stumbled from his fingertips, stammered from his lips. His playing on harp and flute made the birds fall silent, rather than joining him in joyous chorus as they did with his fellows.

But Sundeath strove hard and his teachers were many and friendly. For every one who quipped and teased, there were ten who set tangled fingers straight, showed a more effective stance for bow or harp, and otherwise gave him reason to hope that someday he might be their equal.

When Sundeath was chosen as the champion who would hunt the unicorn, he was thrilled and delighted, for he was well-aware that many surpassed him in every way. When later— mostly from the giggles of coy damsels as they pulled away from him, accepting his poems and bouquets, but not his embrace—Sundeath gradually came to realize that he had been chosen not for all the achievements he had mastered, but for the one he had not.

Blushing, Sundeath realized that he had been chosen as champion of the Seelie Court because he was yet a virgin.

Angered, he sought at first to rid himself of this unwelcome qualification, but he found none within the Seelie Court who would accept his embraces. He might have lain with a human maiden, but his mother spoke to him, pleading his forbearance.

"Sundeath," she said, stroking his golden locks as she had when he was still toddling about on chubby legs, "do not squander what you have. Time enough for that when the unicorn has been captured and its blessings brought to grace our land."

Sundeath frowned. "I have read of the blessings a unicorn can bring. They are wonderful, true, but do we really need them?"

"We will benefit, yes," the enchantress said. "Moreover, our enemies, those monstrous wretches who mock us by calling themselves the 'Un' Seelie Court, will be denied those same benefits. Think on this as well. If you win the contest, the unicorn's life will be spared. Our hunt ends in captivity, theirs in death and brutal mutilation."

She went on to describe how the pale blue horn of the unicorn would be sawn from the poor beast's skull, how the beast would be hung so that its corpse could drain, how it would be skinned, then butchered.

"They make armor for their champion from the hide," she concluded, "and feast upon the flesh and organs. The bones are made into a cage in which they keep their most dishonored prisoners."

By these words, Sundeath was convinced that retaining his virginity so that he might hunt the unicorn was the right and noble thing to do, no matter the extent of the personal sacrifice expected of him. Even so, he looked for reassurance that his suffering would end.

"And after the unicorn is captured, Mother," he said, giving her the title that many a fair elf longed to be granted, ranking it above "princess" or even "queen," "who will care for it?"

She laughed lightly, hearing the question that underlay the question. "Oh, then the unicorn is tended by a fair host of tiny winged fairies. Like the flowers they so resemble, these take their pleasures in other ways than lovemaking. Therefore, their company is not abhorrent to the pure and dainty unicorn."

So satisfied, Sundeath directed all his thwarted passion into his studies, determined that when the time came for hunting the unicorn none would say that he had been chosen for the one quality he did not possess, instead of for the many he did.

So he crafted the Harp of Desires and wove the Rope and Net of Gentle Persuasion. So he made himself a hunting knife of crystal and steel. He laid enchantments great and small upon all his gear. Later, he befriended Zephyr, the wisest of the steeds of flame and storm. Finally, he became wise in every bit of lore regarding the unicorn, so that when the time came he could bring the beast safely to its new home in lands ruled by the Seelie Court.

When the seers came, their silken robes whispering with excitement as they hurried to bring the news that the gate into the realm of the unicorn was opening, Sundeath was ready. He passed through the center of a faery ring, emerging into lands where a member of his kind could venture only once in many long years.

Standing beneath a sky that shown with pale light and a moon that gleamed black, Sundeath read the signs and omens. Swinging into his saddle, he set Zephyr's gilded hooves upon the proper path. Taking out the Harp of Desires, Sundeath set his fingers upon the strings and began to play. His hope was to draw the unicorn to him, taking it from the path of danger long before the champion of the Unseelie Court could so much as frighten it.

As Zephyr paced with measured tread along the forest trail, Sundeath played the song of his heart's desire, focusing upon the task set before him, and touching the string called Longing and the one called Love and the one called Comfort.

He was rather surprised when, coming to a wide glade encircled by ghostly stands of silver birches, what emerged from the curtain of pale green leaves was not a unicorn but a coarsely built but muscular horse. Upon it rode a woman of surpassing loveliness, armed and armored as for battle or the hunt. A tiny dragon with scales that glittered like rubies was perched upon her shoulder. Leaning against her ear, it peeped in alarm. As if shaken from a dream, the woman started, then with one smooth motion drew the long sword that hung at her side.

Without word of challenge, she drove her heels into her ugly steed and to Sundeath's shock and dismay came charging toward him.

When the music first touched her ears, Blackrose wondered on what instrument it could be played. Although her ears told her the music sounded something like harp song—although far more delicate and elegant than any harping she had heard within the rough confines of the Unseelie Court—some sound strange and unfamiliar danced between the notes.

Vaguely Blackrose turned the kelpie's head to follow the music, persisting even when Flamewing flew in loops and circles about her head, reminding her with hisses and spits that she was departing the unicorn's hard-won trail.

For his part, the kelpie made no comment.

Whether this was because he, too, was interested in the source of the music or because of the perverseness of his kind, Blackrose neither knew nor cared to know.

When the kelpie bore her from the cover of a forest of thorn into a lush glade beneath the darkness of the full moon and Blackrose saw the harpist, something twisted within her heart.

He was fair as not even the highest of the Unseelie Court were fair, with hair of sunlit gold. The eyes he raised from his harping to gaze upon her should have been brilliant blue but surprised by being violet. He was finely shaped in face and body. These were well-displayed, for he wore no armor, only a close-fitting suit of tawny fabric overlaid by a leaf-green cloak.

Blackrose, who shared her people's hunger for beauty, felt a longing to have him as a treasure for her own. Fury lit her in the next moment, for she recognized now what unknown instrument the harpist had played. She knew the music of her own solitary heart.

How dare he toy with me! she thought. *Sorcerer! Enchanter! Bind my heart and so take me from the field . . . I think not!*

Almost more swiftly than these thoughts could be shaped, Blackrose spurred her heels into the kelpie's flanks. Drawing her sword with less effort than a cat unsheathes its claws, she raced across the field to eliminate her enemy while he remained weaponless.

The man yelled, whether in fear or in answering

challenge Blackrose could not tell. With his left hand he drew the harp close to his body for protection, while his right hand smoothly drew his dagger from its sheath. A crystal blade caught the pale light of the sky and glimmered as he brought it around to block her sword.

Blackrose expected that fragile blade to shatter, but it held as if reinforced with steel. Even so, dagger is no match for sword. Her longer blade glided across the back of the man's hand. No blood beaded forth, not even a scratch marked the perfect skin. From this she knew that her opponent was protected by enchantments as she was protected by honest leather.

The momentum of this first clash had carried her past her intended victim. Now Blackrose wheeled the kelpie for a second attack. As far as she could tell, that crystal knife was the man's only weapon. She felt certain she could overwhelm his protective enchantments.

The man's dapple grey horse was taller than the kelpie, slender and graceful, although with a broad chest that promised strength as well as grace. The kelpie, however, was no horse but rather a fey creature, ornery of temperament as was shown by its wicked eye. Although the kelpie preferred to shape itself into the semblance of a somewhat stocky pony, for reasons of trapping the unwary it had long ago mastered more comely shapes as well. Now it adapted itself to the new challenge, becoming as large as the Seelie horse, but far stronger in build.

Transformation completed, the kelpie carried

Blackrose back into combat, trumpeting its own challenge to the pretty stallion. The Seelie champion had not moved from his place near the center of the thorn tree-lined meadow. He had tucked away the harp. Now with one empty hand and the tip of the crystal dagger, he traced patterns in the air. His lips were moving in rapid sequence and Blackrose recognized the building of a spell.

"Flamewing!" she cried. "Distract him!"

The little ruby-scaled dragon dove from where in had been anxiously circling, plummeting like diving hawk directly at the Seelie champion. When a few feet away, Flamewing spat fire, then wheeled up and out of reach.

The fire did not touch the champion but transformed instead into a shower of sparks that framed the man within a halo of red, orange, and yellow. Nor did the dragon's attack seem to interrupt the champion's concentration in the least. His lips continued to move, the tip of his dagger to trace elegant and complex patterns in the air.

Undeterred, the kelpie thundered forward, his heavy hooves tearing divots from the turf. Blackrose readied her sword in one hand. With the other, she drew a long dagger, double-blades paired like serpent's fangs either to cut or catch.

When the kelpie brought her close, snapping with square yellow teeth at the pretty dapple grey hide of the Seelie horse, Blackrose brought her weapons into play. She sought to catch the crystal dagger between her own's double blades, while bringing the sword in, hoping at least to shear the man's arm off at the shoulder, although she would have preferred to pierce him through his heart.

Neither goal was achieved. Even as the dragon's fire had been diverted before it could sizzle and burn as intended, so her weapons struck against a ward that had been invisible until it lit in reaction to her strike.

Golden light flashed in protest at her violence, paling to something dimmer when, despite the fiery pain that vibrated right into her very bones, Blackrose persisted in her attack. She knew something of wards, knew from long hours of training that they could be broken and once broken were very difficult to reinstate.

Then what will he do? she thought with vindictive fury. *He came prepared, yes, but when all that he has prepared is spent, surely he will fall victim to my sword—or if not to the sword, to a dagger, an arrow, an axe, even to the blows of my hands and the tearing of my teeth.*

But she felt very odd as this thought arose, very odd indeed. Her tutors in the Unseelie Court had schooled her well in such techniques and never before had she hesitated to use them. Indeed, she had defeated a six-armed giant when he went renegade. He had held her in a crushing embrace, but the battle had ended when she had pushed out his eyes with her thumbs.

But now . . . Now . . . What was happening to her? Why did she feel this curious desire to retreat rather than persist?

Enchantment! she thought. *Enchantment, perhaps*

*lingering from the music of the harp. I'll beat my way
through his wards . . . I'll eat his eyes, rip off his lips with
my teeth, and hold his heart in my hands.*

Sundeath was very glad that he had invoked his
wards before beginning his ride through the unicorn's realm. He had thought to delay, for such magics did diminish in power over time, but in the end
caution had won. After all, he knew he was not the
only one who sought the unicorn. He must remember that the unicorn's sharp horn was not the only
danger he faced.

This attack, though, was completely unexpected.
He had thought to fight the Unseelie Court's champion after the unicorn had been captured. So it had
been with the last such competition and the one before. For all they cheated and schemed, those of the
Unseelie Court had to rely on traditional means of
tracking. The great magics were not theirs. At best
they might bring some ensorcelled creature with
them, perhaps one like this lady's dragon, which
possessed a sharp nose and keen eyes and wings to
sail above the trees and so glimpse the unicorn in
some distant fastness.

Those of the Seelie Court, however, could lure the
unicorn to them, even as Sundeath himself had
sought to do. Once the unicorn caught sight of the
enchanter, other, older magics would take hold. This
double luring was a technique that rarely failed, saving the lives of the elegant beasts and winning their
blessings for the Seelie Court.

What went wrong? Sundeath thought as he began etching a spell against the whiteness of the sky. *I played and sang. Instead of my heart's desire this wildcat was brought to me.*

That wildcat was even now thundering across the sward toward where he sat upon Zephyr, trusting the horse and his wards to defend him while he prepared a spell. Her steed had grown to match Zephyr in size and strength, though doubtless not in elegance or wisdom. Another evidence of cheating, but cheating on the part of the Unseelie Court was so expected that had they not cheated it might be considered a form of cheating unto itself.

She held paired weapons in a manner that said without need of words that she knew how to use them. Despite the fearsome grimace that twisted her perfect lips and narrowed those long-lashed eyes to slits, she remained the loveliest woman Sundeath had ever seen. In contrast to her, the fey damsels of silver and gold and all the hues of the flowers of summer and spring faded to something perfect and lovely yet somehow half-alive.

Lips still shaping the words of the spell that would set upon her the chill of the north wind, the iciest heart of winter, Sundeath looked upon the face now inches from his own. It was alight with pain as she struggled against his ward, alight, too, with the golden glow of the damaged spell. She could break it, would break it, he did not doubt.

What she could not know was that this was but the first layer of his protections. How would she feel when she realized that the agony that burned in her bones had been as for naught? Would she run? Would she continue her attack even if it would mean her death?

Truth came to him as the final words of his spell took shape upon his lips. Truth that shook him and transformed his magic as it transformed him.

He had called for his heart's desire and his heart's desire had come to him. He desired not the unicorn, but what capturing the unicorn would win for him. That prize was not only passion but the rapturous union that would make of that passion more than a passing pleasure. His desire was for his other self, the other who would make him more than he could ever be alone.

He had called and she had come. If she died now, he would have slain her. And so he would slay himself . . .

Realization transformed his spell. Instead of the piercing ice of winter, the spell wrapped about the lady and her steed an avalanche of snow. Soft and smothering, it bound both in its embrace. It would not hold them long, but perhaps long enough for him to speak a few words.

Her head extended above the drift which curled about her as if a cloak of thick white fur. Her dark brown eyes were alive and fierce, reminding him of those of a hawk perched upon the falconer's wrist, at rest, but never tame.

"Lady Champion," he said, his tone haughty and tinged with mild disdain, "I thought our contest was for the unicorn, not to prove the worth of sword against spell?"

He spoke so, although he longed to utter far different words, to speak as sweet as honey, because he suspected that she would never believe him if he spoke the truth.

Those hawk's eyes, darker than those of any hawk, fringed with lashes he longed to brush with his fingertip, narrowed, seeking a trap.

He held his breath, waiting for a retort that did not come, then went on. "I have long trained to prove I could capture the unicorn and bring it back alive to my court. I do not doubt you have trained as well for your own mission. I offer you this. We are here together. Let us hunt in company until we find the beast and see which of our arts will win. Otherwise, what manner of a challenge would this be?"

The snow was melting, falling from her with a swiftness that argued some enchantment in her own armor. In a moment, she would be free. Would she reply with words or weapons?

As Blackrose struggled to break the ward, she knew she could not possibly succeed before the Seelie champion released his spell. She hoped that the charms against such magics worked into the runes that ornamented her armor would be sufficient to turn it aside.

When she had given her order to the duergan, she had demanded protection from fire and water, earth and air, these in any of the forms they take. She had not thought to ask for protection against the sort of sweet-singing charms that the harpist had used—a foolish oversight on her part, for such deceptions were well-known in the Unseelie Court and made a lie of love and longing.

Of course, the duergan had not volunteered any suggestions. Like the kelpie, they were helpful on their own terms, no others.

She saw the enchanter's violet eyes searching her face even as his lips shaped his spell. She wondered what he was looking for, what weakness he sought. He would find none in her. Her marrow burned as the ward strove to force her away, but she pressed ever on.

The cold wet snow that knocked her back and wrapped her in a freezing embrace was welcome at first, for it cooled the heat that was boiling her blood in her veins. Despite this, immediately she began to fight free. She was so concentrated on her battle that she hardly realized when the harpist began to speak. His first words were lost to her, but she heard clearly the second part of his speech.

"I have long trained to prove I could capture the unicorn and bring it back alive to my court," said a voice deep and masculine, despite being as melodious as the notes of his own harp. "I do not doubt you have trained as well for your own mission. I offer you this. We are here together. Let us hunt in company until we find the beast and see which of our arts will win. Otherwise, what manner of a challenge would this be?"

Blackrose could feel that the runes etched into her armor were working against the snow. Did this arrogant sorcerer realize that she would be free within a few moments? Was he prepared for the renewed onslaught of her attack?

Something in those violet eyes told her that he did and was. Strangely, this made her respect him just a little, even as she was infuriated by his arrogance.

The kelpie beneath her would not be free as soon. Best delay for a moment.

"Do you trust me to hunt beside you?" she asked the Seelie champion.

His lips curved just a little. "I trust that you would prove yourself a better hunter than the others the Unseelie Court has sent into the field these challenges past. I studied the lore of past contests. It is long since the unicorn's horn was brought back to your monarchs' realm."

Blackrose stiffened. She knew this only for the truth, but her pride was pricked—both to prove to the Unseelie Court that she was better than those who had come before her and to prove to this arrogant sorcerer that she could best him.

And why shouldn't I agree? Champions before me have told how always the Seelie champion found the unicorn before them so that their battle was not with the beast but with the other—and that other having the advantage of the unicorn on his side. Why should I not learn from their failure?

She gave the Seelie champion a winning smile.

"I like your spirit," she said, and realized with some shock that she meant this. She hastened on, lest she admit to something else she had not known. "And I accept your challenge. Let us seek the unicorn together. When we find it, then we will see what flies faster, your net or my arrow."

"I agree," the other said. "I am called Sundeath, son of the sorceress Silver Lily and Oakheart, a knight of the Rade. May I know what to call you?"

"I am Blackrose," she said, "and who my parents are is of no matter."

She shook the last of the snow from her shoulders, felt how the sealskin of her armor had protected her from the damp. Beneath her, the kelpie kicked itself free of the last clinging drifts, muttering imprecations between square teeth. Flamewing came down and twined itself around her forearm, hissing and whistling in gusts of confusion.

"Then, Lady Blackrose," Sundeath said, promoting her, although she would not for this world or any other have told him so, "let us ride together, and seek the unicorn."

Yes, Blackrose thought. *Let us seek it. I am not being soft. After all, who says my first arrow must be for the beast? A better target would be your back.*

They rode together in what rapidly became concord, not merely company. The kelpie rode shoulder to shoulder with the fey steed, muttering insults at Zephyr, who chose to ignore them. Little Flamewing fluttered about them, dancing on the winds and even going so far as to attempt to rest on Sundeath's shoulder.

To Sundeath's delight, they discovered much in common. Like him, Blackrose had been the one child born to her court in many years. Her closest age-mates had been weird goblins and water sprites. His had been a maiden some five years older. Although they had been friends, when he had been selected as champion, that friendship had ended.

Solitude had been a common state for both Sundeath and Blackrose. Now, finding someone who honestly understood, the words flowed between them. At first they came in spurts and starts, like a candlewick catching fire, then with the heat and intensity of a roaring blaze.

Sundeath learned of Blackrose's hard childhood, of the honors she was ambitious to win. Blackrose was told of Sundeath's sense of betrayal when he learned he was wanted most for what he had not done, rather than his many gifts.

Blackrose proved as prickly as the rose that gave her part of her name—quick to take offense, but ready to accept apology. Sundeath, for his turn, found himself sometimes struck dumb by his desire to declare himself to her, a declaration he knew to be impossible.

Despite this strange accord between them, they did not neglect their quest. Sundeath did not dare use the Harp of Desires, for he did not know what song he might play unintended. Instead, he used the crystal dagger to etch a compass rose against the sky so that they might set their course.

However, direction is only worth so much. Blackrose's sharp eyes found the hoofmarks barely pressed into the grass of a small glade when he would have mistaken them for old deer tracks. After that, she never lost the trail.

They came upon the unicorn all too swiftly for Sundeath's liking, although the search had taken them many hours. The white sky had shifted to pale orange highlighted with yellow. The black moon had given way to a blue sun that gave clear light but created weird shadows.

Was it these shadows that hid the unicorn from him, although it stood directly in their path? Or was it that it looked so little like what he had thought they sought? Sundeath had believed he knew what unicorns looked like. After all, until a few years ago, the prize of the last hunt had dwelled in the environs of the Seelie Court. Yet that creature, horse-like, its arching neck wreathed with garlands of daisies, its horn wound round with silken ribbons, bore little resemblance to what stood poised on the trail before them.

Delicate in build, solid enough to cast a shadow, nonetheless, there was something translucent about its slender body. Zephyr, Sundeath's steed, was said to be born from fire and wind. By the same logic, the unicorn shared the heritage of wind, but in the place of fire it owed kinship to clear running water, ungraspable yet solid enough to drown the unwary. Through this flowed light, ebbing forth from a pale blue horn, illuminating wild eyes.

The unicorn looked back at them over tensed shoulders. It seemed prepared to flee, yet wide nostrils scented the air inquisitively. Tentatively, as if bound by some compulsion outside itself, the unicorn began to take stumbling steps towards them.

While Sundeath sat stunned, still trying to weigh his conflicting visions of the unicorn, Blackrose was bending her bow, reaching for an arrow.

Her hands shook. Perhaps something in her rebelled against shooting at such a creature, but she loosed the arrow nonetheless. Instead of piercing the unicorn's breast, the point coursed over its hide, slicing a narrow furrow that oozed blood.

Compulsion broken, the unicorn fled, silken mane and tail flowing out behind it, pale blue horn glowing faintly against the shadows. Yet even as it fled, it looked back at them fascinated, even though the price of that fascination was its life.

The kelpie immediately gave chase, ruby-bright Flamewing bursting from Blackrose's shoulder into flight. Never one to lose a race, without waiting for command Zephyr broke into a gallop, easily catching up to the kelpie. So the champions thundered side by side, wind whipping their hair. Although it kept looking back, the unicorn outdistanced them, barely, never leaving their sight.

As they tore along, Sundeath found himself frantically thinking. *This hunt means so much to Blackrose, far more than it could mean to me. Should I let her win? No. She would know and that would kill any faint liking between us. Besides, my failure will doom the unicorn. How can she bear to put out such loveliness for mere ambition?*

*   *   *

Blackrose held readied bow and arrow, but she did not shoot again, aware that wind and distance would defeat even her skill.

Now would be the time to take out Sundeath, she thought. He rides by my side. Flamewing has tested and his first ward is down. Surely he has other protections, but they may not stop an arrow.

Yet she did not loose the arrow. Instead, she heard herself saying, "How can you bear to take such a creature and bind it into captivity? If ever there was freedom born, that is the unicorn, yet your people would pervert it into its own antithesis."

She could tell Sundeath was shocked, but his reply remained courtly, as had been all his speech to her.

"How can you say that? You would slay it! From what I have heard, your people would devour its flesh, make cages from its bones, and you yourself would wear its hide as armor. We at least would give it its life!"

"Life!" she spat. "Imprisoned freedom? You call that living? We would kill it, yes, but never take its freedom. When we dine upon its flesh, we take that spirit into ourselves. The cage from its bones is cruel because it retains the memory of perfect liberty. As for the armor, what greater honor can a killer give than to live embraced by the memory of what she has done?"

Sundeath stared at her, his violet eyes wide. "Yet no matter what honors your people offer, the unicorn would no longer drink fresh water or breathe the bright air."

"And each breath a torment," Blackrose retorted, "each swallow unable to ease a throat parched for a headier brew."

As if reined in by these dueling words, the kelpie and Zephyr had slowed their steps. Without speech, the two champions slid from their saddles until they stood facing each other no more than an arm's length apart.

The unicorn also paused. Its flanks heaved with effort, but its nostril furled, not to take in breath but as if drinking in some heady scent that mattered more to it than life.

Blackrose was aware that her arrow had slipped from her bowstring, that she felt no desire to reach for her sword. Flamewing had settled onto the kelpie's head and was making small noises of confusion, long neck arching back and forth between the unicorn it knew was their prey and his mistress.

For his part, Sundeath did not draw the crystal dagger, nor did he make any move to toss net or rope over the advancing unicorn. Instead he spoke, his voice so soft that even Blackrose's keen hearing could hardly catch the words.

"You're right. I hardly knew the unicorn when I saw it, so different was it from the creature that goes by that name in the Seelie Court. Death would be kinder."

But Blackrose, thinking of the stiff white armor that hung in the champion's hall in the Unseelie

Court, of how the last champion had died of what all said was some sort of unassuaged grief, thought differently.

"No. Freedom cannot be preserved at such a cost. The prize is yours if you would take it. Look! The unicorn walks to within a hand's breadth."

But Sundeath did not touch the unicorn that now nuzzled at his sleeve.

"There is," Sundeath replied, "another prize I would rather win."

He reached out a hand that could have grasped the unicorn's mane and touched Blackrose's cheek. "You are lovely beyond any I have ever seen. I have already lost my freedom. How could I take it from another?"

Blackrose felt herself unexpectedly smiling, her heart lightening, unfolding from tight buds she had not known bound it.

"There is one way we could set the unicorn free," she said softly. "For there is one weapon each of us bears that we could exchange and so seal our agreement to give the prize to neither of our courts."

Sundeath's eyes lit with joy, their violet losing its shadows and becoming merry. He grinned at her.

"From what I have heard, that exchange is not one to give once and never again, not if its full delight is to be understood."

Blackrose laughed, her blood rising in her cheeks. She stepped so that she could wrap Sundeath in her arms. She felt his heart beating against her, even through armor and clothing.

"This will not do," she said, fumbling with straps and buckles, finding her fingers unexpectedly clumsy.

"No. It will not." Sundeath took off his cloak of silken leaves and spread it on the ground. Her cloak of moss and shadows joined it.

Zephyr moved off to graze. The kelpie snorted with disgust and wandered down the trail, Flamewing still on its head. Only the unicorn remained, hovering over two who, having divested themselves of clothing and equipment they had taken years to acquire, were now exploring each other with an intensity that forgot all witnesses.

After a while, the unicorn shook itself as if astonished, sniffed the wind in puzzlement, found not what it sought, and fled.

Neither of those entwined in each other's arms noticed its departure. However, their dreams, when at long last they slept, were filled with a brilliant figure made of light and wind and water, running free.

THE GREEN MAN

Amber Benson

The night was a living thing, black and squalid, its ragged inhalations enfolding the girl like a muted chorus as she made her way through the wood, her eyes busily scanning the ground for exposed tree roots and other obstacles. Whirlwind fists of frigid air raged against the trees, hellbent on ripping foliage away from branches and sending leaves spinning inside its eddying currents; while raindrops, fat as blood-filled ticks, fell in glistening sheets of refracting liquid, whistling their progress like the slashing of claws on silk as they buried their corpses into the mossy humus.

But none of this bothered the girl. She was inured to the harshest of elements, the *intention* inside of her compelling her forward despite the inclement weather. It was as if she were tethered to the thing by a gently retracting string, so not even the freezing water that sluiced down the hood of her cloak, caressing her face and making her whole body shiver, distracted her from her goal.

The blue woolen cloak she wore was not meant for the coolness of an autumn night, let alone the torrential winter downpour that now engulfed the girl. It gave her meager protection against the bitter cold, openly inviting the icy chill to seep into her flesh, wrapping its sinewy embrace around her bones as if it could find a permanent home inside her. She had grabbed the cloak from the back of her stepmother's black walnut carved armoire, knowing the piece of clothing wouldn't be missed. The heavier winter cape she usually wore—the fleece-lined one that had belonged to her own mother before she'd died—still hung from its hook in the hallway. If anyone had noticed it draped there—though she doubted anyone had—it would only reinforce the idea that she was safely tucked in bed with the blankets pulled up tight to her chin, lost and dreaming inside the Land of Nod. They would never have believed she would dare traverse the dark of the forest without the cape's protection; a thirteen-year-old girl with her soft, childish hands and innocent face out there in the dark, nearly naked against the elements, braving the storm to commit an unspeakable crime?

It would seem implausible to any adult.

They might have viewed it in an entirely different light if only they knew the truth, the sordid reality of the world the girl had inhabited since the day her father married that *woman*; the creature who, for the last seven years, had made the girl's existence one of utter misery—then, and only then, did the act she perpetrated seem within reason. It had been born of desperation and the need to protect something smaller than herself; something that could not protect itself.

As if in tandem with her thoughts, she felt the tiny bundle in her arms squirm and she realized that the baby she carried with her had awoken. She could sense its hunger, its need for warmth and affection, but she could do nothing for it until they reached their destination.

"Quiet now, little one," she cooed, but she found her voice ripped away from her, lost in the wake of the wind and rattling leaves above her head. The storm had picked up again, the cold air slicing through the thin fabric of the cloak, but she took comfort in the fact that the child was protected, warm and safe inside the fleecy brown blanket she had stolen from its bed.

The baby hadn't cried when she'd come into the room to take it—the baby never cried when *she* held her—and it had been easy enough to swaddle the child in the fleece, wrapping it up safe and tight. Even the rain could not harm the babe; the girl saw to that by keeping the child tucked tightly against her breast underneath the protection of the cloak. Of course, she knew none of these precautions would have lasted had the journey been a longer one—and she thanked the Goddess the tree which marked the entrance to the Sídhe was less than a league from the river at the edge of her father's property.

It was strange to think that getting to her destination—in the pitch of night by way of the icy windswept forest—was proving to be the easiest part of her endeavor, while the actual abduction itself had been the trickiest. Fraught with the most risk because her stepmother was the lightest of sleepers, assured to hear even the faintest creak of foot on stair or rustle of skirt against skin. The girl's heart had lodged in her throat as she made her way across the hall, her breathing barely a whisper as she tried to keep the shaking of her hands to a minimum.

She'd never dared to defy her stepmother before— even when she'd tried her best to please the woman all she'd been met with was pain and humiliation. She could only imagine what her stepmother would do if she were to discover the girl tip-toeing across the thick slats of the wooden floor in the dead of night, her eyes wild with fear . . . and determination.

The girl had already decided should she be discovered during the course of her attempt, she would put an end to the charade once and for all. To this end, she'd taken the poker from the kitchen hearth, concealing it within the folds of her skirt as she made her way upstairs after a tense and silent dinner with her stepmother and father. As she'd held the poker tight in her hand, its leaden weight a talisman against discovery, she'd issued a silent prayer to the Goddess that the precaution of carrying such a weapon might be for naught, that she wouldn't have to use its heft to destroy the woman who had made her life such a misery.

At dinner, her mind focused on what lay ahead; she hadn't given much thought to her father or what her plan might mean for him. As usual, he had been quiet and withdrawn, paying her little attention as they'd eaten, lost in the rich folds of his own imagination. He practically lived for his work, so that his daughter hardly ever saw him outside of mealtimes—and even then he frequently took his dinner in his workshop, a place that was inaccessible to both his second wife and daughter. The girl knew her father was brilliant, that the king paid him great sums of gold to build the strange inventions he dreamed up, but she had never been close to him, never understood what it was exactly that her real mother had found so appealing about the man.

Not that she had ever really tried to know her father. Especially after he'd done the unthinkable and remarried—barely three months after her mother's death—allowing that horrid woman, the one she now had to call *stepmother*, unfettered access to their life. It had irked the girl that the marriage hadn't been for love; that her father had been goaded into the match by her grandmother, a wizened old crone of a woman whose marked fragility belied the formidable character that lay hidden underneath. Luckily, the girl was only forced to endure the old woman once a year at Christmastime—which was still one visit more a year than the girl would've liked.

The girl could remember a Christmas visit when

the old woman had caught her playing with a straw dolly that her mother had made for her before she'd died. It was a representation of the Goddess, one of the life-giving personality facets of the Great Mother called Astarte. The girl had adored the doll, thrilling at its strange, silvery hair and tiny aster seed eyes and mouth. The dolly had been her most favored possession; going everywhere with her and even cuddling up beside her while she slept.

But when her grandmother had caught sight of her otherworldly dolly that cold winter's night, her eyes had flared with recognition and before the girl's bewildered gaze the old woman had made the sign of the cross, her hands like claws as she traced the powerful symbol into the air. Then in a tremulous, sibilant voice, one the girl barely recognized as human, the old woman had called the dolly "an abomination to God."

The girl didn't understand; the dolly was only a gift from her dead mother, it wasn't something to be feared—but then the old woman had done something unthinkable, something the girl's mother would never have allowed had she still been alive: the witch had torn the bedraggled dolly—the only thing of her mother's left to the girl besides the acorn charm—and pitched it in to the Yule fire. The dolly had caught the flame instantly, its straw body and aster seed eyes glowing orange as they incited the Yule log to burn even brighter, creating a miniature inferno inside the wrought iron grating of the sitting room fireplace.

The girl had understood from an early age that her grandmother was a selfish creature and she'd pitied the old woman this glaring weakness, never despising her for it. Even when the girl's beloved mother lay cooling underneath her newly settled gravestone and the old woman had lectured her son about finding an able-bodied woman to run his household and provide a feminine influence for his young, impressionable daughter—and to the girl's consternation he'd listened, marrying the first woman his mother suggested to him—even then she hadn't hated her grandmother. But with the destruction of that cherished dolly, the old woman had made a bitter enemy for life—and the girl had vowed never to forgive her, or her father, for their cruelness.

Her mind swirling with painful memories, the girl reached the towering oak tree just as the baby began to fuss in earnest. Under safety of the tree's canopy, she unwrapped the babe so she could kiss its forehead.

"It won't be long, I promise," she said, nuzzling the child to calm its fussiness. The baby instantly relaxed at her touch, yawning and then closing its eyes to sleep again.

As she stared down at the sleeping child, she remembered the last time she had come to this place. It had been a few days before her mother's death, the tragedy that would soon follow etching the memory into her brain forever, so that even now the remembrance brought tears of pain to her eyes. That it had been seven years since her last visit was superfluous;

the girl knew the way as if she'd ventured there yesterday.

They had stood on this very spot: her mother, tall and willowy, with a shock of sunfire hair and eyes greener than a cat's, holding the girl's hand and pointing to the rough hewn trunk of the giant oak.

"This is where I come from, Daughter," she had said, her voice thick with a honeyed pride that made the girl squirm.

Whenever her mother had spoken of her childhood home, there had been a longing inside of her words that'd spooked the girl. She'd instinctively known that given half a chance, her mother would undoubtedly return to the world of the fairies, leaving her daughter adrift in a human world fostered upon lies and half-forgotten truths.

It was an idea that had chilled the girl.

As mercurial as her mother may have been, there was no guile in the woman. Instead, she possessed an almost animal honesty, something that was inherent in her every action or word, so that the girl always knew exactly what her mother was thinking. Unlike her father or the servants, whose intentions were so complex they were hard for the girl to unravel.

"The fairies will help you should you ever have need of them," her mother had continued, her voice the timbre of silk. "You have their blood in your veins and that will be enough. Though only once will they heed your call—so use the gift I give you wisely."

The girl had been so little that she hadn't known how to respond and, instead, merely nodded her blonde head, her own green eyes wide with wonder.

As she'd watched, her mother had grasped the end of her necklace and yanked, breaking the thin filament that encircled her throat. The charm it had borne, a small stone acorn that her mother had worn around her neck for the whole of the girl's life, fell silently into her mother's outstretched palm.

"This will call them out," she had said, as she'd placed the charm into the girl's open hand, closing the tiny fingers around it as though within their fleshy pads they possessed all the protection the world had to offer.

Three days later, her mother was dead, thrown from the back of her own horse, a timid creature called Buttercup that was the sweetest of all the horses in the stable. The girl had not understood how so fine a horse could've done so much damage, but that was to remain a mystery that she would never solve. Her mother had been out riding alone in the woods, without even a servant to keep her company. The accident, if that's what it'd truly been, was not witnessed.

The following morning her father had had the beast slaughtered, the efficiency of the act frightening the girl. She'd wondered then—as children filled with guilt and incomprehension are wont to do—if she, too, would've been dispatched so competently if she'd been the one at the helm of her mother's death. She'd also wondered how much forewarning her mother had had of her own death, if that'd been why she'd taken the girl to the oak tree and given her the charm; that she'd known this would be her only opportunity to do so.

Yet another mystery the girl would never solve.

Now that she stood at the entrance to the Sídhe, the world hidden behind the majestic oak tree beckoning her forward, uncertainty overwhelmed her. Up until that very moment, she'd been so sure of herself and her plan; now she felt lost. The idea that there would be no going back once she'd put the thing into motion had not worried her in theory, but to hand the child over to the fairies when one was actually doing the deed was a very different thing.

The girl swallowed, her mouth dry as she contemplated her options. She could turn around and go back the way she had come—or she could move ahead with what she'd originally intended and let the cards fall as they may.

It was the babe, itself, that made the decision for her. It kicked out at her from beneath the blanket, its tiny foot catching her in the forearm as if it were bestowing a benevolent kiss. It was as if the baby were saying: go on, do this thing for both of us. It is our destiny.

"I know it's for the best," she whispered as she pressed her lips to the babe's ear. "I know it."

Only once will they heed your call, her mother had warned.

*　　*　　*

Over the years the girl had endured numerous beatings at her stepmother's hand, but she'd never dared waste the gift her mother had bestowed upon her. She could survive the physical pain; knew that once she was sixteen her father and grandmother would marry her off and she would be rid of them forever. She had prayed to the Goddess every night since she was six years old that she might marry a man of true kindness—and were she to find that the suitor chosen for her was a tyrant? Well, if that came to pass then she would gladly use the charm and damn the consequences.

But those thoughts belonged to another girl from another time—one who understood nothing about true fear. Fear for her own sanity, and that of her newborn sibling, had driven the girl to this desperate place; had finally forced her hand enough that she'd dared to waste her one chance and call out the fairies to do her bidding.

Clutching the baby tightly within the crook of one arm, the girl raised her free hand and wrapped her fingers around the stone acorn that had hung like a talisman around her throat for so many years. Repeating the same gesture as her own mother seven years previously, she grasped the charm and snapped the thin piece of string that held it into two, letting the weight of the charm fall into her hand. It was as if she were holding a tiny block of ice in the coolness of the dark, wet night, and she shivered. She had prepared nothing. Her mother had given her no words to say, no charm to incant; just the small piece of cold, dead stone that she now held in the folds of her palm.

As she stood on the threshold of this immutable moment, the girl almost laughed, hysteria burbling up inside of her as she contemplated the dastardly thing she was about to do.

In truth, it was odd for her to think how innocently all the pain and suffering had begun.

Her first blood had come in the middle of the night, the pain ratcheting up her spine like a vise, waking her from a deep and dreamless sleep. She cried out, the noise barely a *hush* in the silence of the room, and then covered her mouth as the sound melted into the shadows. She didn't dare sit up or move in any way, hoping that her cry would go unnoticed, but luck was not with her. She stiffened as she heard the soft *creak* of her stepmother unfolding the covers and climbing out of her goose down bed in the room next door.

Her stepmother did not share a room with her father—he preferred to keep his own suite of rooms in the other wing of the house, so he never found his sleep disturbed by the scream of an ill child or a hungry babe. He left his only daughter completely at her stepmother's mercy . . . and the woman was merciless. Her stepmother never said exactly how she felt about being left to while away the nighttime hours alone, but by her actions, the girl could guess that she did not suffer the indignity gladly.

The door to the girl's room opened silently, a shaft of candlelight illuminating the way as her stepmother, her soft brown hair loose around the shoulders of her white cotton nightdress, stepped inside. The girl squeezed her eyes shut, hoping her stepmother would think she was asleep, but instead she heard her stepmother's light tread continue as she crossed the divide between the doorway and the bed.

"I know you're awake."

The voice was low and measured, the trill of a purr languishing just beneath the dulcet tones, as her stepmother sat down on the edge of the bed, depressing the mattress with her weight.

The girl opened her eyes. She knew better than to outright lie to her stepmother—this only brought you a beating much more quickly. Best to stretch out the truth a little instead and hope her stepmother would choose leniency.

"I had a bad dream," the girl answered, trying to keep her voice as even as possible. The ache in her belly had grown worse and she could feel the wetness pooling between her legs. She just wanted her stepmother to go away and leave her to her pain in peace.

"About what . . . ?" her stepmother asked, her golden-brown eyes curious. "About what did you dream?"

"I don't remember," the girl whispered, avoiding her stepmother's piercing gaze.

There was only silence as the older woman pursed her pale pink lips. The girl understood what would come next—what always came next—but still she sought to stave off the attack with meaningless words.

"I'm sorry. I didn't mean—" the girl began, but her pleas went unacknowledged as two strong hands grasped the edge of the comforter and ripped it away from her prone body.

"No!" the girl screamed as her stepmother grabbed her arm and dragged her from the bed, a smear of bright red blood staining the place where she'd just lain.

At the sight of so much blood, her stepmother relaxed her hold and the girl broke free, clambering to the floor, her white nightdress now a red swirl around her legs.

"What is this?" her stepmother asked, as she reached out a long, thin finger and pressed it into the center of the bloody stain.

The girl trembled, her mouth dry as a wooden board.

"Well . . . ?" her stepmother said, her curving body casting long, dancing shadows against the whitewashed walls in the flickering light of the candle.

"I don't . . . " the girl began—then stopped cold as she noticed the calculating look that had overtaken her stepmother's angular face and wide, expressive mouth.

The girl understood that her stepmother was a beautiful woman when not viewed through the filter of intimacy; for those who knew her only in passing thought her to be a bastion of innocence and light. At

twenty-three, her stepmother did possess the lus-
cious beauty of a newly plucked rose, but the girl
was privy to what lay underneath the veneer of the
freshly blooming exterior—and it was the wicked
soul of a black-hearted witch.

"Come here."

The two words dropped like icicles, shattering
into a million pieces on the floor.

The girl shook her head, fear swallowing her
tongue and rendering her mute.

"I said . . . *come here*."

Shaking like a newborn foal, the girl stood up and
took three tentative steps toward her stepmother.
She could feel each individual purl of the white knit-
ted rug beneath her feet.

"Closer."

It was a command—and the girl could do nothing
but obey, her stepmother's charge ingrained in her
since she was six years old.

"That's a good girl," her stepmother cooed, reaching for the girl's hand and pulling her close, the two
feminine bodies mere inches from one another like
orbiting planets.

"You're a woman now," her stepmother intoned,
her breath warm and spicy like cinnamon as it settled inside the girl's nostrils. "Just like me."

She leaned forward and kissed the girl firmly, yet
sweetly on the mouth. The taste of her stepmother's
lips was heady and ripe, making the girl swoon as
blood leaked from between her legs with every pulse
of her heartbeat.

Her stepmother released her hand and the girl tensed, waiting for the slap she was certain would follow. Instead, she felt her stepmother's hand tenderly snake up the side of her waist, following the curve of her ribcage where it met her breast. The hand paused there, over the small mound of barely ripened flesh and cupped it, gently rubbing the nipple to attention with the meat of her thumb.

The girl bit her lip, the feeling of pleasure at the hands of her persecutor confusing to her, the strange intimacy illogical to the girl.

The girl stood in place, legs locked and rigid, not knowing what to do. If she tried to flee, the rage she might induce would be terrible; if she stayed, well, somehow that was even worse.

"No," the girl hissed, finding her voice again. "Leave me alone!"

But as she tried to push her stepmother away, the older woman grabbed the girl's hair and yanked it hard, tearing at her scalp.

"Shut your mouth," her stepmother said, dragging the girl back to the bed by her hair and shoving her onto the mattress so hard the girl cried out. With rigid fingers, her stepmother tore at the thin material of the girl's nightdress so it ripped apart, revealing the girl's naked torso.

The girl sobbed as she was forced back into her bloody bed and held there against her will. She squeezed her eyes shut as if that would stop the quick, searching fingers from driving themselves into the smooth softness of her flesh until she cried out in agony and guilt—and then she was alone again, tossed aside like a used rag, as salty tears of fear obscured her vision and she fell into a chasm so dark and deep it seemed endless.

The girl shivered, remembering the many times her stepmother had touched her during the intervening months—until her father had suddenly reclaimed his second wife, making her so heavy with child that she no longer possessed the strength to overpower the girl.

The pregnancy had been the girl's saving grace and she'd rejoiced at the benevolence of fate—but then, without warning, a terrible thought had entered unbidden into her mind and she'd been unable to shut it out, no matter how hard she tried. It was the knowledge that when she left the household, there would be no one to protect her baby sister from the cruel whim of the mother they both shared—one by marriage and the other by birth. This eventuality was what had driven the girl to such a state of frenzied fear that she'd stolen the infant from its crib and made the journey to the fairies' lair in the dark of night with only a thin summer cloak to keep her bones warm.

It was why she now stood among the roots of a monstrous oak tree, a tiny acorn charm numbing a hole inside the padded palm of her hand.

Her blood thrumming like a melody inside her skin, the girl let loose a scream, the sound echoing through the darkness like wildfire. Compelled to let the charm loose, she grasped the baby tightly under her arm and raised her free hand over her shoulder, letting the charm sail into the plumage of leaves above her head in a graceful, sweeping arc.

Immediately there was a fierce rumbling beneath her feet and the girl stepped away from the network of tree roots, working hard to keep her balance. Above her the oaken overhang of branch and leaf burst into crystalline blue flames and the rain, which had deluged the girl during her journey, suddenly ceased.

"Ah, a wanderer from the human world," a disembodied voice hummed behind her, precise and masculine.

The girl looked around uncertainly until she spotted its owner—a tall, reedy man in a green suit and matching neckerchief—leaning against the trunk of a nearby tree. The blue flames that had lit the sky only moments before began to dissipate and the girl used this last bit of illumination to commit the man's features to memory: pale blond hair, a straight nose, and two of the greenest eyes she'd ever encountered. As she squinted against the dying light, she thought she glimpsed a shock of wavy green hair as coarse as strands of trailing vine atop his head, but as the darkness grew and blotted out the light, everything took on a muted, gray tinge and the girl could not be sure.

"Who are you?" the girl asked, wary of the man.

The man grinned at her and bowed his head.

"I'm a distant relation—on your mother's side," he added. "But you may call me the Green Man."

To her amazement, she saw that he was holding her acorn charm, casually throwing it up in the air and catching it again with a fluid ease that impressed her.

"My mother said were I ever to have need of your help—"

"Not necessary," the Green Man interrupted. "I know what you seek."

This gave the girl pause. Whether or not the Green Man knew what she wanted, she had come this far and she was going to ask for what she needed with her own tongue. She deserved that—if only that.

"Then you know I want you to take the baby and give me a changeling child in its place," the girl replied. "One that will suck the very life from the human babe's mother until she withers away to dust."

The Green Man raised an eyebrow, but nodded.

"It can be done . . . for a price."

The girl's smile faltered then fell away entirely.

"You become my bride," the Green Man said lightly, knowing this bargain would please the queen of the Seelie Court to no end.

He waited patiently as the girl thought over his offer. He watched her as she considered the bargain, wondering if her stepmother's death was worth this sacrifice, but, in truth, what the girl did not know was that the decision had been made long before she'd grabbed the baby from its woven birch crib and set out into the darkness.

It had been made the moment the girl's mother

had left the Sídhe to follow her human lover into the human world—six long years without a queen, the Green Man mused. Now it seemed only right that the half-human child would return to the land from which its mother had come; like returning a missing piece back to its lawful owner.

"If I say yes then the babe will remain with me, unharmed?"

The Green Man nodded, willing to sweeten the bargain.

"As you wish."

The girl cradled the baby in her arms, love for the tiny thing blooming inside of her like a rose. She didn't need to think any more.

"Then I accept."

The Green Man extended his hand and they shook upon the deal.

He would send one of his hobgoblins over to her father's mansion house that very hour, where it would place a vengeful changeling child into the white birch crib and then quietly slip away into the night, with no one in the house ever the wiser.

As for the girl, well, the Green Man had been dedicatedly listening to her prayers for many, many years and as he stared at her gloriously beatific face, he believed it would be very easy to give her exactly what she had always prayed for.

True kindness.

ANNE

Michelle Sagara

He has come, as he often comes these days, to one of four bars around the corner from the large educational institution in which he spends most of his waking time. He comes not to drink—although for the sake of his table and the attitude of the various bartenders and barmaids, he does; alcohol has never held much sway over him, one way or the other. He's aware, because he drinks so conservatively, that the same can't be said for most of the bars' many patrons, but given his early childhood, he's always known this. It's not to socialize that he visits; he comes to watch her.

She has never been a beautiful girl. She is too round, too short, too uncontrolled; her voice, when she speaks, is rougher, lower. She's also a little on the old side, and the lines around the corners of her eyes and lips—lips the color of her skin—are etched there, now. But he watches nonetheless, fascinated, and willing to be so.

She is nothing like his mother. His mother was slender, tall, her hair long and utterly straight in its fall, no single strand out of place, a curtain of perfect night. Her cheekbones were high, pronounced, her skin the pale of porcelain, and unblemished. No wrinkle graced her eyes, her lips, her brow; even in her rage, she was flawless. Not for his mother something as simple as sweat; not for his mother this noise, this convivial chaos—although even in the chaos, she had an eye for pain and the ugly secrets that sometimes spill out alongside the alcohol.

Surrounded by the pale lights of a bar, the scent of sweat mingling with perfume, aftershave, and alcohol, he remembers his mother; the memories are fragmented, the way the memories of the young often are; they afford him no joy. He lifts his glass—wine, red. Behind the bar, a sweatband across her forehead—and necessary—she is working. She will work for three hours, maybe four, serving drinks, her smile tired and worn around the edges, her hands blocky and strong. Tonight, he thinks. Tonight she will join him. He wants that. He knows how to dial up charm; he knows how to push buttons, invoke responses: he spent years in his mother's shadow—how could he do otherwise?

But he has done none of that here, as if the process is at least as important as the result. He drinks, he watches—carefully—and he waits. It's mildly surprising, how hard it is to wait. He was never patient in his youth, but had thought, until now, that patience had developed, slowly and inevitably, with the passage of time and the accretion of bitter experience.

Tonight, she works the early shift. It is a definition of early that he feels does injustice to the word, but injustice is a fact of life, large and small. She disappears, relieved of her station behind the bar, and reappears without headband or wristbands. But she's clearly been sweating; fine strands of her hair are plastered to her forehead.

She is carrying a large plastic bag, which she almost trips over as she winds her way through the crowd. He rises to offer her help; she waves him away with a tired smile, as if his help in her place of employ is unnecessary. Or unwanted. She is so unusual in that way, in this day: she wants very little and feels entitled to less.

When she gestures—with her head—toward the door, he pays his bill and follows her; she's waiting in the cold night air, her breath suspended in clouds between them. She is also cursing the cold. The cold has never bothered him, although he does find it expedient to wear a coat and gloves. It's a dress coat; hers is puffy down, in a size too large, the edge of her sleeves beginning to fray, the detachable hood long since misplaced.

"Do you need to stop off at your place?" he asks, eyeing the plastic bag.

"No, I'm taking this with me. I'm baking, remember?"

He does. Or rather, he remembers that she

declared her intent; he is only slightly surprised that she meant it.

"Why are you smiling?"

"My mother seldom cooked; she disliked the mess."

She raises a dark, thick brow. "So you ate out a lot?"

"No. We had cooks, some of them very fine indeed."

"It's not the same," is her resolute declaration.

"No, indeed." What he doesn't tell her is that it could never be the same: cooking was for servants, for menials, for those whose choices in life had left them little option.

He doesn't offer to carry her bags; he's made that mistake once before, and besides, the way she holds them implies their contents are precious. Of the many things he learned in his youth, the cost of touching something precious to someone else was perhaps the most severe.

His home is perfect. In this city, with its brownstone and townhouses and harbor, he has chosen to live in the sky—and his condo is as close to sky as it is possible to be. Even in his youth, no buildings reached heights this impressive, and the buildings that came close did so by the dint of architecture, engineering, and centuries of labor.

Or by artifice, but artifice creates places of cunning and guile, not homes.

This, then, is not an act of artifice—but when he

opens the door and stares into the perfectly designed and sparsely decorated interior, he feels that he has not been entirely honest. Nothing is ever out of place here. No doubt his mother would find fault with it, if she knew where he lived and chose to visit, but he cannot think what that fault would be.

Her bags, wrinkled and stretched, don't belong in his apartment, but they come attached to her, and he lets them in. She looks smaller and more tired as she enters the hall, and she hesitates, seeing where he lives, but seeing it in her own peculiar way. "Do you ever come home?" she finally asks, and walks into the kitchen, where she places her bags on the counter, beneath the slate cupboards. She doesn't wait for an answer, or rather, she works while she waits, removing things from the bags and setting them aside in no particular order: flour, sugar, a small carton of eggs, apples, butter. Even milk.

"I come home," he replies, "at the end of every day."

She looks up, and then glances beyond him. "What do you do? Just sit in a chair? Or do you go straight to bed?"

"Pardon?"

"You have no books here."

"Ah. I have some; they are not in the exterior rooms. I have a television. It's on the wall; you can't see it from where you're standing."

"Do you have a housekeeper?"

"I have."

"But not a cook."

He smiles. "No. I seldom use the kitchen."

She snorts. "All this money on appliances—that Bosch costs the earth—to *not* cook. It's a *waste*."

"Ah. You are cooking."

"Yes. You're not helping," she adds, but this time she smiles. "Go—loiter in the living room. I'd tell you to put your feet up, but—"

"I understand the colloquialism. I shall endeavor to relax while you work."

He lies, of course; he watches her. In as much as watching anything is relaxing, she is: she sinks into the center of her activity, and she reaches a place that his entire home can't touch, although she's standing in it. She spills flour; she leaves small, red flecks of apple peel and its sticky juice; she curses as she breaks an egg with a little too much enthusiasm. But she works and as she does, she relaxes.

She has a moment of concern when she realizes how little he uses his kitchen, but she manages to find what he himself can't remember: measuring spoons, cups, baking pans. She mutters about the waste again, asks him if someone else used to live here with him.

"No. I have always lived alone."

This catches whatever part of her attention she's willing to spare. "Always?"

He nods.

"What about when you were a child?"

It's a question he's been asked many times and he has many different answers to give; the same answer, over and over, bores him. Some women want an easy avenue to pity and sympathy, and to these, he speaks of a cold and isolated childhood; some women want to admire his wit and his ambition, and to these, he speaks of the drive for control of his own life, his rise to power, his frequent clashes with the domineering household into which he was born. Some women want to hear stories of wealth and power, and these, too, he supplies; there is no woman—and no man, if it comes to that—who could hold a candle to his mother's power, not even at her nadir.

But she asks the question so casually, he has no avenue of approach; there is just his childhood and the facts of it, multiple and distant.

"I lived in a large household," he finally replies. "In a much larger space than this. You?"

"I lived in a space about this size with a *lot* of people. We were always getting in each other's way— you couldn't take a step without almost tripping over someone." She laughs. "Someone crawling on the floor, or chewing the table legs; there was a lot of swearing, but not too much cursing."

"Did the table legs ever bite back?"

She laughs. It's the sound of her laughter he wants, and this laugh is laced with genuine surprise. "To listen to the kids, yes—but you know, I think that's the first time I've ever heard you say something deliberately humorous."

It isn't. He could tell her—with complete accuracy—every other time he's made the attempt;

he doesn't. She has never appreciated what passes for a sense of humor among his kin. Whereas he? He finds her laughter inexplicable, unpredictable; the oddest things make her almost squeal in delight. They are mostly common things, unremarkable things; even having observed her for so long, he cannot predict with any accuracy what might delight her.

He knows that gifts, on the other hand, cause her to fall silent and withdraw. At best, she is flattered, but flattery pales quickly under the pressure of refusal.

No man would have dared to refuse his mother's gifts, infrequently offered as they were; no man and only one woman in history. Some men were unwise, and accepted her gifts as their due; he was not one of those. When she came with a gift, he looked for barbs; her gifts were often more painful than her punishments, differing only in their subtlety.

Why does this woman make him think so much of his mother?

She is washing her hands in the sink; the soap is one of the few things she doesn't comment on. He knows she is nervous here, and wonders what her own home must be like; she has never invited him in, although he knows where she lives. He's seen her, shadowed by the lights in the second floor room above the street; she doesn't like any height she can't reach by stairs—and any height that might kill her if she's forced to jump is also not acceptable. She told him this the second time they spoke.

He looked at her blankly, wondering if perhaps she, too, was a refugee from distant, very different lands, but she said, quickly, "Fire. If there's a fire. I'm pretty careful, so I won't set it—but when you live in a building like this, your life is partly dependent on the habits of strangers."

"No part of my life is dependent on the habits of strangers," he told her.

She snorted; it is one of her most common—and least attractive—habits. "Everyone's life is dependent on the habits of strangers; some people just don't accept it, that's all. You get in a car, and you're dependent on other drivers obeying the laws of the road. You're dependent on people you've never seen for your food—unless you happen to grow and hunt all your own?"

He has done both, but does not feel the need to share.

Yet after she'd closed the bar down, her words had clung to him, like cobwebs, fine yet persistent. Where there were webs, there were often spiders, and harmless spiders were a modern invention, or an invention of cars, cities, and cold, cold winters. Yet there seemed no venom in her words, no intent to harm or weaken him; she was frustrated, yes, but she was often frustrated.

And she showed it so easily, revealed it so guilelessly. Really, she had no control at all.

What did his mother show?

Displeasure, with a small compression of lips and

sometimes with a dazzling, perfect smile. Pleasure, with a similar smile; those who did not know or understand her often mistook the one for the other, to their detriment. She shed no tears except once, only once, and she did not rage, although she exposed her fury: it was ice and storm, and it promised death, or rather, an end for which death would be a paradise, a blessing.

She did not show joy, if she ever felt it at all, and no sorrow touched her face, except once—and all who were witness died thereafter, all but he. Once, he had mistaken exultant, wild triumph for joy. Once.

But watching this woman bake, he knows that there is joy in what she does, and it requires no death; she takes delight in blending these odd and unpleasantly messy ingredients into something that resembles edible food. She approaches it not as a vocation and not as a cause; nor does she approach it as a foe with which to do battle and over which to triumph.

She finds joy in the idea that what she makes will be eaten, that it will be enjoyed.

He has pointed out that this joy is ephemeral; it will not—cannot—last. She laughs; she laughed then.

"Nothing lasts forever. If we were all stuck in the moment of our single brightest day, we would never learn anything, never grow, never find new joys."

"Nor would you find new sorrows and new pain. Many, many are the people who wish never to have loved at all when love falls to ruin and despair. You must see them, night after night, in your place of employ; tell me I am wrong."

"Oh, you're not wrong," was her quiet—and oddly thoughtful—reply. "But that's what happens when we're in pain—it's our whole world. It's all we can see." She hesitated, and then said, "You're young. I'm not."

He didn't argue, aware that the lack of demur is a lie of omission, and quite comfortable with the fact.

"To be older—like I am—is to realize that it's not all pain; it's just what we're looking at at the time. We expose ourselves to pain when we open ourselves up to life. But we *also* open ourselves up to joy. It's joy that we need, to survive."

He glances at the dripping mess she has made of all her disparate ingredients and says, "This activity brings you joy?"

"Yes, Mr. Spock, it does."

"And you feel that this is necessary for survival?"

"Yes."

"You are incorrect."

She sighs, brushes hair out of her eyes with the backs of her hands, leaving a trail of flower in the gesture's wake. "I suppose you'll tell me—"

"I have some personal experience with what is necessary for survival, yes."

She looks over his shoulder, at the expanse of his perfect home. "Maybe I chose the wrong word, then. Without joy, we can keep going. We can keep our heads down. We can keep putting one foot in front of the other." She turns her back to him and begins to spoon the mixture into the tin cups of the pan. "But that's not living. That's not life."

"What is life to you?"

She shakes her head. "It's little things, really. Like baking. Or singing. Or painting, not that I'm any good at the last two. It's—just—" she shrugs.

While she works, the small ones come out of invisible corners, drawn by her constant motion. If he's being truthful, so is he, but they're almost mindless in their greed and desire for what she prepares. He frowns at them, in warning; there are reasons he has never taken to the cooking that so entrances her.

But she doesn't see them. She doesn't see the way they cling to her shadow, hugging its lines, their faces upturned, calculating. They know only that she is baking for the joy of it, that she intends to share—and they stand on the outside of her circle, joyless, uncertain as to how to cross it, how to make themselves known. What she wants to give, they want to receive, but they have never, ever been good at asking.

Asking is not a trick that many of his kin have ever learned. They travel from the extreme of outsiders everywhere: wanting, desperately, to be on the inside, and despairing over their invisibility. That despair will drive them to small acts of malice in the end; they are not capable of large, not these. They cannot think of themselves as unworthy—not in comparison to the big people—so they must think of the big people as unworthy, ungrateful, deserving of punishment.

He clears his throat, and they freeze in place, as if by being utterly motionless they might pass beneath his notice. But he has gone through the effort of making his home as perfect as possible in order to be free of the small ones; they do not do his laundry, they do not clean or sweep or keep his windows closed—or open; they offer him no necessary service because he has allowed room for *none*. By this, they should know they are both unnecessary and unwanted, and they should leave him in peace; let them find someone else upon whom to shower their unappreciated largesse.

It is always a fine game; if one accepts their labor, one must pay them in the coin of their desire. People think of it as barter—and it is—but they do not understand what the coin of that barter is: the small ones desire, always, to be feted, appreciated; they desire gratitude, and it had better be genuine.

They did not do this in his mother's home. They would not dare; they might be permitted to occupy themselves in their constant chores, but something as menial as housework and tidying was beneath his mother's notice. Once, she overheard their small congress, and she summoned them all, from the furthest reaches of her lands. She destroyed one in three, without exception, in icy silence, and they did not dare to speak her name again for decades, not even in their malicious and hurt whispers.

He clears his throat again. He has not seen them

in a very long time, by design, and he is surprised that they dared to come here. They are still frozen, like rabbits in the headlights of approaching cars, and he would kill them as vermin if he thought she could continue to be so blind. But she turns. "Yes?"

He recovers, because he has always done that exceptionally well. "You failed to finish. What is life, to you? If it is not the love that others seek—"

"Love means different things to different people," she says quickly. "When you use the word, what do you mean? I can't help but notice that you never leave the bar twice with the same woman, and you seem to live here alone."

"Ah, but I do."

"Really? Who?"

"You."

She laughs. She *laughs*. She feels no threat at all, no danger. "I meant someone you're actually interested in."

He retreats into artifice, as it has served him so well. "I have been interested in every woman I have accompanied out of your bar, but they are not interested in me, in the end."

Her eyes widen; they narrow just as quickly. "You're joking," she says, in a tone of voice that implies that she thinks he's lying.

"They are interested," he continues, "in wealth. They like the address, they like my clothing, they like my car. They are not as impressed with my position at the university, but are willing to accept it." He smiles; it is a careful smile that treads the edge between a grimace of pain and genuine amusement. "They are not interested in me."

He has said this often in the past; it seems to mollify women. It doesn't, however, mollify this one.

"Well, how much of *you* do you show them? How can they be interested in something they're not even allowed to see?"

He is nonplussed, and retreats into defensiveness. "I am entirely myself," is his cool response. "What they see in me, they project."

"Meaning they see what they want to see?"

He nods.

"And not what you want them to see?"

He fails to nod a second time, sensing a trap in her words. She is not particularly artful, not cunning, but she cannot be easily moved once she has focused on a subject. Yet it is not her interest to be seen as an expert, it is not necessary for her to be seen as right; she pursues her small victories for reasons he does not understand.

If he understood them, he would have moved on by now. "What do you mean?"

"Look at this apartment. It doesn't even look lived in. There's no mess, no clutter—and I'll grant you that's attractive. But . . . there are no pictures, no sentimental things—no mugs with funny sayings, no kitchen counter clutter, no fridge magnets. All of your towels match. All of your furniture matches. Your *clothing* matches your furniture."

"And?"

"Your clothing generally matches your car."

"I fail to see—"

"You can't tell me you do that by accident. You *want* to be seen in a certain way; that's the way you're seen." She breaks the two sentences by the action of turning on the stove. "If you want them to see more, there has to *be* more."

"There is more," he says.

"Yes, well. There always is. I meant you have to be willing to expose more."

"You mean, in the way that you do?"

At her feet, the little ones are watching. Their heads move in unison, back and forth, back and forth, as if something portentous is being said. Except for the odd one out; he is watching the pans with an open expression of hunger. Let it be said that they are not starving in the traditional sense of the word; they are plump and short and round in belly, round in jaw; they are barefoot because they prefer it; shoes are a trap.

"No." She opens the oven door, slides the trays in, one beside the other, and rises. "Not the way I do. I'm me; you're you. I could never live in a home this tidy; the stress of keeping it perfect would kill me." She smiles as she says it. "I'm good enough with money that I don't starve; I've never been focused enough to be a lawyer or a doctor or a—whatever you are. Look, I'm not telling you to be *me*—you'd hate that. I'm telling you to be more you. How did we start talking about this anyway?"

"You asked me about the absence of love in my life."

She raises a brow. "You asked about the absence of love in mine."

"Very well. We are both people who are accustomed to doing without love." He shrugs and turns away.

But she hasn't finished yet. "No, we're not." He turns back as she begins to clean. "I love."

"But you live alone."

"It's not just people I love—although I have a lot of friends I *do* love. I love baking," she tells him. "And singing, and painting, and walking. I love listening, and I love—" she laughs broadly, "talking. I love to talk. I love to eat."

"These are not—"

"They're things *I* love. I don't always know what other people love—or hate—about me, and I can't be responsible for how they love or how they don't. But I can love what *I* love, regardless."

"These are the things you mentioned when you spoke of joy."

"Ye–es." She walks to the sink, washes her hands, glances at the floor where the small ones are staring at her, open-eyed and hungering. "You know we're all alone, right?"

He is silent.

"But I can't be responsible for what other people feel or think or love. When I was younger," she adds, checking the clock before she turns to face him, her hands still slightly wet, "I thought that anything I loved—anything at all—must be loved by everyone. If they knew about it, they'd love it the way I did. I didn't understand, then, that *I* didn't love what *they* loved, either; I dismissed what they cared about if I didn't. It was stupid, or selfish, or vain." She laughs; there's a hint of bitterness to it, but it isn't ugly.

"Now? I know that we love what we love, see what we see. Sometimes you'll meet someone who sees what you see—and that's a gift. You can share, then."

"And this sharing is important?"

"I think so. Sometimes it's only little things. Food, baking. Sometimes it's larger than that—children, for instance. But children are much, much more complicated than baking."

He has never cared for children, but deems it wise to keep that to himself.

She knows, however. She knows, but she doesn't judge—and why should she? It's not as if she has any of her own. He is curious now; he has never seen her home, and he wonders how it compares to his. It's not as large, certainly, and not as fine; he doubts that it's nearly as private. He guesses that her furniture is old and worn, that it is mismatched, that her walls and her counters are cluttered. But there is something about her that makes him uncertain.

It's strange. His mother was a force of nature in her own right: if she was in a room, all eyes, all ears, all attention, accrued to her. She loved perfection, always, and beauty; she loved elegance and a certain refinement, although a certain raw power could appeal to her for a limited time. She tolerated cats, but disdained dogs; he had no pets that he can now remember. Once he brought a guinea pig home; she drowned it for vermin, and he did not make that mistake again.

She was what she was: irreproachable, untouchable. He could predict with certainty what she would—or would not—do, but that certainty never gave him any comfort; his mother was feared, and that fear was universal. Did she have pets? Yes: caged birds, brilliant in color; they did not speak when she was in the house, although the moment she left it they knew. They had raucous, ugly voices that in no way matched their plumage, but even they understood the cost of using those voices where they might disturb his mother.

"Have you found no joy in your life? Do your studies bring no joy to you? Is there no music that takes your breath away? No song, no poetry? Do you not hear the stories of strangers and feel moved to tears or rage?"

"No. Their lives are not my life."

"Is there nothing that you want to share?"

He stares at her, although this is risky. She always asks odd questions, but this conversation has taken a turn that he did not expect. She asks the words without subtext, without any desire of her own. He does not know how to turn them, how to make them into something other—because such transformations must have some kernel of truth at their heart. "What do I have to share?" He finally asks, lifting an arm to a perfect room—to a room she has seen as empty, because in truth, it is. "I have money, and it buys a brief happiness for others, but it is like any other drug; habit-forming. It does not sustain."

"Starvation is worse," is her clipped reply. She bites her lip, exhales, and adds, "I'm sorry. I hear a lot of poor rich kids, and sometimes—" she shakes her head. "We all think we'd appreciate the things that other people don't, and we're probably wrong about it. You don't trust people who want your money."

"No."

Her eyes narrow. "Do you trust anyone at all? Ever?"

He laughs. It is the first time he has laughed like this, in front of her, and she takes a step back, hitting the counter and coming to a halt. "No," he says, when he can speak again. "It is not a habit that was ever encouraged. I do not have *faith*."

"I wasn't asking about your religious beliefs—"

"But you *were*, my dear. You simply don't understand how or why." This time, he walks into the kitchen, into the sphere of the space he usually circumvents so carefully. He opens the fridge she both admired and despaired of, and removes a bottle. "I will have wine, I think. Will you join me? You are not working."

She hesitates, and then nods. "I'm not sure it'll go with the muffins," she adds.

"How is trust a religion?" She asks, as she takes a chair, crossing her legs rather than letting her feet touch the floor. She does not sit upright; she lounges, and in these chairs, that should be difficult. He cannot imagine his mother would like a woman such as her. He cannot imagine that this woman would care for her, either. But he thinks it, as if it is relevant, and he opens the bottle with enough force it's a small wonder the neck doesn't snap in his hands, which would be awkward.

"If you are a scholar of human nature, you will have come across the phrase 'every man for himself'."

She grimaces. "It's usually an excuse when an apology would be better."

"And one is to apologize for rational self-interest?"

Her expression is momentarily weary; it says "oh this again." But she is here, a guest, and she accepts the odd challenge beneath the surface of his words. She also accepts the very fine glass he offers her. He seldom sees her drink anything but water, and she hesitates, gazing at the amber wine as if it is a danger.

He waits, and after a moment, she accepts the danger and drinks; her expression changes, brows lifting into her scraggly hairline in silent wonder. When she looks at him again, her eyes are still wide, still round, but they are clearly now. She has always seemed so soft—in line, in build, in word—it is striking to see that there is hardness to her; it comes to the surface as she sets the glass down.

He waits for her accusation, for her acknowledgment, for he is *almost* certain that she knows what she has just imbibed. But as if this were a play, a carefully scripted and memorized act, he picks up the threads of his words.

"No, there is no need to apologize for rational self-interest. It's the definition of 'rational' that I object to."

"How so?"

"Do you think I'm baking for you?"

"You are demonstrably baking for me."

She shakes her head. "I'm baking for *me*. *I* want to feed *you*." She glances into the kitchen and adds, "And anyone else here who happens to be hungry."

They have not followed her to the table; they haven't dared. But they have clambered up on each other's shoulders and are peering through the glass—or making the attempt; some jostling, shoving and pushing is expected, and it occurs. He is shocked when she sets her glass down, pushes her chair back from the table, and goes to the kitchen. It is an act of surrender.

"There is enough for *everyone*," she tells them, her hands balled in fists on her hips.

They fall over, eyes wide with shock; they are now very, very pale.

"Well?"

One of the small ones who is perpetually on the bottom says, "There is *never* enough for everyone."

"Then I'll make more."

"There is *never ever* enough for everyone."

"If you keep pushing and shoving like that, there'll be precisely the same amount for everyone: none. Is that clear?"

Guilty, anxious glances are exchanged.

"I mean it. Pretend I have eyes in the back of my head: I hear any more squabbling and you can all go hungry. If you can work together—"

"Doing what?"

"Getting along. If you can do that, I'll make sure that every single one of you *in the kitchen right now* has something to eat. Deal?"

He says, "They are not a democracy. They are not empowered—"

"Oh, hush, you. I'm perfectly happy to send them all to bed hungry."

"They are not children—"

"They are exactly children; they just happen to have no parents. Deal?"

Nodding and shuffling abounds, and he notes—as she must—that there are now six more of the small ones who have magically appeared in the kitchen. She makes no comment, but returns to the chair and sits. "Honestly, how long have you let them live like that?"

He is, again, nonplussed. When he finds words— and they are never far away—he says, "How long have you been able to see them?"

But she shakes her head and lifts her glass. "How long have you had this particular vintage in your possession?"

"Centuries."

"My answer's similar."

He stares at her. He has watched her for months, and all he has seen is a cheerful but sometimes weary woman of middling weight and middling years. She has no great wealth and no great beauty; she fends off no suitors, except the very drunk and garrulous, and she has not particular outstanding talent. When she sings her voice is not unpleasant, but it lacks power; when she paints, she cannot capture the whole of what she sees. Her hair has some grey in it; she disdains—in a quiet and comfortable way—artifice.

She cannot have seen the passage of centuries.

He drinks, as she has done. "Do you know who I am?" he finally asks.

"No."

"Yet you recognize them?"

"I recognize what they are. I recognized *what* you are, but not who; that's always harder. Time has passed, even for the timeless. Everything has to change, if it's alive." So saying, she glances at the back of her hands, and a brief, rueful smile shadows the corners of her lips. "Do you recognize me?"

His brows ripple in confusion.

"There's no reason you should, but you've watched me for a while now."

"I thought you were mortal."

"Yes, well. I've never lied to you. You never asked."

He is now, finally, suspicious. "Why did you agree to visit tonight?"

"To bake for you," is her prompt reply.

"To bake what?"

"Apple and cinnamon muffins. I didn't expect

you to have a small host guarding your kitchen floors. I didn't take you for the type."

"No more did I," he replies more severely. "Why did you wish to bake?"

"I told you. That's the whole of it. You seem like a person who might appreciate it, maybe. Some day. Probably not today, though."

"Did you—were you—"

"Did I know your mother?"

He lifts a brow. "One could not help but know my mother."

She chuckles. "That's a truth even I can't argue with. Yes, I remember her. Queen of the Dark Court."

It has been so long since he has heard the words, it takes him a moment to realize that she has not spoken in the English he assumed was her mother tongue. He rises stiffly. "Do not—"

"Call her?" She unfolds her legs, straightens her back; on her it looks almost wrong. "My dear boy, how long has it been since you've been home?" There is almost pity in her voice, and he cannot help his reaction; his jaws clench, as do his fists. He is not, has never been, an object of pity, except at his own choosing, for his own ends.

How dare she?

She lifts a hand. "I meant no insult. If I had, you'd know."

If she had, he would not be so angry. Or perhaps it is not her pity that angers him; her question disturbs. "Why do you ask?" is his formal, stiff reply.

"Because I have visited recently. It's not what it was in your youth."

"And what do you know of my youth?"

"It was dark and joyless, but very, very beautiful when seen from the outside." She lifts her glass, drinks, closes her eyes. Her lashes have always been remarkably long, and they are edged in gold, as if dusted. It is the one thing about her face that is striking. "Wait a minute," she adds, opening those eyes. She rises and heads to the kitchen to shoo the small ones away from the oven's door. If they wanted, they could drag her down to their level, like an angry human mob in miniature, but they don't—yet—dare.

She is his guest, if unexpected, after all. He would be forced to kill them, an act which would, at this point, bring him some comfort.

She won't let them touch a thing until she has served him, and she does; it is not appropriate food for the wine he is serving, but nothing about this woman is appropriate. When he accepts her offering—although he does not eat it—she returns to the kitchen and supervises the small horde; she is quick and sharp with her words, but they're not listening to anything but tone.

And her tone is strange; it is both hard and soft, cool and warm. Her expression softens into something very like a smile, and it is an idiot's smile; she is feeding the vultures, and does not understand this. The small ones would fall on her corpse if they thought they could gain by it.

She looks up at him at that moment, her face still softened by smile. "It's what they are," she says, as if this explains her stupidity. "But it's not all they can be." She shakes her head. "Next time, I'll make more."

There will be no next time. He could hardly call her a fool and at the same time invite her into his domain again, knowing what he now knows. "How can you play this game?" He asks, more sharply than he intended. There is no caution now; he is no longer hunter here, and if he is not to be hunted, he must be canny, wary.

"Which game?"

"This one. This feeding, this—this. How can you speak of trust? If you are not mortal, you must understand—"

"What must I understand?" Her voice is still soft, but there is now gravity to the words, weight, something that suggests a hidden majesty. "We want what we want—but surely, even that changes? The women you dine with, the women who visit you—they leave. They return to the world, and their lives, and they are largely unchanged. In your youth, that would have been nigh impossible."

That stings, but he accepts it. "I have had to be careful."

"Why?"

"If they were to disappear, it would attract unwanted attention, and that attention would inevitably destroy the life I have built."

"Why live in this world at all?"

"I could no longer live in hers."

"Ah." She lifts her glass. "Then you should understand me better than you think or know. I could no longer live there, either."

He surrenders, then. "You were not one of my mother's courtiers." It is not a question.

"No."

"Then what? You might have been one of the mortals she adopted as pets—but they aged and died as we watched; you are aged, but you are demonstrably not dead, and more significant, you are here. You are free."

"She did not own me."

He laughs at that. It is wild, unfettered; the small ones scatter at the sound, leaving crumbs across his perfect floors in their haste to be gone. "Did not own? She owned us *all*, from the least to the greatest. We existed to do her bidding or we did not live for long—and even those that attempted to carry out her will were not spared if their attempts came to naught."

"If she owned you, how did you escape? Why are you here, in this city? Why do you live without her mirrors and her tokens?"

He falls silent. Silence was one of his mother's weapons.

It is clearly a weapon to which she is impervious. "Trust is folly," she tells him, her voice almost a whisper. "So much of our lives are the stories we tell ourselves, the truth buried somewhere in the words, if it can be found at all. There is never enough for everyone, so everyone must guard what they have, take what they can; we live behind walls, and arm ourselves for invasion. We cannot give; if we give, people will know how weak, how foolish we are.

"We will die, if we are weak."

He nods. "You understand."

"No. I recite. I heard so much, so often. I was not a member of your mother's court, it is true; I would have seemed too feckless, too soft, a child for her liking in my youth. But even in *my* mother's court, these were the truths we held. We did not disdain humans, as you did, but we didn't fear them. We laughed at them, always. Their folly and their foolishness. They would come to us like thieves or beggars, with their small, tiny stories, their ephemeral pain. They would ask us for things: power or wealth or beauty. Sometimes they would ask for children.

"They weren't foolish enough to trust us, just desperate. But they were never so desperate as to approach your mother's court, your mother's throne."

"Yet mortals came."

"Yet they came. Beguiled, because beguilement was the only road they would travel. She lied to them—but so did we. She entrapped them in the web of their own desire—but so did we."

"Your desires were not hers, then."

"No, none so grand."

"And your court?"

She shook her head. "It is gone, I think. I could not

return home after I left your mother's court; she would have destroyed my people and everything that I might have touched, anyone who might have offered me aid. That was her way," she added quickly.

"When? When was this?"

"A long, long time ago."

He stares at her again, and this time he understands what he saw in her eyes the first time; nothing about her face or her hair, nothing about her form, looks the same. Did she bake in his mother's court? No. No, she couldn't have. He says, "Your hair—was it gold?"

She laughs the way middle-aged women laugh. "Yes, gold and long and fine. Not a hair out of place in your mother's court." She hesitates, and then says, "I lied."

"It's what we do."

"Not me, not any more—but I lied." She reaches across the table and gently cups his cheek; her hands are callused. "I remember you. What you were. I remember."

She leaves shortly afterward, the words hanging in the air between them. He closes—and wards—his door, although the gesture is empty. He knows that should she desire it, he will open the door again.

Only once in his long life did his mother shed tears. They were not for, or because, of him, and they caused the deaths of many, for his mother could not abide weakness, could not acknowledge it. But she did not kill *him*, and he witnessed. Surely that must have meant something?

Surely that must have meant something.

In the days that follow he works, he reads, and he writes. He supervises his graduate students with the same dispassionate air that has always characterized his supervision. Living in a land of mortals has granted him some confidence; they are *merely* mortal; no matter what they might achieve, they will be dust in time; he will endure.

But he *has* endured, and at times, in the empty perfection of his home, he feels that that is all he has done; it is a pyrrhic victory. When did it become that? When he first arrived, he found mortal laughter amusing, in a condescending way; he found their delight in their own cleverness very much like the delight of the small ones: laughable, if he was feeling generous. He is not known for his kindness, but has cultivated an aura of fairness, and he knows how to compel them when it is necessary.

He does not do it now; he watches them at work. Their work is often mingled with play, but he does not see much of the joy she so prizes in their daily activities. He watches them, much more discreetly, at play, and even there, there are equal parts pain and happiness, so much so they cannot be separated. He does not see what she sees and it vexes him.

He does not see the woman for whom his mother shed tears, and that is harder. He remembers her in her youth: she was as tall as his mother, gold to her ebony, but just as fair; her eyes were a shade of blue that verged on emerald in the right light. Her hands were long and fine, and she wore black to please his mother, but when his mother rode with her host, she oft slipped into white and gold and wandered through the gardens.

She was always there to greet his mother upon her return, and she would listen to his mother's stories, terse and perfect as they were; she would play music, a harp or a lute, and she would accept whatever small token of affection his mother brought back for her: emeralds or sapphires, gold; never diamonds.

But it is true: she was not of his mother's kin. It was generally agreed that her prominence in his mother's court was in part due to this: she had no ties to anyone that she might manipulate; her own people were in distant lands, their borders contested by both his mother and the mortals who grew bolder and bolder with the passage of time and their own petty wars. They burned and they destroyed with an abandon that the Dark Court did not show; there was no artistry to their destruction; they were like the locusts their farmers cursed and wept over.

Why had she any place in his mother's court at all?

Why is she so small now, so round, so utterly lacking in grace? Why is her hair so frazzled, her voice so rough, her hands so callused? Why does she seek to command no respect, even the piddling respect of the mortals around her?

He does not understand.

* * *

She looks up when he enters the bar, and she smiles. She is sweating. Sweating! Where once this was just a fact of life, it is now almost an abomination. She is jostled by patrons, touched by bartenders—just a tap of the shoulder, a nudge where words would take longer, but it is the principle of the thing.

Her smile is the smile that he first saw. It drew him; he accepts that now. He examines his past for some hint of her power—for she must have some—and finds nothing at all. It is just a smile, like any other mortal smile. But it fits the whole of her face. Yes, her eyes are lined with dark circles, and there are creases in their corners, but even those frame the smile, adding to it.

"I haven't seen you in a while," she says. "Will you have your usual red?"

Has it been that long? No, months at most, if that. He frowns. "Yes."

Someone further along the bar shouts her name, and she whips around, "Just a second!" There is music in her voice; it is rough, mortal music. Yet she is here, she is now. Did his mother curse her? Is that why she has become so diminished? Yet she is *alive*. He was so certain that she was dead and gone, entrapped and encased in permanence in the ice of the queen's vast, private chambers.

He does not like change. The immortal never do. And this is a change unlooked for, unnoticed; the world has shifted beneath his feet, becoming strange and incomprehensible—and the incomprehensible is death. But he came here for a reason.

He says, "The small ones miss you."

She raises one brow.

"They remind me that you said you would bake more, the next time."

"I can see why it took a few months; that must've taken some courage." She doesn't believe him, but she accepts his lie at face value—and this, at least, is a comfort; it's a court trick, a verbal dance, as familiar as breath. "You never touched what I baked the last time."

"I was—"

"Paranoid."

"Cautious."

"Well, I suppose *someone* was grateful, even if it wasn't you. You're sure it's okay?" She speaks as if nothing has changed, and for a moment, he almost feels nothing has. But then she adds, "You don't really seem to want them underfoot, and they'll come. They'll probably be screeching the whole time, too."

"Do they not visit you in your own abode?"

She glances down at the table-top. "No." She does not meet his eyes again until he changes the subject. He does; he understands when she has closed a door. He understood that the first time he saw her, and learned the nuances of it in the months and years that followed. What he does not understand is what his mother saw in her.

He arranges a date for her visit, and as he leaves—and he does, because tonight, she requires it—he finds himself adding, "You'll come?"

She smiles at him, as if he were a child. "Of course I'll come."

His apartment is still perfect. He considers making it less perfect, and begins to do so, arranging newspapers on the living room table, but surrenders when he realizes that they are placed in an artful, almost symmetric mess. Why he does this, he does not understand; this is *his* domain, small and humble though it is; the rules of hospitality that bind him and his kin, subtle and dangerous as they are, do not demand her comfort.

Yet he wants her comfort here; he wants her to drop her guard, to be herself.

He pauses, newspapers once again folded and in his hand. What does that mean, to be herself? She is not what he thought she was; she is not what anyone who traverses the loud and crowded floors of her bar thinks she is either, if they think of it at all. What has she shown him of herself, in the end? He has watched, and he has seen only what any mortal fool might see.

No, he thinks. He has seen more than that.

The moment she enters his home, the small ones gather. They do not limit their invasion to the kitchen, either, and he is certain—as she said they would be—they are more numerous. They chatter and whisper like squirrels, stopping only when the door creaks, as if they are collectively holding their breath.

But she comes with bags—and bags—and when he takes two of them from her fingers, she allows it—her fingers are white from their weight.

"Hey! You two, get your feet *off* the counter!" This starts the chatter again, the excitement. It spreads from them to her; her smile is open, infectious; she laughs—and he finds himself smiling, as if he were as insignificant as they.

He thought carefully about altering the kitchen before she arrived, but in the end, chose to leave it as she first found it. She enters it with less hesitation than she did the first time, as if the act of baking in it—of being the first to bake in it—has somehow made it hers.

He knows that the only space that is ever a safe space is the space one personally owns; so does she. But she is willing to own this small space—and they know it; it is around her they congregate. He thinks of what she says of her youth, and silently agrees; it would be almost impossible to take a step without tripping on something.

There is, of course, some struggle for dominance and position among the small ones; honestly, with such a large crowd, how could there not be? But she breaks it as calmly—and sharply—as she did the first time; she even sends two of the largest to the corners of the kitchen. What is shocking is that they obey.

And he watches, as he did the first time. There is so much he wants to ask, to know, but he is not certain what price he will be asked to pay, and he knows that nothing is given for free. Nothing.

This time, she doesn't just bake; she cooks. She makes a meal. It is long, and it is late by the time she is finished, but she does finish, her face red and slightly glistening with sweat. When she joins him at the table, he offers her wine. She flinches, and then shakes her head.

"No, thank you—I find my tolerance is much, much lower than it was. I can't—" Her lips thin a moment, as if she feels pain, although her eyes are clear. "It made me remember too much."

"We do not forget," he tells her, in the tone of voice reserved for wayward students.

"No, we don't—but sometimes the memories are memories, and I can pick and choose among them; sometimes they're a little too much like life."

"But your life is now given to joy, is it not?" There is an edge to the words.

"Do you think joy is easy? It's simple, but it's not easy. It's partly a dance, partly a story we tell ourselves; it's partly a place we can reach—but only with effort, and we can never stay there. We visit; we're grateful that the door is open." The corners of her lips and eyes crease as she smiles. "But thank you."

He is silent. "For what?" He finally asks. He is surprised that he's asked.

"For them. I miss them sometimes, even if I spend half the time wanting to strangle them all. They remind me of—" she stops. "Is the food to your liking?"

He does smile then. He lifts fork and he eats, because he knows that's the price of her visit. If she has enchanted or ensorcelled the food, so be it. But as he chews, as the texture and the salt and the sweetness mix on his tongue, he wonders. Such a risk to take. Such a risk and for so little.

While he thinks this, she speaks about work, about her regular customers, about the bus driver who stopped to wait for her while she struggled with her bags. She does not speak of his mother, and he finds that acceptable. This is not a meal he could have had in his mother's court; it is, all of it, mortal.

After he has finished, she rises and returns to the kitchen to supervise, and after, she returns to him. There is a marked change in her, now, but he cannot quite place what it is.

"I was sent to your mother's court as a hostage," she says. "I was *called* an ambassador, but that has a different meaning now than it once did."

"You did not want to go."

"No. I knew of your mother and her kin, and I knew of the damage they could do when roused; many of mine were lost. I hated her," she adds, in her soft, clear voice, hatred absent from every syllable. She walks away from the dining table and toward the living room. "There really *is* a TV here. Do you watch it?"

"Yes." His tone must alert her, for she glances at it more sharply. But she sits on the couch, and after a moment, she slides her feet beneath her and leans into the corner cushions. He joins her, taking the chair, putting a physical distance between them greater than the table provides.

"Do not make me get up and come in there!" she shouts, when the small ones begin to shriek. They are laughing, and their laughter, like the laughter of all of their kind, is sharp and pointed. Or it can be; it sounds . . . odd, tonight.

He waits, now.

"I hated her," she repeats. "I had seen her three times in my childhood, in her armor, at the head of her host; I had never seen her in her own domain, and I fervently wished never to do so. But I was chosen. For years, I was taught the arts of her court. I was taught how to play and sing in a manner that might—might—please her. I was taught the art of language and words. I—" she shook her head.

"I was taught the same," he replied.

"Yes, you were. But you lived in that court; it was your home. It was not mine."

"It was—"

"It was not mine. Nothing in the domains she rules can belong to anyone else. Nothing," she added, her voice dropping, "can even belong to itself." She lifts her hands and examines them. "I didn't understand why I was chosen until I was brought to the foot of her throne. Then I saw her, and I saw—" She lowers her hands. "She was beautiful."

"You expected otherwise?"

"We have different standards of beauty, you and I. I wasn't raised in your court, remember. Beauty just *is*. The small ones can be beautiful. Oh, don't give me that look. The pixies in the flowerbeds can be as beautiful as the flowers they tease; the small, warty gnomes that live in branches, and resemble their trees, as if they've grown together over time, are astonishing in their season.

"Yes, they're small, and often very single-minded—but theirs is a malice of minutes and hours, not of centuries, and they exist to make homes for themselves."

"So, too, did my mother."

"It's not the same, and you know it." She closes her eyes and sinks backward. "She was beautiful to *me*. Not because I must fear her—fear was a given, and not because of her power, also a given—she was just . . . what she was. Night and Winter and endless fury. But winter is beautiful in its time. I hadn't expected that. I hadn't expected that anyone could grow to love the cold."

"You speak of love?"

"It's a turn of phrase," is her quick reply. She stops, shakes her head, eyes still shuttered. ". . . Yes. I speak of love."

"You—you *loved* my mother?"

"Is it so hard to understand? She was loved—"

"She was feared."

"Not by everyone."

"By everyone."

"You didn't fear her."

"I? I feared her most of all."

She says, "Your fear and their fear were not the same." Her eyes are open, and they are emerald, they are almost incandescent. He realizes that she is crying, and he turns his face away, aware of the cost of witnessing something so profound.

"I stayed by your mother's side."

"I remember you now."

She nods. "But when she waged her bitter wars against the mortals, when she raided my mother's kin, I was left alone. I could not return to my own home, of course. I could not walk our roads, for she would know. I walked, instead, on mortal roads, and it amused me to do so. I granted small wishes, placed small curses, watched births and deaths and war and famine. You understand these things?"

He nodded.

"Have you only watched people?"

"Pardon?" He doesn't understand the question. She has seen him leave the bar with women of various ages and descriptions innumerable times.

She repeats the question, waiting, her eyes now dry. "It's what I did for centuries. I watched. I only watched. I watched the changes. I watched their gods rise and fall. I listened to their stories, and sometimes when their stories bored me, I made certain they would tell different tales. I grew, I thought, to understand them. Like you, like your mother, I understood their follies and their weaknesses well. But not all actions can be explained as folly or weakness, although perhaps in the end that's what they amount to."

"There is very little that mortals attempt that cannot be ascribed to folly. Look at how their choices oft end: in humiliation and despair."

"If they ended in joy and wonder," she replies, "would it signify anything, to you? They're all dust in the end. Not a single thing they make or do will outlast them."

"Exactly."

She shifts in place, rises, and retrieves a blanket—from where, he is not certain. It is not particularly fine; it is a common quilt, and by the looks of it, made in a period in which quilts were a necessity of mortal economy and not an artistic cloth tapestry. "By that measure, we're *all* creatures of folly."

She wraps the blanket around herself, on his couch; he almost objects, it is so dingy. But he has survived these long years by being sensitive—or powerful enough that sensitivity is not required; he is not certain that the latter applies here. Her words also rob him of outrage at something so minor.

"What did we seek, in the long, long centuries of our lives? What, that they do not, in their scant years, also seek? You've studied them; you consider yourself a scholar of humanity. For what did you study? To manipulate them? To find better ways to amuse yourself?" She watches him steadily, like a cat might.

"Tell me you have done otherwise."

"It is not an accusation; it's a statement. We're not mortal. Their folly and our folly are different. We have the luxury of time. We don't face age and growing fragility; our bodies do not fail us except by design or the curses of the more powerful."

"And you were so cursed?"

She blinks. Looks at her blocky, callused hands, and surprises him: she laughs. It is rueful, this laughter, but without edge. She does not answer the question; instead she says, "Ah yes; even mortals have their fixed notion of beauty, and they cling. Have you adopted only hers?"

"Hers?"

"Your mother's."

Has he? Beauty is not subjective; it is a fact, a force, like his mother.

"Did you not watch the mortals age? Did you not find it fascinating?"

"No. Not when I realized that age is their weakness."

She shook her head. "Weakness is our entrance. If they had no weaknesses, they would just be . . . us. I walked mortal roads," she added, and this time she lifts the patchwork blanket. "And I came to understand one truth of mortality well."

"And that?"

"They are changed by ownership."

His lift of brow is derisive. "Did *you* not visit the mortals in my mother's court?"

"In her lovely, lovely cages? Ah, yes. You mistake me, or rather, I haven't been clear. They are changed in either direction. What they are owned by changes them, yes; how could it do otherwise. But what they *own* also changes them.

"And for a time, toward the end of my tenure at your mother's court, I had grown less cautious. I did not live as you live now, because I had other options, other choices—but I held the mortals in no great respect, and I did not value their base cunning; I thought I understood the whole of what might motivate them. I made, in short, a mistake."

The import of her words sink slow roots; they flower in epiphany. "You were trapped."

She nods. "Indeed, I was trapped."

After a long, long pause, he says, "Did you tell my mother?"

"I could not, in my captivity."

"And after?"

Her gaze falters for the first time. She smiles, yes, but it is bitter, devoid of the warmth that characterizes so many of her easy, impulsive smiles. "What do you think? What do you honestly think?"

He nods; in a similar situation, he would have said nothing; not to his mother, nor to the rest of her court. But he would not say anything now, either, in the heart of another's domain—not unless compelled by a power far greater than his own. He wants to ask her how, or by what, but senses that it is superfluous. The fact she has shared, and she is not the only one of her kind to be trapped by the merely mortal.

"You must want something from me," she says, as if she can hear the whole of his thought, "and at that, very badly; you ask me no questions."

He nods; both statements are true.

"My captor was not an old woman, not wise in lore; she was a slight, pretty girl, too pretty for her village. She had only a brother, for kin, and he was a bull of man, unkind and very much enamored of his drinking and his standing in the town. I did not think she would survive for long; she was the type of young woman that men covet, often openly, and she had no wealth with which to buy her own safety.

"Your mother was, at that time, in the north, near the Isles," she added.

"Where your own people dwell."

She nods. "I understood the necessity of her wars, but I could not easily stand by and watch and wait, so I was reluctant to return to her court. I could not raise hand against her," she added. "I had tried, once, and I had failed." She speaks calmly. "And so I felt some kinship with this girl, and I watched her from afar, and one day, when she was washing clothing by the brook side, a man came from the village to catch her unaware.

"She was not strong, and he was not kind. She wept in silence after his departure, and I chose that moment to appear before her. I could see the whole of that man's fate and hers. It is an old story," she added quietly. "The man went directly to the young woman's brother. Her name," she added, "was Anne. He told the brother what he had done, and made an offer for her hand in marriage; her brother accepted on her behalf, for he felt he had no other choice; what other man would have her?

"But Anne? She came to me. She did not ask anything of me then; she wept and she raged, but as the days passed, she quieted. She made this quilt, but not then; she made it years later, and she made it for another, not me."

"It is yours now."

"Yes. The one she made it for is long dust; I could preserve the quilt, but not the mortal. Anne quieted, and when she was quiet, she sang. She spoke of her mother—long dead—and her father; she spoke seldom of the brother she feared. And she grew round with child, the unfortunate girl, for she very much wished to reject her suitor and remain unmarried; with a child, she could not do that; her brother would not have her in his house for fear of what others would say of him.

"I pitied her. Perhaps that was the start of it. But how could I not? I was a cage bird as well."

"She married the man?"

"She did. You wonder, now, why this is relevant, but be patient, and you will understand the answer to your many questions. She married him, she bore a child; she did not die of it, although it was close. The child was not a son, but a daughter, a girl very much like the child I imagine Anne herself might have been. Mortal children are wrinkled and ugly at birth," she added, "but also strangely beautiful in their utter helplessness, their complete fragility; she thought to hate the child, but she could not.

"I neither hated nor loved her then; she was merely a mortal child, and I had no need of one at that point. I was content to leave the babe where she was, with her mother. But her father was difficult. He had all the foibles and follies of mortality, but none of the unexpected grace; he was proud in the way of the fearful, very like the brother. He was not good with words; his persuasion took the form of fists, and he was not always careful to make certain his bruises would pass undetected.

"So Anne was pitied, and she was shunned. She had her home to keep, and the child; she had a husband who she feared and hated as humans fear and hate. It was a life like any other mortal's life. But I watched it blossom. I watched it grow both thorns and flowers. In my fashion, I gardened there, although I did not know it at the time.

"The child grew," she added, after a long pause. "I found her difficult; she was very like the small ones who've taken over your kitchen, but far, far more fragile; no punishments suitable for the small ones could be visited on her; she would not survive them. Her mother found her frustrating, but—joyful. It was to be my first experience of that strange state of joy, for much of Anne's misery was also directly due to the child.

"When the child was five, her father nearly beat her to death. It was then that I intervened; I lead him away in the dead of the night, enticing him onto the wild, old roads. The moon was at its height then."

"She asked this?"

"Of me? No, never. I do not know if she understood who or what I was; she did not ask, and I did not offer."

"You chose this?"

"Yes."

"To save the child."

"And to save Anne."

"But—"

"Yes. It was an act of folly and anger. But I could no longer stand by and bear witness; I could curse him, and had, but the effects made Anne's life more difficult, not less. I did not tell her what I would do; I merely acted, and left him wandering in the wild, where any stray creature might come upon him. But then, they were alone. They were grateful to be alone, for a while, but it was not an easy life. It was then that I began to teach Anne some of the ways of plants; how to bespeak them, how to cajole them. She needed food, and while I was not above the theft of food for her sake, I was by then aware that the cost was high."

"You taught her."

"I did."

"And she repaid you by trapping you in her world."

"She did."

"Were you not angry? Were you not enraged?"

"I was. But I also knew your mother's campaign would be long, and I would be free ere her return; Anne was mortal, and the mortals of that time lived a scant few decades. She did not think she could live without me. I concurred. But her death, when it came, a scant handful of mortal years later, her daughter but ten years of age. Anne knew she was dying; I did not deny it. But she called her daughter into her room, and while her daughter wept openly, she told her—"

"She bound you to her daughter."

"In a fashion, yes. I had thought she would attempt to give her daughter my name."

"She did not?"

"No—and it surprised me. Instead, she did the unexpected."

"And that?"

"She gave her daughter to *me*."

He was silent for a long moment, and when he spoke, he allowed his confusion to show. "She was knowledgeable enough to entrap you, and you say she loved this child, but she gave the child *to* you? Did her dying strip her of all sense?"

"I thought so at the time. There was no one—not even me—that she loved as she loved that child, and oft no one she resented half so much; it was complicated, the one and the other existing side-by-side, a human alloy." Her gaze sharpens as she watches him; he does not understand why. "But I understood that the gift was in equal measures blessing and burden; the greatest source of her joy and the greatest source of her sorrow, bound together. Yet I could not refuse her."

"She commanded you?"

"It was a gift. It was a mortal gift. I could have refused."

"Then why did you not do so?" He frowns, now, thinking about his mother's court. "This was—it was just before you left."

"It was decades before I left, in mortal count, but yes, in ours, it was brief."

"You—you did not bring the child to court; you could not have kept her a secret. I heard of no such—"

"No. I did not bring her to court, not then, and not later."

"But if you accepted her as a gift—"

"There was no place for her in the court, as there would have been no place for Anne. The court was not my home, do you not understand that? It was where I lived, but I lived as you lived: in her vast and expansive cage. I could live in that cage; I would have chosen it, in the end, because of what I felt for your mother. But what I owned, your mother owned—and I did not choose to surrender Anne's only child into her keeping." She smiles again, a tired, mortal smile. "Although there were certainly days to follow when I considered that option seriously.

"We buried her mother in the garden, and from her grave, a tree grew. It grew overnight, and perhaps that was unwise, but it comforted the child, who would often rest beneath its bowers or climb its branches. She was not Anne, although she had some of her looks and bearing; she was brighter, happier, less constrained. But so, too, might Anne have been in a different life.

"I stayed with her. Sometimes I let the small ones in, and they would tend the house; I paid them their due, although the child learned what they liked and would often skim milk or flour for their use. She had no friends, and that was my fault; I—like all of my kin—hold tight to what I own, and I held her too tightly, too long. I did not wish her to suffer her mother's fate."

"She was mortal, she would—"

"I did not wish the brief span of years allowed her by her very nature to be those years."

"Why would you care?"

"I really can't explain it." Her voice is soft, and there is sorrow in it. "Except in this: I owned her, yes, and she owned me; whatever it was that existed between us bound us both."

"It was not a binding; you said yourself the child's mother did not make that attempt."

"It was not a binding of word and power, no, but it was strong and subtle and in the end. It changed almost everything. I learned what Anne learned in the long and hard sleepless years: to find joy, to make it. It was Anne's gift to me—I believe that now. To learn to understand her joy, and what love can be, even if it begins unwanted." She pauses, tightens her grip on the blanket; her hands are less blocky now, her fingers longer and finer; her hair has straightened and it is, as he remembers, the color of pure, spun gold. "I learned, also, the measure of her pain and her fear in a way that I had never understood it.

"I understood how to manipulate it, of course; who among us did not? But to feel it, to live it? No. And I believe that I would not understand her joy if I had not come to understand her sorrow. I learned both, tending to the child. I held her while she wept, and I held her—when she could be held at all—

while she ambled about the house like a restless cat; I listened to her laughter and her chattering, and I taught her what I thought she needed to learn.

"She would not allow me to destroy her enemies, large or small; what I did, I did without her knowledge. She was not her mother, in that regard; she was not canny, and far too trusting—and perhaps that was my fault. She could have asked for the moon, and I would have attempted to retrieve it for her, abandoning the night skies—but she asked only for me. For my time, my constant attention, my acceptance.

"And when she was of Anne's age, I guarded her. The small ones guarded her. We kept vigilant watch against predators, and in time, she found a man she could love, and we deemed him almost worthy." She laughs as she says this, her laughter clear and high, as unlike the face she now wears as—as almost anything could be. "But before their first child was born, your mother finally returned to court, and I was called away.

"I returned to the strangeness of the court. It was as it had always been: eternal, ageless, free of disease and blemish and unpleasant noise. She came to me in her armor, her sword sheathed, and she brought—ah, she brought rubies, the color of light seen through blood. It was as if she knew.

"I was not different; I thought I was unchanged. I appeared before her as I now appear before you: eternal, immortal, hers." She lifts her hands to her face for a moment. "It is true that I loved your

mother before Anne. It is true. But it is the love of
our kind; it is not lived in, it does not transform. It is
regard and—and distance. She did not need me, and
I did not need her. I needed only avoid her rage and
her fury; I needed only to stand, to observe, to be
caught a moment by her utter, perfect power, her
perfect beauty. It was . . . peaceful, for a day. For two.
It was peaceful and quiet.

"But I could not remain in that court for long, for
Anne's daughter was aging with every passing day;
she had so little time left her, and your mother had
forever. Surely, surely, in her councils of war and her
plans for conquest, a few years here or there would
not be missed?"

He is utterly silent, watching her. She is no longer
mortal, not to his eyes; he cannot see the barmaid in
her perfect, porcelain skin at all. Yet the barmaid lingers in the quilt, which has not changed; dingy,
patchwork, colors faded, it shrouds her shoulders.

"But of course, that is not the way of the queen.
She followed me. When her son was born—Anne's
daughter had three children—she followed me. She
did not interfere, not then, but she watched me, for I
attended the birth as midwife. I did not come as I am
now; I arrived as you first saw me; it was a comfort
to her husband, and to his wife, I think, for if she
loved me, she was also mortal, and some fear lurked
in her. I helped deliver her son; I was careful in the
disposition of his birth caul, and I protected the child
against our own. Then I gave him to his father, and I
spent some time at the side of Anne's daughter. She

had aged so much in my absence; I had missed the birth of her second child entirely.

"But I told her my queen had come, and I could not leave the court as often. The small ones remained by her side, and in her house, as was proper, and she made certain that her husband and her children paid them the respect and regard they desired. When I rose to take my leave, when I left their home, your mother was waiting on the path.

"She was smiling. It was a smile of brittle rage. My hands were not entirely clean of blood and after-birth and human sweat. 'So, this is what you do when you leave my side? Tend to mortals like the meanest and lowest of their kind?' I thought she would kill them all."

He is surprised that she did not, but he knows she did not. Somehow, he knows.

"Yes. I stood by your mother's side for centuries, and asked nothing of her but her presence, her per-mission to stand in her perfect shadow. That night, I asked her for one and only one thing: that she spare this family and its descendants. It did not ease her rage, and I feared that she would refuse me—but had she, I would not be here now. I would have died before I allowed her to cross that threshold. She re-turned to the court, and she did not summon me. I was not allowed to enter her chambers.

"It was hard," she says quietly. "And perhaps, had I abandoned my mortals entirely, she would have forgiven me and we might have continued as we had begun. But—their time was so *short*. In the end, instead of attempting to mollify her, I travelled to Anne's daughter, there to watch her children grow, as Anne's daughter had before her.

"Your mother watched me. She could not—did not—understand what they gave me, or why I wanted it. Perhaps it was the latter. But she thought me changed." She glances at her hands, now. "I thought she was wrong—and that was my mistake; your mother was so seldom wrong about anything. But she watched, she waited, and in time, Anne's daughter also passed away; she was much older, in mortal years, than her mother had been, and she was less terrified, for her own children had children and homes of their own. She gave me this blanket, because Anne had made it, so long ago, and it was one of the few things that remained of Anne in her home.

"And I brought it to court, and I hid it, and I grieved." She looks up at him, her eyes once again luminescent. "She called me Mother," she says softly. "I thought she was addled and wandering, and told her, gently, that I was not Anne—and she said, rather crossly, that she *knew* that.

"And time passed. I did not go into the mortal world so often, and when I did, it was only to catch a glimpse of her children, and her grandchildren. But . . . there was no joy in your mother's court, and I understood, as the decades passed, that I—I missed it. I tried, but the court is too cold and too perfect and it requires a subtle labor into which one puts passion, but not what mortals call 'heart.'

"She came to me, when the moon was at nadir,

and she stood where you are standing now, and she said the mortals had all but destroyed me. I told her no, I tried to explain—but there are some experiences that defy explanation; you understand the explanations only when you have the experience. Do you understand, now, where this is going?"

He is holding his breath. He thinks he has been holding his breath since she entered the apartment. "What happened to the small ones?"

He has surprised her, and yet, he has pleased her as well. "They remained with Anne's family. With her daughter, and then, in ones and twos, with her grandchildren. One day, perhaps, they will leave, but they are all there now."

"They did not return to you?"

"I could not give them, not entirely, what the mortals could. Is that not the way? If mortals offered us nothing of value at all, we would be sundered; we would live in worlds that do not, and will never, touch. I know what they *can* be, because I have seen it; small, they are large and ferocious." But she lifts a golden brow. "You have not answered my question."

"I—I—no. No, Lady, I do not know."

"She desired the experience, to better understand her loss—but she was the queen, and not the least of her hostages; she could not bear to take a mortal child as her own, not in the way I had done. Why bring a mortal babe into her realm? She had done so countless times, and it had never moved or changed her. I told her that I had not lived in court with a mortal; I had lived in their homes—and this she could not do.

"We have no children," she added softly. "It is a truth which you must understand and acknowledge; if we are enamored of that brief flash of youth, we steal them. We do not make them. Why, then, were you born at all? And how?" She finally rises. "There is only one of our kind who has borne a child. Your mother. She could not do what I did, and she could not bring herself to be bound in *any* fashion to a home not her own.

"Do you remember your childhood? I remember some of it. It was not Anne's childhood; it was not the childhood of Anne's daughter. It was, like the court, slow and cold and joyless. We were not, any one of us but you, children. We did not run and play and we did not desire the open affection, the vulnerability, of our creators. But you? You were different.

"You *were* a child. You are still your mother's child. What you wanted, we did not want; what you feared, we did not fear. Can you not see that, now?" She is radiant, tall, beautiful; she is what she was in the childhood that they both remember. "We none of us wanted her love, until the end, and only one among us, besides you, could."

"You speak of yourself."

She smiles. "Yes. I said I love to talk, didn't I? But you left your mother's home, her court, her lands. You left her."

"I left after you did. Why did you leave?"

"Because I wanted what she could not give me,

and I could not return to her side until I no longer wanted it so deeply, so completely. It is not her fault, and not her failing; it is entirely my own, and I have struggled to learn how to give *myself* what I need." There is no lie in her voice, or her words, but looking as she does now, he doesn't expect to hear one; she is as flawless in her presentation as any one of his mother's court might be. Yet she is here, and he cannot think what she might gain by it.

"And . . ." he walks to the window, to look—as he has often looked—down. "Why did you return? You said you had returned and my home is not what it was?"

"I have learned much from mortals in my time here, I have experienced much. I returned to her because, for the first time in her long history, she had need—of me. She had, I think, no joy of it, and I regret that; but she had need."

He swallows. "What did she need?"

"She needed me to find you, of course. To find her son, who left her, inexplicably, to live in the realm of mortals, as a mortal—just as I had done."

"She asked this?" He cannot keep the shock from his voice.

But she shakes her head as he turns. "No, of course not. She is your mother. She could no more ask than come herself, and if she came, it would be to break and destroy; she knows it, as we know it. She could not give you what you wanted—what you needed—because she had no experience of it; she did not know how. She will never, I think, know how." Her voice is soft. "She will never be able to surrender that much.

"I told you—I never expected to love her. I did not expect to find her beautiful: I was wrong. She was beautiful—to me—the way things that are beautiful are: she was entirely herself. She is what she is, and she was always that. She is not capable of being what we want, what either of us grew to want or need. But she has changed, slowly, and almost imperceptibly. She has changed."

He is staring, now; he cannot help it. "How?" he finally demands—or means to demand; it comes out as a plea.

"She needs, and she knows that I know it. Yet she has not repulsed me, and she has not destroyed me. That is a start—and it is a small, small start, and it may not be enough for you. I will make no attempt to compel, but—if you can, visit her."

"She will never allow me to leave again."

"I am here," was her soft reply. "Her home is a cage, but there are gaps between the bars, and seeing them, she has not—quite—closed them."

"She has you," is his bitter reply. "She has always had you, even then. She cried for you. Men died because of it. She has never—" he cannot bring himself to say it, to expose it, although he is certain she knows.

But she smiles, and it is a sad, wise smile that is entirely out of place on the face she now wears. "It is not the same. I loved her, as we love, but I could not leave my only daughter, a child I did not bear and did not want." Pulling the blanket across her shoulders, she heads toward the kitchen; as she walks, she dwindles and shrinks, losing elegance and height and even hair. "I'll clean up here. Call her."

He closes his eyes. "She—she wanted me? She wanted to bear me?"

"Oh, yes. And, in the way of things, she had days where she bitterly regretted that choice, and days where she exulted in it. She is what she is, but in as much as she has ever been capable of love, she loved you."

He turns from her to the television on the wall, lifts his hand and gestures.

There she is: the height of perfect Winter, in her aerie, surrounded by the only pets she now keeps: her silent birds. But they are *not* silent now, and she has clearly not destroyed them. He watches her for a long, long moment. And then, almost helpless, he whispers a single word, and she turns, and their eyes meet.

ABOUT THE AUTHORS

Amber Benson co-wrote and directed the animated web-series, *Ghosts of Albion*, (with Christopher Golden) for the BBC. The duo then novelized the series in two books. Her first solo novel, *Death's Daughter*, was released in 2009, and the sequel *Cat's Claw*, in 2010. As an actress, Benson spent three seasons as Tara Maclay on the cult hit show *Buffy the Vampire Slayer*. She has also written, produced, and directed three feature films, including her latest, *Drones*, which she co-directed with Adam Busch and will be released later this year.

Paul Crilley is a Scottish speculative fiction writer based in South Africa. His work has appeared in numerous anthologies, including *Dr Who: Destination Prague*, and *Under Cover of Darkness*. His first young adult novel *Rise of the Darklings, Book One of The Invisible Order* series, came out in 2010. The sequel, *The Fire King*, was published in September 2011. He also worked on the computer game, *Star Wars: The Old Republic* and writes for television.

Sarah A. Hoyt has published over a hundred short stories, in venues ranging from *Asimov's SF* and *Analog Science Fiction* to various anthologies. She's also the author of over twenty published novels. Currently, she is writing the Daring Finds mystery series (*Dipped, Stripped And Dead*, *A French Polished Murder*, *A Fatal Stain*) as Elise Hyatt, the Shifter Series (*Draw One In The Dark*, *Gentleman Takes A Chance*, *Noah's Boy*) and a space opera series (*Darkship Thieves*, *Darkship Renegades*) under her own name. More information and samples of her work are available at http://sarahahoyt.com.

Kerrie L. Hughes is a freelance writer, editor, and artist currently residing in Green Bay Wisconsin. She has run away a few times.

Mary Robinette Kowal is the author of *Shades of Milk and Honey* (2010). In 2008 she received the Campbell Award for Best New Writer and has been nominated for the Hugo and Locus awards. Her stories appear in *Asimov's SF*, *Clarkesworld*, and several Year's Best anthologies. A professional puppeteer and voice actor, she lives in Portland with her husband Rob and a dozen manual typewriters. Visit her website www.maryrobinettekowal.com for more information about her fiction and puppetry.

Jane Lindskold is the bestselling author of the Firekeeper series, which began with *Through Wolf's Eyes* and concluded with *Wolf's Blood*, as well as many other fantasy novels. She lives in Albuquerque, New Mexico.

John (J. A.) Pitts learned to love science fiction at the knee of his grandmother, listening to her read authors like Edgar Rice Burroughs and Robert E. Howard during an eventful childhood in rural Kentucky. *Black Blade Blues*, the debut novel in his urban fantasy series, was released in the summer of 2010 and the mass market edition is now available. *Honeyed Words*, the second in the ongoing series, was published in summer 2011. He is currently working on the third book in the series slated for summer of 2012. He has a BA in English and a Masters of Library Science from University of Kentucky. When he's not writing, you can find him practicing martial arts with his children or spending time with his lovely wife. John is a member of the Science Fiction and Fantasy Writers of America.

Ever since writing her first fantasy story at the age of eight, Jenifer Ruth has wanted to be a writer. Once a middle school English teacher, she is now pursuing her dream of writing while living with her family in Reno, NV.

Lilith Saintcrow was born in New Mexico and lived a nomad existence as a military brat, writing as soon as her fingers could curl around a pencil. She currently resides in Vancouver, WA, with her children and a collection of cats.

USA Today-bestselling writer Dean Wesley Smith has written over a hundred novels and even more short stories. Not only does he write thrillers under another name, but he also wrote the only two original

Men in Black novels.. For more information about his work go to DeanWesleySmith.com.

Rob Thurman is the author of the Cal Leandros Novels, the Trickster Novels, the Chimera Novels and has a story, "Milk and Cookies," in the Charlaine Harris & Toni LP Kelner anthology *Wolfsbane and Mistletoe*. Rob lives in Indiana, land of rabid, blood-sucking cows as far as the eye can see. Protecting the author's house and home is a hundred-pound adopted Lab-Great Dane mix with teeth straight out of a Godzilla movie and the ferocious habit of pissing on herself and hiding under the bed when visitors arrive. Rob hopes to be the first to write a post-apocalyptic fey Western, but in this business you never know. Reach the author at www.robthurman.net.

Michelle Sagara West writes as both Michelle Sagara and Michelle West; she is also published as Michelle Sagara West (although the Sundered books were originally published under the name Michelle Sagara). She lives in Toronto with her long-suffering husband and her two children, and to her regret has no dogs.

ABOUT THE EDITORS

Martin H. Greenberg is the CEP of Tekno Books and its predecessor companies, now the largest book developer of commercial fiction and nonfiction in the world, with over 2,250 published books that have been translated into 33 languages. He is the recipient of an unprecedented four lifetime achievement awards in the science fiction, mystery, and supernatural horror genres—the Milford Award in science fiction, the Solstice Award in science fiction, the Bram Stoker Award in horror, and the Ellery Queen Award in mystery—the only person in publishing history to have received all four awards.

Russell Davis has written and sold numerous novels and short stories in virtually every genre of fiction, under at least a half-dozen pseudonyms. Some of his more recent novels include work in both *The Executioner* and *Room 59* series, as well as a forthcoming project for StoryPortals.Com. His short fiction has appeared in anthologies such as *Imaginary Friends*, *Law of the Gun*, and *Under Cover of Darkness*. He also works as an editor and book packager, and has created anthology titles ranging from westerns such as *Lost Trails* to fantasy such as *If I Were an Evil Overlord*. A past president of the Science Fiction & Fantasy

Writers of America, Russell now writes and edits full time, as well as teaching for Western State College of Colorado. He lives in Wisconsin with his wife and children, and in his copious spare time, he tries to get some sleep.

Tad Williams

SHADOWMARCH

SHADOWMARCH
978-0-7564-0359-6

SHADOWPLAY
978-0-7564-0544-1

SHADOWRISE
978-0-7564-0645-5

SHADOWHEART
978-0-7564-0695-0

"Bestseller Williams once again delivers a sweeping spell-binder full of mystical wonder." —*Publishers Weekly*

"Tad Williams is already regarded as one of fantasy's most skilled practitioners, and this latest work more than confirms that status." —*Amazing Stories*

"Williams creates an endlessly fascinating and magic-filled realm filled with a profusion of memorable characters and just as many intriguing plots and subplots.... Arguably his most accomplished work to date."
—*The Barnes & Noble Review*

To Order Call: 1-800-788-6262
www.dawbooks.com

DAW 47

Celia Jerome
The Willow Tate *Novels*

"Readers will love the first Willow Tate book. Willow is funny, brave and open to possibilities most people would not have even considered as she meets her perfect foil in Thaddeus Grant, a British agent assigned to look over the strange occurrences following Willow like a shadow. Together they make a wonderful pair and readers will love their unconventional courtship."　—*RT Book Review*

TROLLS IN THE HAMPTONS
978-0-7564-0630-1

NIGHT MARES IN THE HAMPTONS
978-0-7564-0663-9

FIRE WORKS IN THE HAMPTONS
978-0-7564-0688-2

And don't miss:
LIFE GUARDS IN THE HAMPTONS
(Available May 2012)

To Order Call: 1-800-788-6262
www.dawbooks.com